Praise

A gripping Young Adult fantasy story, brimming with danger, magic and intrigue, set in a richly imagined world, with a superb cast of characters.

– Mary Simms,
BookCraic

Dorothy Winsor's novel presents an intriguing and well-drawn world, with a very likeable lead. An exciting, adventurous, and thoughtful YA fantasy novel.

– Dr. Una McCormack,
New York Times Bestselling Author

A delightful coming-of-age story about finding out who you are when everything about your life is changing; when you can't go back but aren't sure you see a path forward; and when the gifts you've counted on most may turn out to be not to be the ones you need to save the people counting on you.

– Rachel Neumeier,
author of Winter of Ice and Iron

Dorothy A. Winsor is a meticulous writer who expertly balances intelligence and delight.

– Saladin Ahmed,
Hugo, Nebula, and Gemmell Awards finalist

Journeys: A Ghost Story, is a very good tale that, without any real surprises, still manages to surprise. There's a well-wrought aura of melancholy that permeates the story, even in the funny moments. Another author I'll keep an eye out for in the future.

– Fletcher Vredenburgh,
Black Gate Magazine

[In Finders Keepers*], the action is brisk, emotions are deep, and the moral message is subtle but strong, providing excellent depth for all readers, young and not so young. Great story – I loved it as an adult and think it is a wonderful book for older kids and young adults. Five Stars.*

– Melinda Hills,
Readers' Favorite

For Meckinock

I swear to use my work to share the vision the dragon
shows me.

I will treat that vision with reverence and care.

I will bring the best of myself to my work so it is all I can
make it.

I will not allow my work to lead others away from the
dragon's truth.

I will be ever faithful to my craft.

—Crafters' Oath, The Dolyan Islands

The dragon of Kural was said to have red-gold eyes that
gleamed like glass with light shining through it. He loved
learning, insight, glass, and spies.

—*A History of the Dolyan Islands* by Mara of Basur

Chapter 1

THE PIECES I'D cut for my stained-glass window glowed on my worktable. My fingers itched to put them together. Behind me, the door to my workroom opened, and my mother entered. "It's late," she said, pushing a sweat-darkened strand of hair off her forehead. "Time to quit and eat something."

"I finished cutting the pieces," I rushed out. "I'm ready for you to approve them."

Her tired face broadening in a smile, she put one arm around my shoulders. "You're not excited, are you?"

I rewarded her with a laugh. "How could you tell?"

She squeezed me close, then let me go. Face sober, she bent over the glass shapes, running her gaze slowly along the table. She had slipped into her role as craftmistress. Even though I was her daughter, the glasswork had to be right. Not that I'd want it any other way.

I clasped my hands first in front of me and then in back.

"I feel you staring at me," she said without turning. "Go bring in some wood for the furnace."

She might be craftmistress now, but that tone of voice was pure mother. I refrained from rolling my eyes and left her to her inspection. The big workshop was empty when I walked through. The furnace, banked for the night, still glowed with heat. The tools had been put away, and the other glassmakers were gone. I stepped out into the chilly yard. The oncoming late winter darkness left just enough light for me to see as I gathered an armful of wood from the shed and started back inside.

As I reached the doorway, I glimpsed movement near the gate and recognized the solid, middle-aged form of Miriv, my mother's deputy and the woman she loved. A man I didn't know was talking to her. When he saw me, he stopped.

"Who's that?" he asked.

Miriv glanced back. "None of your business. Clear off. You're not welcome here." She strode toward me, mouth tightly set.

"Tell Calea I was here," the man called after her. He was still standing by the gate when Miriv put her hand in the small of my back and hustled me inside.

I dropped the wood in the box next to the furnace. "Who was that?"

Miriv shrugged. "Someone your mother used to know. How's your window coming along?"

I lost all interest in the man. "I'm about to find out."

"I'll make you some eggs." Miriv set a pan on the brazier.

I hurried into my workroom where my mother still bent over the table. She was nothing if not thorough about glass. The work was good. I was sure of it, but I wasn't certain how she'd judge it. She'd been tense lately. She'd worked well into the night at least twice. I didn't know if she was worried about something or just driven to finish a project. In my nearly seventeen years, I'd seen her both ways. I had time to notice a new burn hole in the sleeve of her red glassmaker tunic before she straightened.

"You changed the design I approved," she said.

I grimaced. I knew I shouldn't have done that. I was still an apprentice. "Rhyth's representative asked me to make their island larger than the others. I didn't think it was a big enough change to need your permission." Also, I'd been afraid she'd say no. Sometimes she oversaw my work down to the littlest detail, as if she assumed I might be doing it wrong before she even looked.

"The design is dragon-inspired," she said. "You altered it to please a powerful buyer."

Her face was unreadable. I couldn't tell how seriously she thought I'd gone wrong. My stomach tightened with worry. "Miriv says sometimes I indulge myself in work that's too fanciful for anyone else to appreciate. I was trying to be practical with this one."

"Be careful, Emlin," she said, voice sharp. "The dragon doesn't force his inspiration on us. We have to be open to it. And if you trifle with what he gives, he may abandon you."

In my opinion, she was being overly dramatic, but since I wasn't a fool, I kept that thought to myself. "This is still the same idea. And you have to admit, it will be beautiful."

She stared at the glass pieces on the table, chewing her lip. Finally, she sighed. "Yes, it will. You can go ahead."

"Thank you!"

She kissed my forehead. "Still, I prefer the window you made for the Great Bookhouse. It could have been made by no one but you, and I know the Sage is thrilled with it."

"I had to give that to them because no one would buy it." I was still annoyed by that, but even apart from the oddity of some of my work, stained-glass windows were hard to sell. Most people couldn't afford even ordinary window glass, and those who could often didn't want to reduce the light by adding color. Unfortunately, stained-glass was the only work the dragon inspired in me. So, two months' work, and I'd had to give it away.

We were apparently finished. My mother untied her leather apron and lifted it over her head as I went to look at the window pieces again.

"A man was here asking for you," I said.

"Who?" she asked, voice muffled by the apron.

"I don't know. Miriv says you used to know him. By his accent, I think he was Lyzian." Lyz was the island closest to Kural. A number of their merchant ships had been in our harbor lately. "Maybe he wanted to buy glass." If my mother's distraction came from worry about the business, a new order might cheer her up. Not to mention making life easier for the rest of us.

The silence was so complete, I glanced back to make sure she hadn't left the room. She was still there, standing motionless, the apron twisted in her hands. Maybe it was an effect of the moonlight washing through the room's window, but her face looked ashen beneath its usual bronze color.

"Are you all right?" I asked.

She loosened her grip on the apron. "Of course. Tidy up." She went out to the main workshop, closing the door behind her.

So much for the idea that news about the Lyzian would make her less tense. Oh well. She'd settle down eventually.

I put away my various knives and files, hung up my apron, and followed her out to where a plate of scrambled eggs and a hunk of bread waited for me. As I wolfed them down, my thoughts turned to the ceremony that would happen on my birthday next month. With it, I'd earn the right to wear a crafter's ring. After that, I'd no longer be an apprentice. I'd be able to design my own patterns and projects with no one's approval. It was time. I was ready.

I washed my plate, put it away, and started up the stairs to my room. As I passed the set of rooms belonging to Miriv and my mother, my mother's tense voice penetrated the door. "But what's he *doing* here?"

"I told you, I don't know." Miriv sounded exasperated.

After a beat of silence, my mother said, "It's my night to watch the furnace."

The door jerked open, revealing her with Miriv close behind. My mother narrowed her eyes at me. "Did you want something, Emlin?"

"No, no." I backed away, embarrassed at having been caught eavesdropping.

"Go to bed." My mother turned back to Miriv. "You too." She kissed Miriv's cheek. I went on upstairs, and before I closed my door, I heard my mother climbing down to the workshop. Surely they'd been talking about the man Miriv met at the gate. Both of them were more upset than I'd have expected if he was just a customer, no matter how big an order he might place. But it was clear neither of them thought he was my business.

How interesting.

I WOKE FROM a dream of flying – a dragon dream – a sign the dragon asleep on the Heights was remembering the days he soared overhead. I wished I could go back to the dream, but I needed to use the privy. Reluctantly, I slid from under my warm covers, shoving my feet into my slippers before they touched the cold floor. I was almost all the way down the stairs when I saw my mother buttoning her cloak under her chin. I halted. She couldn't be leaving. It was her night to feed the glasshouse furnace. If it went out, it would take hours to grow hot enough to make glass again. She'd have docked the pay of anyone else who left that post.

To my utter disbelief, she opened the door and left. That went way beyond her dealing with something that made her tense. That was downright shocking.

As soon as the door closed, I rushed down the stairs, grabbed my own cloak from its hook, and followed her. Whatever the matter was, it had to be important for her to leave the furnace. The man at the gate flashed into my mind. Maybe she was going to meet him. I couldn't resist the chance to learn something about this man from her past. The mystery was just too enticing.

Fumbling to wrap myself in my cloak, I followed her as she walked rapidly along Wood Road until she reached the bottom of the steps leading up to Merchant Street, where the road narrowed up against the wall supporting the higher street.

A man emerged from the dark next to the steps. "Well met, Calea. How have you been?"

Sheltering in a house doorway, I recognized him as much by his Lyzian accent as by his appearance. Excitement bubbled in my chest.

"As Miriv undoubtedly told you," my mother said. "I don't want to see you."

That was not what I expected her to say.

"Just for a moment." He put his hand on her arm, but she shook off his touch.

"I have no time for you," she said. "None. Go away and

do it now or I'll call the Watch."

He backed off a yard. "I'm on Kural for a while," he said. "I'll try you again." Without waiting for an answer, he climbed the stairs to Merchant Street.

Not a customer, then. She'd sounded like she did when talking to me or Miriv. This was personal. In the back of my head, I'd been thinking he might be an old boyfriend. She'd had one or two in the years between my father's death and the blossoming of her affection for Miriv. If he was, she didn't have fond memories. I knew a bad breakup when I saw it.

My mother pulled her cloak tighter around her and walked on even faster than before, probably even more aware than I was of the furnace waiting to be fed in the glasshouse.

Now she led me into the big square in front of the palace. So she'd had a goal other than seeing the man. She crossed the square and spoke to one of the night guards while I pressed into the gap between two houses.

In the dark, the dragon-work wall around the palace glowed like a pink pearl. I hardly ever got to see it like this because I hardly ever went out at night. In one of my earliest memories, though, my mother was holding my hand in the square and telling me the tale of the dragon breathing fire over the palace soon after it was built. When the fire faded, she said, the glow remained, a sign that the first drake of Kural and his dragon were bonded, the way the fire and stone in the wall were. I'd been fascinated. She'd struggled to keep me away from the fire in the glasshouse furnace for days afterwards.

The palace guard opened the gate, and my mother vanished inside. Leftover rain on the cobblestones oozed through my slippers, making my toes curl up in protest. The moments slid past. The square remained quiet but, hidden behind the houses on the steep hill down to the beach, the surf pounded. I shifted, uncomfortable because, waiting like this, I couldn't avoid noticing that I still needed to use the privy.

In front of the palace, one of the guards moved, and I pulled farther back into shadows. He opened the gate, and my mother's voice pierced the dark. "Good night."

"Good night, Mistress Calea." The guard's voice bounced off the buildings surrounding the square.

Footsteps tapped across the cobblestones, and she appeared, walking briskly toward Merchant Street, apparently going straight back to the glasshouse. I still had no idea what had drawn her out tonight, and now I had new questions about the Lyzian man. Now though, I needed to beat her home. She'd be furious if she knew I'd gone out in my nightclothes, snooping on something she obviously meant to keep secret. If I waited until she struck off into Wood Road, then ran farther along Merchant Street, I could take the stone steps down the hill, and get there first.

I padded softly after her, keeping to the shadowy edge of the street. The shops lining it hunched in on themselves, quiet and dark. When we were almost to Wood Road, I sped up to draw close and be ready to run once she'd turned off. My foot skimmed over a broken cobblestone, sending a chunk rattled off into the dark.

She whirled to face me. "Emlin?"

From the mouth of an alley on the right, a patch of deeper darkness lunged out. My mother jerked away from it, but an arm shot out to hook around her waist and draw her close. She gave a choked-off scream and fell forward, thudding face first onto the street.

For a disbelieving moment, I froze. Then my body came to life, and I ran to them. The man planted a foot on either side of her hips. He grabbed her hair, yanked her head back, and put something to her throat. Starlight glinted off metal. I grabbed his arm, my hands closing around bunched muscle. He smelled of wood smoke. With an oath, he flung his arm wide, knocking me to the cobbles.

"Help!" I shrieked, scrambling to me feet. "Somebody help."

The man turned toward me, his brows black slashes over the top of the kerchief covering his mouth and nose. A spot of color gleamed like glass in the darkness: a stone red as a drop of blood in the earring at the top of his right ear. Warm fluid ran down my legs. Somewhere close by, a Watchman's whistle shrilled. Cursing, the man tore off into the darkness. I hurtled myself across the filthy street to where my mother lay, face up now, open eyes reflecting the stars.

"He's gone," I gabbled. "He's gone."

I laid one hand gently on her cheek, then stared at the dark smear I'd made. Now I saw the cut across her throat, saw the blood, black in the moonlight, the smell of it tingeing the night air like the metals the glasshouse used in its dyes. One of her hands lay in a puddle of it, fingers curled up like the petals of a flower.

I tried to scream again, but the blood smell had soaked up all the air in my chest. Then the breath came in a long, wobbly inhale, and I began to cry.

The Watchman's whistle sounded from the direction the running feet had gone. I pushed myself to sit up, snot running from my nose. "Help!" I shouted again, though part of me knew the moment when help would matter had passed.

Night Flights 1

Kural's dragon is dreaming of the color blue: the pale blue of a summer sky, the murky blue of the ocean after a storm. The blues swirl in his head like a contrapuntal song. He stirs and tries to shrug, but his wings are pinned.

Chapter 2

"E MLIN?"

Heart pounding, I startled awake to find my fellow glass maker Renie bending over me. The familiar slanted ceiling of my room rose above her. I blinked. What was she doing here? Hadn't she gone home? Light flooded through the window at the foot of the bed. It must be morning.

I stared at the bandage wrapped around her head, binding back her straight, dark hair and making her face look thinner than ever. Someone had been hurt... but it wasn't Renie, was it?

The previous night's events poured back into my memory. I sat up, gasping for air, pain clogging my throat. My mother was dead. Someone had killed her. That had really happened.

"I'm so sorry to disturb you," Renie said in her gentle voice. "A Watchman has come to ask you about last night. Miriv wants him to do it in Calea's—" She stopped and started again. "In the office with her there. Can you come down?"

I blinked at her, fishing for words that would make an

answer. My brain muddled through the problem. I finally swung my legs out from under the covers while Renie grabbed a shawl from the foot of the bed and draped it around my shoulders. My slippers had gone missing. I vaguely remembered Miriv carrying them away the previous night. The soles had been stained dark. I shuddered and gulped.

Renie helped me to stand, took my arm, and guided me out of my room as if I were an old woman. I felt like one, like pain had bent all my bones.

I clutched the rail as we went down two flights of stairs to my mother's office, where Miriv waited, her red shawl wrapped over the nightdress she'd been wearing when the Watch brought me home the previous night. Her face and body sagged. The door to the bedroom she'd shared with my mother stood open. The blankets were rumpled, but Miriv looked as if she hadn't slept at all.

She held a hand out to me and drew me into the chair next to hers. "Renie, would you bring the Watchman up?"

Face scrunched in worry, Renie left.

"What happened to her head?" I asked. It was stupid, but Renie being hurt confused me.

"A tile slipped off the roof while she was bringing wood in this morning." Miriv let go of my hand to pour me tea from the pot at her elbow. "How are you doing?"

The surface of my tea rippled, making me realize my hand was shaking. I set the cup on my mother's desk, then clasped my hands in my lap. "Those tiles are heavy."

"I know. She was lucky it just grazed her."

I caught myself thinking someone should tell my mother so she could order repairs. I closed my eyes, as if that would shut out the now-empty place where she had always been.

"I suppose I should see if there's a leak," Miriv said vaguely.

Miriv would have to run the glasshouse now, I realized. She'd been my mother's deputy. This would be her office now. Her rooms, alone.

A knock sounded at the door, and Renie escorted a Watchman in. He was gray haired and wore an officer's sash. In sending him, the Watch was treating this murder as important. Of course they were. My mother had been Kural's craftmistress. The Watchman's shoulders hunched as if he were uncomfortable.

"Is it all right?" He pointed to the chair on the other side of the desk. When Miriv nodded, he sat and took out a wax tablet, ready to make notes. He aimed his sober gaze at me. "Tell me what happened."

I stumbled through an account of what I'd seen. Miriv took my hand again, her grip so hard it hurt. I didn't explain why I'd gone after my mother, and he didn't ask. I wasn't sure I knew any more. The thing that had happened was so big that it wiped out everything else.

"So you didn't recognize him?" the Watchman said.

I shook my head. "He had a kerchief over his face. He wore an earring," I said, suddenly remembering. "With a red stone. In his right ear, I think."

The Watchman wrote it down without comment. Many men wore earrings. He was finding me useless. "This man who stopped her, could he have followed her to the square?"

"I don't know. I didn't see him go after her." I lifted my free hand helplessly. "You know who I mean, Miriv. The one who came to the gate. Who is he?"

She drew a breath and talked to the Watchman rather than me. "His name is Dain. Calea knew him years ago."

"Was there bad blood between them?" he asked.

"I don't think so," Miriv said. "He's Lyzian and hasn't been on Kural in years as far as I know."

"I'll talk to the palace guards. Maybe they saw the killer." He stood. From his pocket, he took something small and laid it on the desk. "I think this belongs to you now, lass."

I stared at my mother's crafter ring, the one she'd always worn on her right forefinger. Indeed, once the dragon accepted her as a crafter, the ring would have fit her finger tightly enough that she couldn't take it off. Around the outside curled the etching of a dragon. I'd never seen the inside, but I knew what was inscribed there too, the final words of our oath: *Ever faithful to my craft.* The cremation would have been this morning. Miriv and I weren't expected to go, of course, but the other glassmakers would have. The fire that consumed her body would have left the ring.

The Watchman said, "I'll let you know what I learn. I'm sorry to have disturbed you." He bowed and took his leave.

I clutched my mother's ring hard enough that it bit into my palm. Cold anger knotted in my chest. Whoever did this wasn't going to skip happily away into the rest of his life. Not if I had anything to say about it. "She knew this Dain?" I asked Miriv.

"Years ago. He might as well have been a stranger yesterday."

"But how did she know him? Were they enemies? Could he have wanted to hurt her?" I bit back a question about them being sweethearts because I was afraid it would hurt Miriv.

She shook her head. "I don't think so. When he came to the gate last night, he sounded... friendly."

"But my mother was angry when she talked to him."

"Emlin, believe me when I tell you that Dain is unlikely to have killed her," Miriv said. I wanted to ask more, but she was crying now.

"Do you want me to stay with you?" I asked. The tears swelling behind my own eyes were pressing hard. If they slipped out, I feared they'd go on forever. Miriv and I would weep in one another's arms endlessly, both of us broken open by our loss.

So, I was ashamed but relieved when Miriv said, "I'd like to be by myself for a while. Do you mind?"

"No. You do what you need to do." I hugged her and went back to bed, but not to sleep. I'd been right that once I started to cry, I wouldn't be able to stop.

I SPENT THE next month – the mourning month – crying, sleeping, and spinning questions in my head. The Lyzian man – Dain – the night he showed up, neither Miriv nor my mother had wanted to talk about him, at least not to me. That meant he mattered somehow. Maybe he was an old boyfriend, maybe not. Judging by my long knowledge of her, Miriv had told the truth when she said she didn't think he was the killer, but his appearance struck me as too big a coincidence to ignore. Had he worn a red earring? I wasn't sure. He could have followed her. He would have had time to hide in that alley while she was in the palace. And when she left, the guard had called her name loudly enough that he would have known she was coming. Something had drawn her out when she never should have gone. Someone wanted her alone in the dark where she'd be an easy target.

The day the mourning month ended, I got up, braided my hair, and dressed for work. It was time to get moving. I'd asked every day, but the Watchman hadn't come back yet. If he didn't come today, I'd go to Watch Headquarters and make them tell me what they'd found about Dain or her trip to the palace or anything else. I needed to know. I owed it to my mother to make sure that whoever hurt her paid a price.

At the last moment, I put on the blue glass beads my mother had made for me to wear on my seventeenth birthday, only a little over a week away now. At a ceremony then, I was supposed to take the oath, get a ring of my own, and become a fully-fledged crafter. That would be my deadline. Before I could move on, I would find my mother's killer.

Chapter 3

M IRIV WAS ALONE in the workshop when I came down
the stairs. I fell into her open arms. For a moment, we
stood that way. Then I pulled back, wiped my cheeks, and
said, "Let's make some glass."

"Eat first." Miriv put a bowl of porridge in my hands. I
ate quickly and escaped into my workroom before Renie
arrived from home or Gillis, who slept in the room below
mine, got up.

The glass I'd made before my mother was killed shone
on the table, right where I'd left it. The girl who'd worked
there then felt like a stranger to me. With care, I picked up a
piece. I'd blunted the edges after I cut them, but the many
tiny scars on my hands showed that glass had taught me to
treat it with respect. I fit the piece into the pocket of the lead
strip I'd cast in that other life, nestled it into its proper place,
and tapped four nails into the pattern board to keep it from
moving. Tension eased out of my shoulders. Shaping this
bright picture kept my mind away from other images
haunting my head.

From the workshop next door came the roar of the
furnace and the muffled talk of the other three women

blowing glass. I worked on. Cooler air and the smell of fish and seaweed washed through the open window behind me, telling me the tide was out. Eyes on my work, I chewed my lip and rolled a bead on my necklace against my breastbone, my fingers rasping over the tiny symbol on the biggest bead. C for Calea. My mother's mark. I reached for another piece of glass so I could not exactly forget her, but, I hoped, feel alive again myself.

The workroom door snapped open. "Emlin," Gillis began.

The glass piece slid from my fingers and pinged onto the table. "Dragon fire!" I bent to examine it, but my hand had been raised only an inch, and the piece looked unharmed. I spun to glare at Gillis in the doorway. As usual, dark curls had escaped from her fishbone braid. They clung to her flushed cheeks, still childishly round despite Gillis being only a month younger than I was. "Don't startle me like that!" I cried.

"Doo," she said, using a word she'd learned from the old granny who'd run the orphanage she'd lived in. "Doo" seemed to mean anything Gillis wanted it to. "The piece is all right, isn't it?" She stepped closer and eyed my window. "I knew you'd work again. You're too gifted to stop."

She was trying to smooth my ruffled feathers, of course. She was good at that with everyone, including me. Being angry at Gillis was as useless as being angry at a kitten. "I'm sorry I grouched at you. Did you want something?"

Her eyes widened. "There's a Watchman here to see you. Maybe they found the killer."

I gripped the edge of the table. "Did he say that?"

"No. Miriv asked, but he said he was here to talk to you." Gillis held the door to the workshop open and waved me toward it, face pink with excitement.

Before I could move, the same city Watchman who'd come before pushed past her. He pulled off his uniform cap. "Lass."

I held up my hand to ask him to wait. "Gillis," I said, "would you ask Miriv to come? She needs to hear this too."

"The new craftmistress?" the Watchman asked.

I nodded, not bothering to explain that Miriv and my mother had loved one another. It would be cruel to shut Miriv out.

Mouth pursed in a pout, Gillis went back into the workshop and, a moment later, Miriv came in. She closed the door and stood beside me. I wrapped my arm around her waist, noticing that her face had grown thinner in the last month, and the lines around her mouth had deepened.

"What have you learned?" I asked the Watchman.

"Not much, I'm afraid. No one else has reported trouble. We've concluded he was just a thug who saw a woman out on her own in the night and took his chance to rob or rape her."

Miriv rubbed her hand across her eyes.

"No," I said. "That's wrong."

He shrugged. "No other explanation fits."

"But he didn't try to rob her or... or do anything except kill her." I heard the shrillness in my voice as he edged a step backward. "She'd been in the palace. Did you ask them why she was there?"

"They said she was delivering glass."

"Not possible. She'd never leave the furnace just to make a delivery." I turned to Miriv. "Right?"

She shook her head. "There are no orders for them in the account book. I looked because I wondered the same thing."

"I have no reason to doubt the palace," the Watchman

protested.

I could well believe he didn't want to accuse the palace of lying to him. "How about Dain? Could he be connected?"

"He turned out to be the Lyzian trade representative," the Watchman said. "Given how long it had been since he last saw her, we don't think it's likely." He moved toward the door, ready to be done with this difficult conversation that I was making even harder.

Too bad for him. He wasn't the one who'd seen his mother murdered. "Is that all you're going to do?"

"It's natural to want something like this to make sense," he said, "but it doesn't. It was just one of those terrible things. I'm sorry." He yanked the door open and strode through.

I spun to face Miriv. I hadn't waited a month to be fluffed off like that. "The man is an idiot and a coward."

Miriv bit her lip. "Maybe he's right. Maybe she was just unlucky to be there when the killer was."

"I don't believe it." I thought of a question I'd mulled over during my mourning month. "She had something on her mind. Do you know what it was?"

"No, and believe me I've racked my brain. Whatever it was, she refused to talk about it." Miriv drew a wobbly breath and patted my arm. "It would be better for you to stop thinking about this if you can. Calea is gone. It's you I worry about now." She went back to the workshop, closing the door behind her.

I pressed my hands and forehead against the door. Just one of those terrible things. No. I had been there. I'd *seen* it. The man had gone straight for her. He'd been waiting. Waiting for *her*, not any random passer-by.

Miriv was worried about me – my inability to move on, I guessed. But I wanted, *needed*, to know who had killed her and why. The Watch had been no help. What could I do that they hadn't done?

I drifted to my worktable, eyeing the glass pieces waiting to be fitted into a pattern. I was good at that. Fitting bits into a whole was the form my dragon inspired work took. I just needed to do the same with pieces of information about my mother's death.

I rolled a bead against my chest. I could see if anyone at the palace would talk to me when they hadn't talked to the Watch. I'd met the steward when I last delivered glass to the palace. Maybe he'd see me.

And I'd find Dain and learn why he'd come to see my mother. I'd have to be careful. He could be dangerous. Someone certainly was.

A loud clang and cry erupted from the workshop, shattering my thoughts. I bolted into the bigger room. The furnace door hung crookedly from its lame hinge, and Gillis rocked on the floor, swishing her arm in the water bucket and jabbering, "Doo! Ow!"

Miriv bent to look at the arm, then glanced over her shoulder. "Run and get the salve and bandages, Renie. Hush, Gillis. You work with glass, you get burned." Her voice was firm, once again that of the new glasshouse craftmistress with responsibilities to see to.

Renie bounded up the stairs to Miriv's office. She must have come in while I was in my workroom because it was the first I'd seen of her since the morning after my mother was killed.

"I thought Kedry was sending the ironmonger to fix that door." I wrapped my leather apron around my hand and heaved the door back into place. So close to the furnace, the warm-soup heat of the workshop made me dizzy. Kedry owned the glasshouse and was lucky my mother and Miriv were both honest managers, because he neglected the place shamefully.

"He must have forgotten," Miriv said.

"Again," I said.

Renie came running back with bandaging, a towel, and a jar of salve. She handed them to Miriv.

"Let me see, Gillis." Miriv drew Gillis's arm from the water and patted it dry.

Gillis pressed her lips together and made muffled squeaky noises. She had a right to, in my opinion. The red streak on the back of her forearm was already lifting in a puffy blister.

"It's all right, Gillis," Renie said soothingly. "The salve will help." She came next to me to watch Miriv treat Gillis's burn. I felt better just having her close by. Three years ago, Renie had married and moved out of the glasshouse to live with her husband, Tae. I still missed her gentle presence. The first time I liked a boy who didn't like me back, it had been Renie I turned to for sympathy.

True to form, she asked, "Are you all right?"

"I'll be fine. How's your head?"

"It's healed except for an annoying scab that tears if I'm not careful when I brush my hair." Renie touched my shoulder. "I take it the Watchman didn't tell you anything useful."

I glanced at Miriv, still frowning over Gillis's arm. She had enough worries without knowing what I meant to do. I maneuvered Renie into the corner near the furnace. "Do you know anything about my mother and a Lyzian named Dain?" I murmured.

She too dropped her voice. She was six years older than I

was, but she'd been young when she came to the glasshouse and remembered well enough what it was like to need secrets. "I never heard of him. I'm sorry." Her forehead scrunched. "I know she was preoccupied. I thought she might have a project on her mind, but then she went to see the Sage which made me think she wanted counsel, so I left it alone. Truthfully, I thought it might be about you or Miriv."

"She went to see the Sage? When was that?"

"Maybe two days before she was killed."

I mentally added visiting the Sage to the list of things to do. I couldn't see how yet, but maybe knowing what was on her mind might help me find her murderer.

Miriv ran her finger around the bottom of the salve jar to scrape out the last onion-scented fingerful to spread across Gillis's arm. "Emlin, if you're ready to go out again, it's your turn to do the marketing. If not, I can do it."

"I'll go." I untied my apron. The market was in the palace square, so a visit there would give me a chance to start my hunt by asking the gate guards some questions.

"Kedry is coming by in two days to pay us. I'll talk to him about the furnace," Miriv said. "The roof tile too."

"Good." The idea of leaving the hinge broken and roof unrepaired even for two extra days made me wild. There should at least be order inside the glasshouse. When I was six, I'd once grabbed a poker and tried to run after two neighbor boys who'd thrown stones at our gate. I felt that same frantic protectiveness now.

Miriv pushed a strand of gray-threaded hair behind her ear and stood up.

Gillis rose too, face brightening. "When you're in the market, would you buy jaja fruit? I hear the Rhythian ship finally brought some in." That was Gillis. Emotions washed through her and were gone like summer storms. I'd always thought that readiness to feel was what gave her glasswork such emotional appeal.

I hung up my apron, then fished in the bowl where the three of us who lived in the glasshouse kept our shared food money. I had to chase a coin across the bowl's bottom and up the side, trying to hook my fingernail under it. Not much there. Good thing we'd all be paid soon. My mind on what I might ask at the palace, I grabbed the marketing basket and found Miriv blocking my way, holding out two gulls.

"From the glasshouse funds," Miriv said. "When you're in the market, buy some Lyzian burn salve."

"The Lyzians are making medicines again? I thought their crafthouse closed."

"The rumor is it's open again," Miriv said. "If it's the same as it used to be, no one can match their salves."

If Dain was the Lyzian trade representative, maybe their reopened crafthouse was why he was on Kural. I considered whether in visiting my mother, Dain could have been just a man looking up an old friend while he was here. No, I decided. Miriv and my mother had sounded too strained when they talked about him.

Behind Miriv, Renie had picked up a blowpipe, ready to gather molten glass to shape into one of the vases she and Gillis had evidently been making. Gillis was already chirping about something, only occasionally twitching her burned arm, as if trying to shake off the pain.

"I'll see what they have." I went out into the yard, then ducked back in again. "Did Kedry pay the sand merchant? There's not much out here, and you know he won't deliver again until he has his money."

Miriv blew out her breath. "I'll ask him."

"Curse the man." I skirted the shrunken sand pile, heading across the yard. Our gateposts still fluttered with white mourning ribbons. In the space between the posts, I halted. This would be the first time I left the glasshouse since I saw my mother murdered. The good part of the world, the part that sheltered my friends and my work, the dragon-blessed part lay at my back. Someone had harmed not just my mother, not just me, but us, and that needed to be set right. I touched one of the blue beads on my chest and started for the market.

Chapter 4

WHEN I CLIMBED the last step to Merchant Street, a man stepped out of the shadows in front of a shop selling fine leatherwork imported from the crafthouse on Bria Island. "Fair afternoon. It's Emlin, isn't it?"

My heart kicked against my ribs. It was as if he'd emerged from my blood-soaked memories. I'd seen him only on the day my mother died, but I recognized that high-cheekboned face, that curly dark hair. Dain. I flicked my gaze to his right ear. He wore no earring now, and I'd have to get closer to see if the top of it was pierced.

This was good, I told myself over the sound of my pulse panicking in my ears. I wanted to talk to him. I'd just been planning to talk to the palace first. I looked along the street behind him and felt reassured to see a pair of women heading off toward the market and a young man in a scholar's gray tunic drooling over the goods in the pastry shop's window. I wasn't alone on a dark street this time.

I managed to make my mouth move around some words. "What are you doing here? What do you want?"

Dain patted the air between us. "Easy. All I want is to talk to you."

I tightened my grip on the marketing basket's handle. "How do you know my name?"

He gave me a smile he probably meant to be unthreatening. Up close, I could see his teeth were pale pink, suggesting that he'd once chewed thoi, though he didn't smell of it now. "I asked around. I used to know your mother. Perhaps she mentioned me? Dain?"

"Never."

He shook his head. "You look so much like her, I'd have known you as hers anywhere."

"You saw her that night. You were waiting for her." *The way you were waiting for me just now.*

"Ah. Well, yes. As I say, I used to know her. I can't tell you how sorry I am about what happened to her, and how much I regret letting her walk away alone that night." The space between his brows wrinkled. "Does the Watch know who killed her?"

A good question. Maybe he was worried that they suspected him. "They've decided it was just a street thief."

Behind him, the young scholar bumped into a woman leaving the pastry shop. "Sorry! Sorry!" he cried and scrambled to help her scrape up the cake that had fallen from her basket.

"She didn't seem happy to see you," I ventured.

Dain grimaced. "Things may have ended badly between us. Man-woman things, you know." He cocked his head. "But perhaps you're too young to know these things don't always work out. You're what, fifteen?"

"Not quite seventeen," I said stiffly. I wasn't sure if he'd killed my mother, but as I'd suspected, they'd parted on bad terms. I didn't find that reassuring.

He dragged his hand down his face and seemed to think

27

for a moment. "Listen, I'm on Kural for a while as the trade representative from Lyz. For Calea's sake, I'd like to get to know you. I've rented a place on the road zigzagging down the hill to the harbor. The house with the purple front. You know it? I don't think Miriv will let me near the glasshouse, but maybe you can come and visit me."

Meeting him in private seemed like a bad idea. "I could do that. We could maybe go for a walk."

"Good," Dain took a half-step closer. "I regret not protecting Calea, and I feel as if I owe it to her to do better by you. If you ever feel unsafe, you're welcome to come to me." He put a hand on my shoulder.

My whole body stiffened.

"Excuse me," a pleasant male voice said, and Dain snatched his hand away.

I looked past him to see the scholar, a smile crinkling the corners of his gray eyes. "Am I going the right way to reach the Great Bookhouse?" He extended his hand to me, making a bony wrist stick out of a sleeve with a smear of cake near the cuff. "I'm Addy, visiting from the little one in Vinan. Little bookhouse, I mean. In Vinan. I'm pleased to meet you."

Automatically, I put my hand in his and had it enthusiastically pumped. It was probably good the boy held onto it extra long. My knees were so wobbly, I wasn't sure I'd have stayed upright otherwise. I hated myself for letting Dain frighten me. "I'm Emlin. This is Dain." It felt unreal to be introducing this man I didn't know and still suspected of murdering my mother.

With an eyebrow raised, Dain let Addy shake his hand too an extra four or five times.

"I'm sorry to interrupt," Addy said. "You two are probably heading for the market or something, but if you could give me directions first, I'd take it as a kindness."

Dain smiled and stepped aside. "Emlin can tell you. I need to be on my way. Remember what I said, Emlin. The house with the purple front above the harbor." He strolled off and vanished into the leather goods shop.

Air flowed back into my lungs. I cleared my throat. "You want the Great Bookhouse?" I pointed ahead to where the palace tower rose over the surrounding rooftops, the gape-mouthed gold dragon at its top glinting in the sun. "The bookhouse is on the other side of the palace. If you use the tower as a marker, you should be able to find it."

He grimaced. "I already tried that and got hopelessly turned around, which is how I wound up here. There are so many more people here than in Vinan."

I couldn't help smiling. Being from Vinan would explain why he was turned around in Kural City. Vinan was in the most rural part of Kural Island. There were jokes about Vinanians not knowing how to find a public privy in the city or what to do on their wedding night. "I'm going as far as the palace square. You can come with me if you like, and I can point you on from there."

"Thank you." He sounded relieved.

I had to admit I felt some relief too. Dain evidently didn't want to talk in front of someone else, which meant that with this boy's company as a shield, I could reorganize my scrambled brain and plan what to do. With Addy loping along at my side, I strode away from the shop where Dain had gone. Grief burned behind my eyelids as we crossed the place where my mother died. I was going to learn who killed her. I was going to make him suffer.

Chapter 5

"I APOLOGIZE AGAIN for interrupting you and your friend," Addy said.

"He's not my friend." When Addy raised an eyebrow, I remembered Dain's hand on my shoulder. "He knew my mother," I added, apparently shortly enough to discourage more questions.

We moved from the cheese maker's stall to the baker's, where I handed over a gull and stowed flat discs of bread in my basket. Food shopping first, then talk to whoever would see me at the palace. And the burn salve, I reminded myself. I wasn't sure where that booth was. I'd keep an eye out.

"You probably want to know why I've come to town, though you're too polite to ask," Addy said.

"I assumed you might want to see more of the world than the Vinan bookhouse. Maybe it's a little, um, dull?"

"Oh, no. Well, yes, sometimes it's dull, but that's not why I'm here. I'm supposed to look for books we don't yet have in Vinan." He waved in the general direction of the harbor. "Some of them come off the trading ships. I thought I'd look at the ruins on the Heights while I'm here too. Never pass up a chance to learn, eh?"

I had to smile at his enthusiasm. It was soothing to be in the company of someone who knew nothing about what had happened. It felt like permission to forget for a while. "I expect the Sage buys anything worth having, assuming they can afford it."

"Bookhouses aren't what they once were on any of the islands," Addy said. "It's a pity. Every island's dragon loves learning. Where are we going now?"

"To buy jajas."

"I love jajas," he said, surprising me not at all. Everyone loved the luscious fruit, and it was hard to come by.

As I expected, the jaja merchant's pennant fluttered over a booth near the palace gates. A handful of would-be buyers hung about nearby, but the table was empty, and the fruit seller was nowhere in sight.

"Is that the palace?" Addy gawped at the building, which had to be the biggest he'd ever seen. "Why aren't the walls glowing?"

"They are. It's just hard to see in daylight."

"The Vinanian sage wants me to look at the palace library if I can. Will the guards let me in?"

"I doubt it. As you'd expect, they don't like strangers wandering around the palace." I approached the gate guard, my palms growing clammy. "Excuse me," I began, trying to sound casual. "I heard there'd be jajas for sale today. Do you know if that's true?" I'd decided to start the conversation with something trivial.

The guard looked at me sideways and down his nose. I thought he wasn't going to answer, but grudgingly, he said, "Trouble unloading them at the docks I hear."

That seemed only too likely. My mother had complained endlessly about how badly the harbor repairs were going. The guard's voice tickled something in the back of my mind. "Weren't you on duty here the night my mother – Craftmistress Calea – died?"

Next to me, Addy let out a soft grunt.

The guard grimaced. "What of it?"

"Did she say why she'd come so late?" I heard the urgency in my voice and bit my lip. I didn't want to sound accusatory.

He looked away. "Delivering glass, she said."

I still found it hard to believe she'd leave the furnace just to make a delivery, but I supposed she could have told the guard that. "Do you know who she saw?"

He shook his head. "She'd come with glass before. I just let her in." His voice was tight too. He knew he'd sent her name echoing around the square.

"Could you send word to the steward that I'd like to speak to him? Tell him it's Emlin, Calea's daughter." When he hesitated, I added, "I know him. He'd want to see me, I'm sure."

"I'll send word," he said. "Come back in a while and see what he says."

"Thank you." If anyone could answer my questions, it would be the steward.

I turned to leave. Addy must have heard our conversation because the space between his brows was wrinkled with sympathy. Somewhat surprisingly, he had the sense to hold his tongue.

"We're almost where you want to go," I said. "If you take the street that runs through the archway there and then the second left, you'll come to the Great Bookhouse."

He looked where I pointed. "Would you mind if I tagged along a little more before I go? A country boy like me won't get another chance to see Kural City." He turned to look at the palace tower again, and as he did, he managed to back into me. Fending him off, I skipped out of the way. He wore scuffed boots rather than the polished shoes I'd seen on scholars from the Great Bookhouse. "Sorry," he said wearily, like a man who'd said that a lot. "I apologize for my clumsiness. I offended a dragon as a child, and I sometimes think it's a dragon's idea of a…" He trailed off as if groping for the right word.

"Punishment?" I suggested.

"Joke," he said sourly.

I could see why a young man might find perpetual clumsiness humiliating. He had broad shoulders under his baggy grey tunic, and he smelled faintly and rather pleasantly of some spice I didn't recognize.

"Anyway, do you mind if I stick with you for a while?" He flashed me a gleam-toothed smile. "I won't be a nuisance, I promise. I'll carry your packages and tell you scholarly secrets." He reached for my basket, but fumbled and grabbed it only just before it hit the cobblestones. "Would you believe I did that on purpose?"

I was so elated at the prospect of seeing the steward that Addy's sad joke actually made me laugh, but I took the basket away from him anyway while the bread and cheese I'd bought were still in it. "Tempting as that is, I haven't any use for scholarly secrets. You can help me find a Lyzian medicine booth."

We strolled along between a hodge-podge of old-clothes dealers, egglers, cobblers, and flower sellers. As usual, children mobbed the booth selling toys from Velir Island's crafthouse. Voices called to us from both sides, offering bargains. I waved to merchants I knew, but didn't stop.

"You're a glassmaker?" Addy's gaze roamed the booths ahead. "I have that right?"

"I am."

"Have you ever seen the Dragonshard necklace Drake Haron wears? For a glass crafter, I imagine that would be a special thrill. Glass made by Kural's dragon itself."

"Our Drake Haron only wore it for the Flame Testing, and that was before I was born. I assume it's locked up in the tower treasure room. You're right that I wish I could see it though." The pieces of the Dragonshard necklace had been formed on the Heights long ago when Kural's dragon sent molten rock rolling down the hillside. The necklace burned anyone who wrongfully claimed to be Kural's drake. What would it feel like if I touched it? Would I sense the dragon's complex, brilliant mind? I didn't know whether I was more excited or frightened at the prospect.

"In Vinan, people say Drake Haron is ailing," Addy said, "so maybe you'll have a chance to see the necklace when his son becomes drake."

"It's true that Haron's been ill for months, but he's tough."

"So, people have seen him? Have you?"

"Of course not. We're not talking about the mayor of Vinan."

"Sorry. I'm just worried about him."

I immediately felt guilty for squashing him. Truthfully, I found his earnestness charming. "I judge Haron will hang on a while yet." Ahead, I spotted a booth displaying what were unmistakably medicines.

Addy gestured down a side aisle. "If you don't mind, I see something down there that I want."

"Go ahead." He ducked out of sight as I approached the

Lyzian booth. A boy and girl in blue tunics stood behind it. The girl was handing a paper packet to a woman clutching the hand of a small boy. "Chew one every day now," the Lyzian said. "That's the only way to be sure you won't conceive."

Her customer nodded, tucked the packet out of sight, and quickly led the little boy away.

Well, that medicine was new. Assuming the girl wasn't a fraud.

She and the boy both smiled as I drew nearer. "Can I help you?" The boy waved at the bottles, jars, and packets on their table, inviting me to choose.

I eyed their tunics. If they were frauds, they were bold ones in claiming to be crafters. The boy especially had nerve. There used to be more men crafters, and there was no reason the dragon shouldn't call them, but no one *had* to answer the dragon's call and Dolyan parents usually wanted their boys to take over family businesses. Over the years, crafting had come to be seen as women's work. I didn't mind. I rather liked living with other women. "I heard you have burn salve."

"I do have it." The girl picked up a jar and unstoppered it to show me green goo. "Two gulls."

I handed over the coins and stowed the jar in my basket. "Isn't that a crafthouse tunic? Is the medicine house on Lyz open again?"

"It is. Has been for about a month now." She beamed.

"Are you one of the medicine makers?" I tried not to sound accusatory, but if she wasn't, then she shouldn't be wearing the tunic.

"I'm an apprentice. Lyz's dragon breathed its visions into me a few days after the crafthouse opened."

"Into me too," the boy added. He'd undoubtedly noticed

35

that I was ignoring him.

"Then how are you here on Kural?" I knew I sounded scandalized, but Dolyan crafters were bonded to their island's dragon. The crafter had to be from that island for the bond to form. Dolyan law forbade their leaving the island where their dragon slept.

"Our new drake, Jaffen, says we can move around if we want," the boy said. "He says the law about not leaving an island came long after the first dragon riders and was made by drakes afraid of losing the money their crafters brought in."

I was shocked all the way to my toes. They had to be fraudulent. "He has nerve to gainsay that law. It's dragon-given." The girl opened her mouth to answer, but I marched away without listening. The gall of Drake Jaffen!

Addy met me where he'd left me and fell into step. As he drew near, I noticed again his faintly spicy smell. He'd bought a paper twist of honeyed nuts which he held out to me. When I shook my head, he scooped a handful for himself. "Are we going back to the palace now?" He cocked his head like a bright-eyed magpie.

As pleasantly as he smelled, his presence might put the steward off of talking to me. "Can you find your way to the Great Bookhouse from here? You don't need to come with me."

He wasn't listening. Instead, he frowned at the palace tower, visible over the market booths. "There's something going on over there."

As soon as he said it, I realized the raised voices I'd been hearing weren't just normal market noise. Nearby shoppers were lifting their heads and cocking an ear. An old man took the elbow of the gray-haired woman with him and hustled her away.

"Maybe I'll come along to see what's happening," Addy said.

Alarmed now, I hurried down the row of stalls and emerged to see a line stretched from the jaja booth near the palace gates all the way to the foot of the fountain, so close that when the breeze puffed in off the harbor, the stone fish in the fountain blew water down the necks of those people craning to see the front of the line. The single palace guard on duty before had been joined by three more, all watching the crowd warily.

Addy looked from one end of the line to the other. "Are you sure you want jajas?"

"No." *Sorry, Gillis.* "I do have to talk to that guard though."

He grimaced but nodded. I found that with the crowd rumbling, I was glad of his company after all.

I plunged into the square and moved toward the gate, trying to skirt the edge of the line, which grew more ragged every moment. I halted in front of the guard who'd promised to send word to the steward half afraid he might have no time for me now, but he spoke right away.

"The steward says Mistress Calea didn't come to see him, and he doesn't know what glass she might have brought."

Behind me, a man somewhere in line shouted. "I heard there aren't really going to be any jajas here."

The guard's gaze darted in the direction of the voice.

"That makes no sense," I said. "She told you she was delivering glass."

"I don't know what to say," the guard said.

The man hidden in the crowd shouted again. "All the jajas that were unloaded went to the big houses on the hill. I saw them being carted off." A growl arose from the thick column of people.

Addy scrunched the paper around the nuts he'd bought and stuffed them into his old-fashioned belt pouch. "Emlin, maybe we should get out of here."

I'd be hanged if I'd give up so quickly. "She must have talked to someone. Who was it?" I asked the guard.

"Here they come!" someone cried.

Close by, on my left, a large handcart heaped with jajas lumbered out from an aisle of booths. "That's all?" the man who'd been shouting bellowed. "That's not enough."

The line dissolved into a mass of shoving people. I scrambled to keep my feet, but rough hands pushed me toward the cart. Faced by the mob, the man steering the cart turned and fled. Under the pressure of bodies, the cart rocked, and then, through a gap in the crowd, I saw Addy fall against it and tip it all the way over. Fruit spilled out.

A whistle shrilled, and palace guards poured through the gates, clubs raised in their hands. There were so many that they had to have seen the trouble coming. People started running. My heart sped up. Things had just gone from mess to menace.

"Which way are you going?" Addy came panting out of the fray.

I pointed, and he took my arm. We struggled through the thickening stream of panicked people. He yanked me to the right and threw a sharp elbow at a muscular oaf who'd nearly bowled into us. But the oaf was too terrified to back away. He barreled into Addy, knocking him flying. As he was launched backward, Addy shoved me out of the tangle. I bounced off a thick-set matron and lurched to my hands and knees, wrist scraping through the handle of my marketing basket. A foot slammed onto my basket, crushing a corner. A man sprawled across me, knocking me flat. I choked from terror and the weight of him on my back. He grabbed my braid to haul himself across me, making fire sear my scalp. Something tugged at my throat. The man scrambled to his feet and ran. The pressure on my throat gave way, and my mother's blue glass beads bounced off the broken string and rolled under the trampling feet of the crowd.

Chapter 6

"**N**o!" WITH ONE hand, I grabbed the beads still on their string and with the other snatched for the ones that had come off. A boot smashed down, turning a bead to splinters. I was scrambling frantically to where blue glimmered in the crack at the foot of the palace wall, when someone clutched my upper arm and hauled me upright. A guard I didn't recognize raised his club, ready to swing. His eyes were wild, his breath heaving.

Dizziness swept over me; a flash of the same terror I'd felt when my mother's killer stood over me.

From nowhere, Addy lurched against him, knocking him into the palace wall. "Sorry!" Addy cried. He hipped me aside and grabbed the guard's elbow. "People are trying to break down the gate. They need you." He shoved the guard hard, and they both vanished in the churning mob. The crowd was breaking up and fleeing the square. A man ran past me, cradling an armful of jajas and chased not by a palace guard but by a city Watchman. The Watchman stopped long enough to say, "Get out of here!"

"I have to look for my beads!"

"Now!" He pushed me toward Merchant Street, and

when I stopped, he pushed again. "Go!"

I took one last look at the cobblestones and ran for home. No doubt about it. Some of my mother's beads were as lost as their maker. I hoped Addy would be all right.

People occasionally raced past me, all going away from the square. The noise of the riot faded in the distance. Astonishingly, the basket still dangled from my wrist, still holding the salve. The cloth-wrapped bread had snagged on the broken wicker, though the cheese was gone. Gradually, my heart slowed along with my footsteps. But my shoulders sagged with relief when I entered the safety of the glasshouse yard.

I skirted the sheds of firewood, soda ash, lime, and sand mixed with ground quartz pebbles from Kural's north shore. The glasshouse's door stood open and the shutters were folded back against the stone walls, inviting any breeze to sweep away the heat of the furnace. So, there was nothing to muffle Miriv's raised voice.

"It's not right! It's not just!"

I paused in the doorway. Despite the open windows, the sprawling workshop simmered with heat, but the real fire in the room came from Miriv, who was facing down the slick-haired man whose back was to me. Kedry, the man who owned the glasshouse. Renie and Gillis huddled together on the other side of the stone marver table. Renie's face was even paler than usual, and she had her arm around Gillis, who was twisting her hands, her eyes huge. Miriv rounded the table, closing in on Kedry.

"It's not right," Miriv said again. "We've earned those wages, and I know we've sold enough that you can afford to pay them."

"You know nothing of the kind." Kedry spoke with calm

self-assurance. "Anyone in town who ever loaned money is calling in debts. They're worried about that young fool Drake Jaffen on Lyz, who seems bent on taking over every island he can."

I dodged around Kedry and *thunked* the basket onto the table. "You're not going to pay us?"

"Of course I'm going to pay you." Kedry rolled his eyes as if I'd said something idiotic. He mopped his forehead with a lace-trimmed handkerchief, grimaced at its sodden state, and shook the cloth off his fingers onto a nearby shelf jammed with jars of metals for coloring glass.

"He says he'll pay us but less than he's supposed to," Miriv said.

"You're lucky I'm paying you at all," Kedry said. "I should shut this place down. My time would be better spent running one of my father's estates."

For a moment, no one moved but Kedry, who flapped his elbows, unsticking his ribs from the sweat circles on his shirt. Even my tongue was briefly paralyzed by shock. "You'd throw us all out?"

"If you shut your mouth and take what I give you, I won't have to."

"The glasshouse is a gift from Kural's dragon," I tried. "It's not just yours. It's Kural Island's. Closing it would be irreverent."

"I can't help that," Kedry said. "I have to think about myself."

I took a step toward him but stopped, overwhelmed by the smell of his hair oil. I ran a deliberately contemptuous gaze down his yellow silk shirt and trousers. "Which is undoubtedly why you saved enough money to pay your tailor."

Miriv sucked in her breath, and with one part of my mind, I didn't blame her. I was being rude to the man who employed us all. But he'd been rude first, and I'd been afraid enough today. This man had been given a sacred trust and he was treating it as if he could toss it away like an old shoe. Not to mention he was talking about our home and our jobs.

Kedry's face turned purple and not from the heat. "You think you could do better?" He fished a key from his pocket and held it out. "I'd like to see you deal with stingy buyers and greedy suppliers. See how you do when bill collectors start knocking on your door day and night."

The roar of the furnace washed away all other sound. I stared at the key, a sign of ownership by every custom in the Dolyan Islands. A shaft of escaped firelight gleamed off the curly metal end.

"Go ahead," Kedry said. "Take it." He was so sure we wouldn't do it, so sure he and only he owned the glasshouse like he owned that gaudy shirt, like we had nothing to do with what happened here.

I snatched the key and knotted my hand around it. Pulse pounding in my ears, I met Kedry's startled gaze with a look I hoped was less surprised than I felt.

Kedry licked his lips. "I'm happy to be rid of the place." He stalked from the room.

I gaped after him. What had I done?

For a moment, no one moved. Then Gillis and Renie trailed around the sides of the table.

"Couldn't you have waited two days for some money, Emlin?" Gillis cried. "He'd have paid us something anyway. Doo! Now what are we supposed to do?"

"He might not have held that key out in two days," I said.

"If he's short on coin for the bills, he probably wanted

you to take it. But would it have hurt to wait and see?" Miriv slumped against the table, looking weary, as she had since my mother died. She frowned at the crushed basket on the table. "What happened to that?"

"There was trouble in the market, a riot really. I fell and someone stepped on it." An image popped into my mind of the club-wielding guard looming over me. I shuddered. If Addy hadn't blundered along, my blood might be spattered on the cobblestones of the palace square, the way my mother's had been. I dug shaking hands into my pocket for change from the shopping. My fingers met the smooth curve of a bead. I flinched.

Miriv pushed herself erect, probably reading the distress in my face. "Are you hurt?"

"No. I couldn't buy the jajas, though. Sorry, Gillis." I eased the coins around the beads and dropped them in their bowl.

"No wonder you were ready to snap at Kedry," Miriv said. "I never should have sent you out so soon."

"I'm all right. I admit it was frightening, but it's over."

"You're still upset," Miriv said. "I can see it."

Renie came up next to me and hugged me. "I think Emlin was right to take the key. What she said about this place being a gift from our dragon is true. Closing a crafthouse is disastrous for an island. Look at what happened on Lyz when its medicinehouse closed. Their crops failed for two years running, and a plague killed half the pigs on the island."

"Oh," I said, "Lyz's crafthouse is open again, just as Miriv said. I met two Lyzians who claimed to be new apprentices."

Everyone turned toward me, interested in this news about fellow crafters. "So the rumor was right," Miriv said.

"Their dragon is calling again? And a boy responded this time."

"So they said. But they also said they were allowed to leave Lyz, so I don't know how reliable they are." I pulled the basket toward me on the table and handed the jar of salve to Miriv. "Gillis will have to tell us how good their work is."

As Miriv unstopped the jar and offered it to Gillis to sniff, I recalled the apprentices weren't the only Lyzians I'd met today. It would be better not to tell Miriv about Dain waylaying me though. She was already worried about me, and obviously I still meant to question him.

"Is Emlin going to run things now?" Gillis's face puckered. "Is that what it means that she has the key?"

My voice came out shakier than I might have wished. "That wouldn't be right. Miriv's been running things since…" I trailed off.

Miriv groaned. "Emlin, I appreciate your faith in me, but—"

"She's right," Renie said. "You take the orders, and make sure we have the right supplies, and schedule all the work, and keep the order books."

Miriv ran a hand over her face, then took the key I held out. "I'll see what I can do."

"So we'll be paid all we're owed?" Renie asked. "Tae will want to know, and—" She smiled hopefully. "Maybe we'll need it." She wove her fingers protectively over her stomach.

"You're pregnant?" I managed not to add "again." Renie had been pregnant twice in the last three years, but had lost the baby each time. I'd held her when she cried for the last one.

"I think so," Renie said.

"That's wonderful!"

"Let's find out," Miriv said. "Emlin, run up to my office and get the order book and my slate."

I hurried up to the craftmistress's rooms on the first landing, pulled the current order book from its shelf, and rushed back down to the workshop. We gathered around the marver table while Miriv found the page with the current orders and chalked numbers onto the slate. I craned my neck to watch as she added them.

Miriv read the resulting number aloud, then tapped the chalk on the table. "That should have been plenty to cover our expenses." She frowned. "Kedry was entitled to some profit, of course, but if he hasn't paid the bills, he was skimming off more than his due. I'll have to see all our suppliers and find out if what Kedry said was true. If they're unwilling to let us run any debt at all, we're in bad trouble. But maybe they'll take some partial payment if they know we're running things ourselves."

She straightened, spine popping. "I'll also have to look at how much we have coming in. The goods going to Rhyth are supposed to be on that ship by the day after tomorrow. That will bring in some coin, but I can't know yet if it will be enough."

The four of us stood in silence. "Maybe we could give the key back," Gillis said softly.

"No!" I said. "The window I'm making for the drake of Rhyth isn't promised until next month, but I had a lot of the work done before, well, before, and I made good progress this morning. If I work overnight, I can finish it, and it'll have time to dry, so we can send it on this month's ship instead."

"Are you sure?" Miriv said.

I hesitated. Finishing the window early would be a stretch, but I was the one who'd grabbed that key. I ran my gaze over my fellow crafters – grieving Miriv, maybe pregnant Renie, orphan Gillis. If the glasshouse closed, only Renie would have a place to live, and none of us would be able to earn a living. My mother was gone, but I still had my glasshouse family, and I meant to keep them. "I'm sure."

Gillis marched to the shelves and pulled out the fumigant we'd bought to rid the workshop of sand fleas that had ridden in on a delivery the previous month. With her fingertip, she hooked Kedry's sweaty handkerchief off the shelf and onto the floor. She sprinkled it with the powder, and to cheers and a sneeze from Renie, she kicked it out the door. "There. Done with Kedry," Gillis declared.

But as Miriv turned away, I glimpsed worried lines between her brows.

I thought there were probably some between mine too.

Chapter 7

I COULDN'T QUITE believe it, but we'd claimed the glasshouse for our own. Now we just had to keep it afloat.

I put the order book and slate away, then ran farther up the stairs, past Gillis's room to my own, high under the eaves. I had to scuttle sideways along the foot of the narrow bed, neck crooked to avoid the slanting roof. From the chest in the corner, I dug out the carved walnut box that held, among other treasures, my mother's crafter's ring. Carefully, I transferred the beads from my pocket to the box. They clicked together and nestled in a folded shawl like a clutch of robin's eggs. I counted them, then sat back on my heels, listening to the sparrows twitter outside the open window. I'd lost five. I prodded the beads in the box and was relieved to see the one with my mother's mark. I fit the box back into the chest next to her private work journal, where she'd sketched ideas for glass dreams she'd never make now.

Back in the workshop, I found Renie packing the items for Rhyth in small barrels full of straw. With Gillis's help, Miriv was making glass gulls, perched on rocks, wings lifted for takeoff. I slowed to watch. Gillis twirled a glob of molten glass on the end of the blowpipe, rolled it on the marver table until it took on the shape Miriv wanted, then laid it over the elongated arms of the chair in which Miriv sat. Miriv pulled a wooden paddle from the water bucket and prodded the glass, wisps of steam rising to dampen the dark hair on her temples. She nodded, and Gillis blew into the pipe, inflating the gather.

Better Gillis than me. Not that Miriv was likely to ask for my help. The last time I worked on gulls, I'd been the one shaping them until I let my mind wander and twisted one's wings into spirals. My fingers itched with dragon inspiration when I did it, but Miriv had scolded me. I had nothing against the gulls. I just found them boring to make.

Mind already on my window, I passed through into my workroom and closed the door behind me, muting the noise and heat of the furnace. Settling my leather apron over my head, I walked to the big table in the center of the workroom, and inspected my window, ticking off to myself what I still needed to do.

In a sea of the glasshouse's special – and very expensive – blue, circles of clear glass showed each of the twelve Dolyan Islands, stretching from Lyz in the far west to Basur, closest to the Cambyrian mainland in the east. I'd made the islands clear so when light shone through them, they'd look like the stars in the Dragon constellation whose pattern they echoed. And I'd stretched a green and gold dragon over the island chain. The first dragon riders had seen the stars' inverted image in the islands when they flew from their home in the Westlands. The riders had taken it as a sign and settled there, one Drake or Drakaina to each, with their dragons nesting in the islands' peaks.

In the war-torn Westlands, the dragons had searched for these learned, creative men and women, called them together, and fanned their longing for a world that valued knowledge and art rather than power. Sharing their dragons' ancient minds and wisdom, the riders had filled these islands with their learning and their skills. On Kural, that was especially the skill to turn sand and ash into something beautiful by melting them in the fire – the fire of the furnace and the dragon fire I felt in my guts when an idea for a glass design burst into my mind. I'd already fit more than three-quarters of the glass pieces I'd made into the design. Now I needed to put in the rest, solder the joints, weatherproof the window, and let it dry for a day before I framed it. Worry gnawed at my stomach. Despite how confident I'd tried to sound a few moments ago, I was going to be hard pressed to have it ready by the day after tomorrow.

I took up the next chunk of glass and set to work, wrapping lead around piece after piece, building my window out to the edges. My hands and eyes worked without my having to urge them.

Dragons no longer sailed the Dolyan skies, of course. The old riders' many-times-great-grandchildren ruled the islands now. The original riders had used their dragons' gifts with humility and respect. But the lure of power turned out to be hard to resist. Later rulers had grown selfish and quarrelsome, the legends said, so one by one, the dragons had vanished into the hills and fallen asleep. The tale told of them flying again when a worthy partner appeared. Until then, the only sign of them was the occasional smoke of their breath coming from the hills.

That and the work still created by their crafters and scholars. Perhaps the original dragon riders had feared how the future would go. They'd seen the lust for power and violent rule in the Westlands. So in their wisdom they'd built the crafthouses and also the bookhouses whose scholars could counsel any ruler willing to listen. Not that many of them did.

I put the last piece in place and straightened. One final time, I ran my gaze over the design. Until today, I hadn't really known for sure exactly what effect my window would give. I'd created the design two months ago, but even now, I couldn't say where the ideas had all come from. That was what it meant to be dragon-inspired. The work was mine, but it also came from the dragon who worked through and with me.

Alone in my workroom, I allowed myself to smile at what I'd made. The crafter wasn't supposed to preen. The work mattered more than the maker. Still, this work existed only because I'd made it, and it was beautiful. I wished my mother could see it. I'd been trying to live up to her skill for most of my life. I thought maybe this window did.

I swallowed the pain in my throat.

I got out the tin of lye flux and brushed it onto the joints. Then I set the burner on the table, lit it, and put the iron in the fire to heat. I looked at the little pile of solder sticks, hoping I'd made enough. Once the soldering iron glowed, I scraped a knife gently over a place where two pieces of lead met, cleaning it so the solder would stick and set to work. I was just finishing the last joint when the workroom door burst open, and Gillis entered.

"Are you coming to eat?" she asked.

Suppressing my irritation at her barging in again, I glanced at the dark sky outside the window. When had the day taken wing? I set the soldering iron down carefully in its holder and dug my knuckles into my tired back. "After dinner will you help me turn this so I can solder the other side?"

"You've got that far then? It will be done?" Gillis approached the table and studied the window. She looked at me with shining eyes. "It's glorious."

Warmed by our shared satisfaction, I followed Gillis into the workshop and washed my hands in water from the bucket. Renie must already have gone home, but Miriv stood at the furnace, melting cheese wrapped in flat bread. Gillis's stomach gurgled, and she giggled and pressed her hand to it.

"How is the window coming?" Miriv asked, carefully unaccusing.

"It'll be done," I said.

Her shoulders relaxed. "Let's eat outside. It's cooler." She led us out to the table and benches in the yard.

At the sight of a bowl of jajas, I halted in the doorway. "Where did those come from?"

"I forgot to tell you," Gillis said. "A scholar came to ask if you were all right. He gave us the fruit and also bought one of the gulls Miriv and I were making." Gillis gave me a sly smile. "If you ask me, he was too handsome for a bookhouse boy. He had nice long legs. Have you been keeping secrets from us?"

I found myself smiling at a bowl of fruit.

"Try not to be silly, Gillis," Miriv said sharply.

Gillis lowered her eyes demurely. "It's all right, Miriv. Piret's driven every other man clean out of my head."

Miriv's mouth tightened. "He's not for you, Gillis. His father owns a fleet of fishing ships."

"And I'm a Kuralian crafter," Gillis said. "Besides, Piret's not like his father. His father is boring and gray."

I took one of the jajas and was about to bite into it when I saw its underside was suspiciously squashed. I frowned at it.

Surely Addy hadn't picked this up off the cobblestones? Abruptly, the worries eating at my mind dissolved, and once again, Addy made me laugh. I'd known him only a few hours, and yet I was sure it was exactly the kind of thing he would do. And why not? I reached for a knife and started to cut away the bruising.

I STRUGGLED UP out of the fog of daytime sleep and lay for a moment listening to the faint whoosh of the furnace down in the workshop. I'd worked into the night because the glazing putty needed at least a full day to dry, and I still had my window's second side to do. Then I'd need to make a temporary frame to hold it until it was installed on Rhyth.

But while the second side dried today, I'd go to the bookhouse and see what the Sage had to tell me.

I dressed, and then despite the need to get to work, I took a moment to lean out the window, inhaling the scents of ocean and sun-warmed clay tiles. Toward Kural City's center, the palace tower rose. Toward the sea, clouds of dragon breath smudged the sky on the horizon over Lyz. At night, I'd seen fire there for the last few months. Lyz's dragon was stirring, alarming all of us on Kural. As far as I knew, the dragons slept quietly everywhere else in the Dolyans. Maybe Lyz's would drift off again, but maybe it wouldn't, and in the meantime, the idea of a waking dragon seemed to have put fire in Lyz's new drake, too. Rumor had it he was looking to rule islands beyond his own. The man had a desire for power that ran against every hope held by the original riders and their dragons. It was shocking really.

I thought about Dain being Lyzian. If Drake Jaffen

wanted to weaken Kural, a good way to do it would be to destroy the crafthouse linked to its dragon. And a good way to do *that* would be to get rid of its craftmistress, who also happened to be its most renowned glass maker. Jaffen could easily have sent Dain to do something other than negotiate trade deals. I'd try that line of questioning when I talked to Dain.

As I was pulling my head back inside, my gaze caught on something stuck between two tiles down near the edge of the slanted roof. It looked like a filthy bit of cloth. How had that got there? My room was on the fourth floor, and it certainly wasn't mine.

I leaned out to see better. Despite the rag's sodden, dirty state, I could see it was marked with a pattern like a man's kerchief – a kerchief that had maybe snagged on a tile and been pulled from a pocket.

A kerchief like the one my mother's killer had tied over his face.

My breath stopped and I gripped the sill for support as my vision began to tunnel.

It couldn't be his. I was letting my fear create phantoms.

Into my mind flashed the memory of the tile that grazed Renie's head the morning after my mother died. Suppose it hadn't come loose on its own. Suppose someone had loosened it and shoved it down onto her.

I pried my fingers from the windowsill and tried to think rationally. I was being hysterical.

All right then, a voice in my head whispered, how *did* the kerchief get there?

I chewed my lip. I needed to get a closer look at it. The roof was steep, though, and I didn't want to go out the window unless I had to. I looked around my room for something I could use to fish for the kerchief. Without many choices, I settled on a hairpin bent into a hook and tied to doubled-up thread from my sewing kit. I fed it out the window and watched it bump down toward the fabric. When I swung it, the makeshift hook caught the cloth but pulled loose when I tried to reel it in. I tried again, and again the hook failed to stick. Cursing under my breath, I bent the hook at a sharper angle. This time, it held, and I slowly, carefully drew my prize up the roof until I could lean out and reach it. I pulled it in, spread it out, and took a good look.

The kerchief was wet and filthy but hadn't yet started to rot. That fit with it having been left there the day after my mother's murder, when the tile fell. The cloth's pattern was a simple one, red and blue squares, and the fabric was thin and cheap. Hesitantly I brought it to my nose and sniffed. The kerchief's underside still smelled faintly of wood smoke, just as the killer had.

I balled the kerchief in my hand and took deep, steadying breaths.

DOWNSTAIRS, I FOUND Renie and Gillis greeting Miriv just coming through the door. She'd gone out earlier to find out how much we owed our suppliers. Now she plodded across the room and sank stiffly into a chair, rubbing one shoulder. I thought again of how tired she'd looked since my mother died. Her grief was wearing her out.

"What did you learn?" Gillis bounced on her toes, eager for an answer. Despite my fear about the kerchief, I held my tongue to hear it. Miriv's news would decide whether we could go on.

"Kedry owed everyone all right," Miriv said. "He was

truthful about that. And three weeks ago rumors said he owed so much he couldn't pay. So our suppliers went knocking on his door to collect."

"They must have gone after Kedry hard," Renie said. "No wonder he was difficult." She actually looked sympathetic. I had no idea how she managed the generosity that took.

"So where does that leave us?" I asked.

"They were happy to hear we run the glasshouse now," Miriv said. "They're willing to take partial payment for what we need until we get settled."

Gillis and I let out simultaneous sighs of relief.

"What's the matter, Miriv?" Renie asked. "Are you hurt?"

I realized Miriv was still rubbing her shoulder and wincing.

"Not really," Miriv said. "A horse bolted on Thread Street. I managed to dive out of the way, but I jammed my shoulder against a wall."

"Doo!" Gillis cried. "People should take more care. That road is narrow. You could have been killed."

I struggled for breath. "I think it was meant to kill her. I think someone is trying to kill us all." They turned startled faces my way.

"What?" Gillis asked.

"Think about it," I hurried on. "My mother is killed, and then someone drops a heavy roof tile on Renie."

"It fell." Gillis scrunched up her face, somehow still managing to look sweet.

"But what if someone knocked it loose. I just found this kerchief caught on the roof above the shed." I spread it out on the marver table. "It's like the one the man who killed my mother had tied across his face."

"Emlin—" Miriv began.

"I know it's a common kind and maybe it wasn't him, but maybe it was." I thought of something else. "During the riot in the square, a man nearly clubbed me."

"You told me he was a guard," Renie said gently. "He wore a uniform, right?"

I tried to remember. I thought he did, but I'd been reeling with fear, and I couldn't picture him clearly. "Maybe I was wrong. And now Miriv is almost run down in the street."

"Emlin, come with me." Miriv took my arm, steered me into my workroom, and closed the door. She shoved me down to sit on the bench under the window, knelt before me, and pressed my hands between hers.

I flashed on a memory of her crouching like this to tie my shoe when I was small. I could see the individual hairs springing away from the part on the top of her head.

"Emlin, I know you're still in pain over Calea. And neither being caught in a riot nor this business with Kedry has helped. It's all been hard on you. Anyone would be disoriented."

"Miriv, please! Just listen. What if this is somehow about the glasshouse? The place itself, the work we do. It's like someone wants it to stop. You know the rumors about trouble from Lyz. Maybe Drake Jaffen wants us to shut down. *He* could have spread that rumor to Kedry's creditors. Even Dain said there might be danger of some kind, and he's from there."

Miriv's eyes narrowed. She sat back on her heels. "When did you talk to Dain?"

I grimaced. Dain's name had just slipped out. "Yesterday, when I went out to the market, he was waiting for me."

"Why? What did he want?"

"I have no idea. He said he wanted to get to know me.

Because of my mother, I guess."

"Dragon take him." Miriv rose, paced to my table, and stared at my window, though I wasn't sure she saw it. She kneaded her sore shoulder.

"He said I should come and see him if I felt unsafe," I said. "But maybe he's the danger. None of this happened before he came to Kural. And he knew my name which meant he's been asking about me, which is a little frightening. He was even guessing my age."

Miriv spun back to me, face ash gray. "Stay away from him."

I rose too. "Miriv, what's the matter?"

"Stay away! Don't have anything to do with him."

"Why?" I asked. She quivered with tension. I felt as if I were on the edge of a cliff about to jump. "What was my mother to him? What was he to her?"

"Whatever it was, he left for seventeen years, so he wound up being nothing to her, and he's nothing to you either."

"Why would he be anything to me?" Silence stretched between us. I thought about what she'd said. "Dain left seventeen years ago," I said slowly. "Seventeen years ago, my mother was pregnant with me." Despite the heat that always filled the glasshouse, I felt cold to my core.

"Oh, Emlin," Miriv said. "I'm so sorry."

I swayed on my feet. "She said my father was dead! She said he died before I was born!"

"And he did. Or as good as. He left."

My knees gave way and I collapsed back onto the bench. "How could you keep that from me?" I clenched my hands so tightly my fingernails cut into my palms.

"Calea wanted it kept," Miriv said sharply. "If she hadn't,

she'd have told you herself."

"And she *should* have! I had a right to know."

"It was Calea's choice." Miriv's voice was hard. "You're a crafthouse child. You were born and raised in this glasshouse. You're ours. He had nothing to do with you."

I sputtered a laugh. "Oh, I think he did."

"You know what I mean."

"Do you think he killed her?" I whispered, unsure if I was asking Miriv or myself. "Could he cut the throat of a woman who'd been his lover?"

"I don't know." Miriv sagged against my worktable. "Calea always said Dain was a complicated man. It was one of the things she liked about him."

"I need to be alone, Miriv. I need to think about this."

She hesitated, then leaned in to kiss the top of my head, and left the room.

I leaned back against the wall. The sound of gulls wheeling in the harbor drifted in through the open window. Far away, thunder rumbled warning of an approaching storm. As if in response, another part of my new reality struck like lightning. I stood and went to my table to stare at my window. I might be a crafthouse child, but that didn't mean I was meant to be a crafter. If Dain was my father, then I was half Lyzian. Glasswork was Kural's craft. Glass crafters were *always* from Kural. So what did that mean for me?

Thunder sounded again, closer this time. Had I been fooling myself about being dragon-called to make glass? Maybe I only thought I felt him because I was in the glasshouse, and the dragon could be felt here by anyone. I made stained-glass, not the other beautiful objects we sold. I could make most of those things, but I never felt inspired with them, not like Miriv, Renie, and Gillis were. Not like my mother had been.

And my mother knew it. No wonder she'd checked every bit of glass I made so closely, far more closely than she checked Gillis's work. She'd been afraid I wasn't truly dragon-called.

I was supposed to undergo the crafter ceremony in less than a week. How could she have meant to go through with that? What did she think would happen?

My fingers spasmed around the edge of the table. I couldn't think of this now. I had two clear goals: find out who killed my mother, and save the place where my friends lived and crafted. My mother could have been killed because she made Kuralian glass. If someone was trying to kill the rest of us because we did too, then my two goals were really one.

Today, then, I would finish my window and go to the Great Bookhouse. I turned to my shelves to gather the glaze and my brushes. It was time to get to work.

Chapter 8

AFTER OUR SCENE about Dain, I'd had no trouble convincing Miriv I needed to seek the Sage's counsel. As soon as the rain stopped, I followed the same route I'd laid out for Addy two days ago until the Great Bookhouse rose before me, three storeys built from Rhyth Island's red stone. I knocked on the polished wooden door. After a moment, it was opened by a girl of about my own age, wearing scholar gray.

"I'd like to see the Sage please. I'm Emlin from the glasshouse."

The girl pulled the door wide. "Come in. I'll see if they're free."

I stepped into the entryway and wiped my damp shoes on the mat.

The girl led me down a hall with arches opening to both sides, showing rows of shelves for books and cubbyholes for rolled manuscripts. The place smelled of dust and old paper. Other figures in gray sat at tables or stood behind counters spread with their reading and writing. Laughter spilled into the hallway and then the sound of someone shushing it. I kept an eye out for Addy but didn't spot him.

The girl gestured to a bench outside a closed door, rapped, and went in. A moment later, she came out again, and held the door for me. "The Sage will see you now."

As I entered, the Sage moved from behind their desk with their hands outstretched to clasp mine. "Emlin, I am so sorry about your mother." Their voice was even huskier than usual.

I swallowed the throb of grief, focusing instead on our joined hands. The fingers on the Sage's right hand were stained with ink.

"Sit." The Sage pulled out a chair for me. As I settled in, they took the seat behind the desk and leaned toward me. "How are you?"

"I'm… getting better, I believe. But I've been thinking about my mother's last days and wondering what she was doing and thinking. It would make me feel better if I knew." I cringed internally when the Sage readily accepted my excuse.

"Of course. Many people feel that way after a sudden loss."

"I gather she came to see you," I said. "Can you tell me what that was about?" I braced myself to argue if the Sage said their conversation was private and couldn't be shared.

"She didn't actually come to see me. At the door, she asked to see some of our books and manuscripts. But when I heard the island's craftmistress was here, I went to greet her."

That stopped me for a moment. "Do you know which books she asked for?"

"Judging by what she had on the table when I saw her, she wanted to know more around the history of the original dragon riders trying to ensure that the islands would be justly ruled." Mouth pursed, the Sage shook their head, making their long white braid sway. "They'd seen so much war and struggle for power in the Westlands. They wanted none of that here if they could manage it."

"History of just rule," I repeated blankly. Maybe she'd been worried about Lyz attempting to take over Kural. She wouldn't have known Dain was about to reappear in her life, but like everybody else, she'd seen the fire on Lyz's mountain. And she knew that Lyz's previous drake had driven their medicinecrafters off and closed the crafthouse. That would have worried her sure enough.

The Sage smiled. "Yes, but being Calea, she eventually had to think about glass of course. When I found her, she was admiring a picture of the Dragonshard necklace. She'd apparently learned what she wanted to know by then because she closed the book and asked me if she could see the window you made for us."

At the thought of my mother wanting to see my glasswork, my throat closed up again. I found the Sage watching me closely.

"Perhaps you'd like to see it too?" they asked gently.

"If you don't mind," I managed.

The Sage shepherded me out the door, down a hallway, and up a flight of stairs. At the top landing, my window filtered sunlight and sent fragments of color dancing across the floor. We stood side by side, blinking at it.

I had fitted it together from dozens of glass pieces, each one a different shape. I'd dyed most of them in shades of yellow and gold, but a slash of blue slanted across near the bottom and a curve of red arced across the top. A third of the way up, a green shape rose. It took a while for most people to realize it was a person, though I'd left it deliberately unclear whether the person was a man or a woman.

"Is it dragon-inspired?" the Sage asked.

The question thrilled me, implying as it did that the Sage saw me as dragon-gifted.

"I think so. The idea came in a flash as I was waking up one morning. The shadow of a bird flitted across my wall, and I could see the window." I hadn't seen every detail, of course. What I took to be dragon inspiration didn't work that way. At least not for me. But I knew the effect I wanted and knew where to begin. The bits had been frustratingly difficult to fit together in a way that pleased me. The technical trick was to use the lead strips to outline the design but still have them meet in a way that kept the window strong. By the end of a month, I'd overheard Miriv and my mother arguing.

"Calea, can't you guide her to making some sort of order out of that mess?"

"No, I can't," my mother had said shortly. "I think she's grappling with a true dragon vision. Frankly, I'm glad to see it in her."

That last part made sense now. She'd hoped I could be dragon-called even if I was Dain's child.

"It certainly inspires me," the Sage said. "Every time I pass it, I see the beauty and order people can make from seemingly impossible pieces. And then I see that human figure curving upward and bless the understanding we can reach toward if we're open to the dragon's vision for us."

I was so grateful, I couldn't speak. This was why the dragon valued learning and crafts. Sometimes people needed to be reminded of what mattered.

"Thank you," I said. "I should go."

The Sage guided me back toward the entry. Once again, I looked into the side rooms as we passed.

"Looking for someone?" the Sage asked.

Heat rose into my face. "Not really. It's just that I ran

into that scholar visiting from Vinan, and I wanted to thank him for a gift he brought to the glasshouse."

The Sage raised their eyebrow. "I haven't seen any visitors at all. From Vinan, you say?"

Into my head popped an image of Addy poking his nose into every corner of the city while he had the chance. I smothered a smile. "I must have misunderstood," I said quickly.

"I expect he'll turn up eventually." The Sage smiled. "It sometimes takes the young ones a while to find their way here."

"Probably so."

I began the trip back to the glasshouse. As I dodged puddles, I thought about what I'd learned and what it meant for where to look for my mother's killer. She'd been worried about the Dolyans losing sight of the dragon riders' original vision. To me, that suggested she'd heard something about Lyz. Tomorrow I'd make sure *I* delivered the order of glass to the Rhythian ship, take the chance to go to Dain's house above the harbor, and ask why he was on Kural.

Night Flights 2

Gillis is dreaming of wandering a street, barefoot, her stomach hurting with emptiness.

Miriv is dreaming of Calea. She doesn't want to wake up. She wants to stay in this dream forever.

Tae is dreaming of the perfect cradle he will make for his and Renie's baby.

Renie is dreaming of fierce eight-year-old Emlin telling off a customer who had been rude to Renie. She smiles in her sleep.

Emlin is dreaming badly. Her mother is once again bleeding on the cobblestones in Palace Square. Emlin wakes, panting. Her killer, she vows. I'll find her killer.

Chapter 9

WITH THE FRESHLY washed kerchief stuffed in my pocket and my head stuffed full of the questions I meant to ask Dain, I set off to deliver glass to the Rhythian ship. After the delivery, I'd stop at his house and ask my questions.

I scarcely noticed when Wood Road narrowed and crowded me and the glasshouse cart against the wall near the steps up to Merchant Street. A scraping noise came from above, and I glimpsed a rock the size of my head hurtling down the wall toward me. I didn't have time to scream before it passed close enough that I felt a breeze down my back. It bounced and shattered, shooting a chunk big enough to bruise my right calf.

Up on Merchant Street, a shadow moved. Without thinking, I dropped the cart handles and raced up the steps. A thin slit ran between the two shops nearest the steps. I pelted through it and found a ledge overlooking Wood Road. Panting, I turned both ways. No one was in sight. The shadow had fled.

I'd been right. Someone was after us glass crafters.

I was gripping my bruised calf and waiting for my heart

to slow when I looked down and saw the unguarded glasshouse cart, loaded with wares. *Dragon fire*! I hurried back down to Wood Road and took several deep breaths to calm myself before setting off again. I felt danger still poking at my back as I wrestled the cart around a tight corner and guided it down the road snaking to the harbor. I marked Dain's house as I passed, but didn't stop. Maybe he was out getting rocks ready to drop on me. I shuddered.

At the far end of the waterfront, a few fishing boats bobbed at the crumbling docks Drake Haron's son, Symond, was supposed to be fixing. Nearer sat a row of three ships. Kural's own blue and gold flag flew from the masts of the closest two, but the far one showed the flying fish symbol of Rhyth, so that was where I headed. Sailors sharing gossip lounged around the ramp leading to the Rhythian ship, some wearing the kerchiefs of Kural and some those of Rhyth. They all turned as I rattled up.

"I have glassware to go aboard this ship. Who do I talk to?"

One of the Rhythian sailors peered into my cart. "I'm the mate. We've been expecting you." He beckoned to a second man. "Get this on board."

"Wait," I said. "You have to pay me first."

"I've no word of that." The mate waved his man forward again.

I tightened my hold on the cart. "No payment, no glass." I glared at the mate. "I want to talk to your captain."

The mate hesitated, then flicked a finger at a sailor who ran up the gangplank. The breeze carried the smell of seaweed and snapped the flag on the ship's mast. I tapped my toes on the slimy boards under my feet and looked up the hillside to where I could see the purple house. Had Dain knocked that rock loose? Even knowing I was his daughter? I raised a hand to my throat, then dropped it when my fingers found no beads to twist.

After a moment, the sailors around me resumed their talk. "You mark my word," one said. "The fire on Lyz means trouble. It flared up right when their old drake died, and the Lyzians take it as a sign this young fool Jaffen should rule all the Dolyans."

"It'll never happen," a woman said. "Their old drake was a tyrant, but too scared to bother anyone other than his own people. Brave enough to torment and kill them, but only when he was safe behind walls. This Jaffen won't be any gutsier than his father. We're lucky it isn't the other son. Even his own father condemned him as a criminal."

A small woman in a green shirt strode down the gangplank – the captain, judging from the way the Rhythian sailors all stiffened at the sight of her. She scowled at the mate. "Something you can't manage?"

The mate pointed at me. "She has the shipment of glassware, but she says we have to pay her before she'll part with it."

The captain shot me a hard-eyed look. I could smell thoi a yard away. "I already paid Kedry," she said.

I closed my gaping mouth. "When?"

"Early today."

"But—" I let my protest fade. It would be just like weasel Kedry to say the glasshouse was our problem and then take our money. I caught myself grinding my teeth. The captain gestured for a Rhythian sailor to take the glass, but I tightened my grip. "Wait. I know you didn't pay for the window because it wasn't supposed to be done yet. You owe me for it."

The captain frowned. "Our drake's window? Half that price was paid at the start."

"But the other half's due now."

The captain cocked her head, then spoke over her shoulder to the mate. "Go get five dracos from the safe."

"No!" I cried. "You think I don't know what I'm owed? It's ten dracos." Everyone around us had turned to watch, but who cared if they gawked? I refused to let this woman cheat me. "If you won't pay me what the window's worth, you won't have it." I shut out the thought that if she didn't give in, I'd have no money at all to take home.

"We're at the end of our run," the captain said. "We don't have ten dracos to spare."

"What's the trouble here?" a new voice asked.

With their eyes on a point behind me, everyone bowed. I realized I'd heard horses clopping along the road and turned to see Symond, Drake Haron's son, astride a towering black horse, attended by no fewer than eight guards. Symond's handsome blue silk shirt gleamed like water in the harbor. I had the irrelevant thought that unlike Kedry, Symond had taste. I hastily backed up a step and bowed.

"No trouble, sir," the Rhythian captain said.

"She's paying me less than she owes me for a window," I said.

"You're Calea's daughter, aren't you?" Symond said. "I was sorry to hear about her death." His mouth pinched, and for a moment he seemed to think. He pointed his riding crop at the flat package in my cart. "That's the window?" His horse pranced, and he yanked the reins to still it. "Let's see it."

I untied the twine, folded the burlap aside, and tipped the window up so light could shine through the glass and bring it to life.

The Rhythian captain wiggled two fingers at her people. As one of them took the window from me and lifted it out of the cart, I stepped back to see better. It was the first time I'd looked at it in full sunlight. I only distantly heard wheels squeak as the other sailor pushed the cartful of our work up the gangplank. Everyone else fell silent, looking at the window. It glowed with an inner life.

Surely Kural's dragon had called me to do this, I thought desperately, even if I was half Lyzian.

"You're Calea's daughter all right," Symond said. "Can you paint that oversized circle and reduce the size of Rhyth?"

The captain unfolded her arms. "Wait. That window's intended for *our* drake. We already paid half what it's worth."

"The contract says the second half is due on delivery," I said. "Pay me what you owe, and you can have it. Otherwise you broke the contract." I turned back to Symond. "I can."

"How much would it cost me?" he asked.

I was so fixated on getting ten dracos from Rhyth that I barely stopped myself from naming that as the price. "Twenty dracos, sir. That's what it's worth."

He smiled. "Yes, I'd say it is. Bring it to the palace tomorrow morning. Deliver it yourself. I may want to talk to you about buying other things too." His saddle creaked as he readied himself to ride on.

I grabbed at his stirrup, the hard leather of his riding boot slipping under my sweaty grip. "I need payment now, sir." As the words tumbled out, my triumph faded. Assuming Symond gave it to me, I was back to the money for the window being the only gain I took home today. Still, twenty dracos was a solid amount.

Two of Symond's guards sidled their horses toward me, and I hastily released his foot. "Pay her," he told a guard, then spurred his horse toward the dock repairs, followed by the rest of his escort.

The remaining guard dug in a belt pouch marked with Drake Haron's golden gull. She pulled out a handful of coins and dropped them in my outstretched hands.

The sailor who'd taken the glassware on board the ship rolled the empty cart back onto the dock. I tucked the coins in my pocket and rewrapped the window, ignoring both the Kuralian sailors who looked amused and the Rhythian captain and her crew, who didn't. I hoisted the window into the cart and set off back up the steep road.

No doubt desperate to pay his creditors, Kedry had taken our money. Whoever was trying to destroy the glasshouse and glassmakers along with it was doing a good job. I wondered again if it might be Dain acting on Lyz's behalf. Despite any danger, I had to talk to him. But given what I now knew about who he was, I preferred to talk in a place more private than the streets.

In front of the purple house, I hesitated. Dain would be foolish to kill me in the house he'd rented, I reasoned.

Before I had a chance to change my mind, I rapped on the door. It opened to reveal Dain, blinking in the sunlight.

"Emlin!" Smiling, he pulled the door wide. "Come in."

"Can I bring the cart in? The window in it is valuable."

"Of course." He stepped out and helped me maneuver the cart into what proved to be a front room with a fireplace, dining table, and cupboards. It smelled faintly of Dain's breakfast bacon. "Sit and I'll get you some ale." He snatched a note from the table and tucked it into the top drawer of the sideboard.

I stared at the drawer. He hadn't wanted me to see that, which made me crave having it in my hand. He poured two mugs from a pitcher, handed me one, and settled across the table with the other. For a long moment, the only sound was the friendly shouts of sailors down in the harbor. A small green gem dangled from Dain's left earlobe, but he wore nothing in his right, and any piercing in its top curve would have been hidden in the fold.

"Emlin," he began, but I spoke at the same moment and kept going.

"Have you been out this morning?" I asked. *Maybe knocking down rocks?*

"No. I had a late start."

"Have you been busy working on trade? Someone said you'd been talking about Kedry's debts, so I guess Drake Jaffen is interested in glass."

"Who's Kedry?" He drew in his chin.

"He owns the glasshouse. Or did."

"I've had nothing to do with him or his debts. I believe Jaffen is interested in all the island crafts, including glass."

"I thought maybe Jaffen wants the glasshouse closed."

"Not that I know of," Dain said. "Listen—"

"I'm glad for the chance to talk to you," I plowed on, "because so far, the Watch has learned nothing about my mother's death. You were the last one to talk to her. Did you see anyone following her that night?" I saw by his wince that I didn't have to explain which night I meant.

"No." He rubbed his hand over his mouth.

"You didn't go to the palace then? Or maybe stop in the alehouse on the square's corner?"

He sat back, eyeing me thoughtfully. "No, and of course, if I'd seen anyone near her, I'd have been right there making sure nothing happened to her." He took a drink of ale while I debated whether to believe him. "What does the Watch think?" he asked. "A random robber maybe?"

"That's what they say, but I think they're wrong. He was waiting for her." I studied Dain's face, searching again for some sign of guilt. "Who do you think it might have been?"

He threw up his hands. "How would I know? I haven't been on Kural in years. I wish I *did* have an idea. I'd go straight to the Watch."

I dragged the kerchief from my pocket and smoothed it out on the table. "After I ran into you the other day, I found this. I wondered if you might have dropped it."

Nose wrinkled, he prodded the cheap fabric with one fingertip. "No, it's not my style."

I chewed my lower lip. I had to admit he was convincing. I felt the oddity of the situation: I didn't know him at all and yet we were intimately connected.

He leaned forward. "Listen. I have something I need to tell you."

A shift in his voice made me stiffen. We were moving into personal territory, and I didn't want to talk to him about this. "Unless it's about who killed my mother, you don't."

We stared at one another across the table. I saw his face change when he realized I knew.

He picked up his mug and hid behind a drink. "Did Miriv tell you?"

"I guessed and she admitted it."

He ran a hand through his hair. "I owe you an explanation."

"How do you plan to *explain* abandoning her?" I couldn't stand sitting across from him for another instant. I'd asked my questions about my mother's death. I didn't know if he was lying about killing her, but I knew for sure I wanted nothing to do with him as a father. I jumped to my feet.

"Wait." He shoved his chair back and caught my wrist. "Please, Emlin, give me a chance to say some things."

"Let go of me." It took all the restraint I had not to spit in his face.

"If I let you go, will you at least listen to what I have to say?" Dain asked. When I glared at him in silence, he released me. "Please. You're my daughter! I owe you. I owe Calea. Let me tell you what happened. Just sit for a moment or two more. That's all I ask."

He was good at coaxing for something he wanted, I thought bitterly, and probably had been when he romanced my mother too. I sank back onto the chair.

He sat and slid his mug from hand to hand, leaving a wet streak on the table. A corner of the kerchief darkened as it grew damp. "I've thought about Calea a lot over the years. I was working for Lyz's drake when I knew her, though of course until six months ago, it was the old drake, not Jaffen."

"Doing what?"

He grimaced. "The old drake sent me to buy something and once I had it, I had orders to take it to him immediately. That's why I went home when I did."

"And it took you seventeen years to come back."

His shoulders squirmed. "Emlin, I know this doesn't reflect well on me, but I was married."

I'd have stood up if I could, but I wasn't sure my legs would hold me. "Did my mother know that?" He shook his head. I wanted to cry. She must have been so bewildered when he left. "So you were lying from the start." I braced my hands on the table and pushed myself up, leaning hard enough that my untouched mug of ale rocked and spilled, plastering the kerchief to the table.

He leapt up to block my way to the door. "You don't

understand. My wife and I were never happy together. She died last year, and when Drake Jaffen asked me to be his trade representative here, I jumped at the chance mostly because I wanted to see Calea again. I never expected to find a daughter."

"You hurt her. She wasn't much older than I am now." The thought pierced me with sadness. I'd never imagined my mother so vulnerable. She was Calea, a superb worker in glass, the glasshouse mistress. She was my *mother*, the person who woke me in the middle of the night and led me out into the yard to see shooting stars because they were too beautiful to miss.

Dain lifted his hands, palms up. "All I can say is I'm sorry. I didn't mean to, and I'll regret that I did until the day I die."

Again, I tried to decide if I believed him. A man who cheated on his wife, and a good enough liar to deceive my mother. What hope did I have of being able to read him better than she had? "Your regret doesn't change what you did to her. I only hope it was limited to abandoning her. Get out of my way." I backed my cart up to turn it.

"Wait. There's something else I need to tell you." He grabbed the edge of the cart and held it. "Drake Jaffen is planning to visit Kural Island to talk to Drake Haron about naming him his heir."

I scoffed. "Rather than Symond, who's his own son? Our Drake Haron would never be fool enough to do that."

"Nonetheless, he's coming. After they're done talking, I'm going back to Lyz with Jaffen. You're welcome to come along."

I snapped my drooping mouth shut. "Don't be ridiculous. I'm a Kuralian glassmaker. It's illegal for me to leave." I jerked the cart out of Dain's grip, but he still stood in my way.

"One other thing, Emlin. Since I do represent Lyz, it's best no one knows we're related. We wouldn't want a Kuralian to mistake you for an enemy agent."

I froze. "You mean hurt or even kill me? Who? Who would do that?"

He shook his head. "I don't know. But given Calea's murder, you should be careful."

I blew out a frustrated breath. At best, this man was useless to me. "Move."

He stepped aside. "If you change your mind, you're always welcome here." He held the door open, and I rolled my cart out of his house.

Chapter 10

OUTSIDE MY LYING father's house, I paused to simmer down and decide if I'd learned anything useful. "Not my style" he'd said of the kerchief, and that fit with the little I'd seen of him. Still, he'd whisked that note out of my sight, and Drake Jaffen had sent him to Kural. My trip to the bookhouse suggested my mother was worried about Jaffen. Maybe Dain wasn't a murderer himself, but he could know someone who was. He was definitely up to something that he didn't want me to know about.

Steps hurried at my back, and Addy loomed up next to me. His delighted smile felt like it came from a different world. "Glass girl! I'm glad to see you. I've been worried you took hurt in that scramble the other day even though your friends at the glasshouse said you were fine."

I wrenched my mind away from Dain. "Thank you for bringing the jajas. That was kind."

"Let me give you a hand." Addy nudged me aside, took the handles, and started pushing the cart. It wobbled and slid on the cobblestones, roaming the road with a will of its own.

"I may owe you an apology. I told the Sage you were in town, so they know you didn't come to the bookhouse."

He wrinkled his nose. "Oh, well. I expect I can explain when I get there. I saw you coming out of that house. Were you selling glass to the man who lives there?"

"No. Be careful with that cart!"

"What's in here anyway? It's heavy."

"It's a window I sold to Symond."

"Are we taking it to the palace?" He craned his neck to look up at the top of the road.

"To the glasshouse for now. To the palace tomorrow morning." The realization hit me that I'd found a way into the palace after all. I could try again to learn why my mother went there. My breath slowed. Understanding her mysterious trip to the palace would surely tell me something about her murder. She might have said something that would point to the person who lured her out into the night.

Addy jerked the cart back just before it rammed a woman coming out of her front door. "Sorry," he told her. She harrumphed and hurried off.

"Addy, give me that." I pushed him away. "You must have things to do. Books to find." He had no shame over his nosiness, and I didn't want him poking at why I'd been in Dain's house.

"Well, good to know you're all right." Addy halted mid-stride, and I went on. When I glanced over my shoulder, he was frowning after me, one hand tapping against his leg. Gillis was right. He was good-looking for a bookhouse boy. He turned and walked back the way we'd come.

As I passed the steps to Merchant Street, I resolved not to tell Miriv about the falling rock. She already thought I was overwrought. I also shoved any thoughts of Dain – and Addy – out of my head in favor of the glasshouse's more immediate need for the money I hadn't been able to collect. I

79

left the cart in the yard, rubbed my hands on my trousers, and stepped through the doorway into the workshop. The noise of the furnace masked my arrival, but the instant my shadow fell across the floor, Gillis and Miriv turned toward me. Renie hadn't shown up for work that morning and still wasn't there. Miriv had been making gulls, plucking at the honey-soft glass with tweezers to draw out the birds' shapes. She set the one she'd just finished on the marver table.

At the annealer, Gillis broke into a broad smile. "You have our money? Oh, Emlin, let's see it."

I clutched the coins in my pocket through the wool of my trousers. "I have the money for the window. I wound up selling it at full price to Symond, who was there to look at the docks. The Rhythians refused to pay what they owed on it. But that's all I have because the ship's captain already paid Kedry for the rest of our order."

"Kedry?" Gillis said. "But that money is ours."

A sharp crack snapped my gaze to the marver table. Miriv's gull lay in pieces on the table and the floor, broken under the strain of its own heat.

"Dragon fire," Miriv said.

I cringed. Miriv never swore.

"I'm sorry!" cried Gillis, who should have moved the gull to cool in the annealer.

Miriv flung her tweezers on the table. "It's all right, Gillis. We should have known."

"Kedry robbed us," I said. "As surely as if he'd held us at knife point. The man is a gaudily dressed cockroach."

"He took those orders," Miriv said, "and for all I know has the right to be paid for them. I don't know the law, and Drake Haron isn't holding court right now. Until he does, we have no choice but to make do. Let's see what you have,

Emlin."

I emptied my pocket onto the table. Miriv sorted the coins into piles, making one large one first, then four smaller ones.

She pointed to the biggest pile. "That's for the suppliers. It's what they agreed to take for now. It's a blessing you got double what we expected for the window, Emlin, or we'd be short."

I looked at the other piles. "For us?" It was the first time I could see exactly what Kedry had done to us.

"Doo." Gillis bit her lip. "That's less than Kedry would have paid us." She looked from me to Miriv. "How will we live on so little?"

"Hush, Gillis," Miriv said sharply. "If the rest of us can manage, you can."

Gillis's chin trembled. "Of course. Excuse me." Head lowered, she rushed up the stairs. The door to her room *thunked* shut.

My fury at Kedry churned my stomach to sickness. "Can we put off giving the suppliers anything?"

"I doubt it. This was the minimum I could get them to agree to." Miriv poked one of the piles aside. "We'll send Renie's to her."

"Why isn't she here?" I asked.

Miriv let one of the little piles slide through her fingers and clink back on the table. "The healer said she might have better luck with this one if she stays home for the first few months. Tae came around to tell us."

Renie's being gone would reduce the amount of glass we could produce and make it even harder to catch up with Kedry's debts. It didn't bear thinking about. I finished stoking the furnace just as Gillis came down the stairs.

Though her face was blotchy, she held her head high. My respect for her rose. "It'll be all right," I said, trying to sound certain. "Symond said that when I delivered the window tomorrow, he might want more things too. Come on, Gillis. I'll help you make some of those gorgeous goblets."

She frowned. "They all have to look alike, you know. People want them to be a set."

"I know. I'll be careful this time."

"There's nothing wrong with them being a set," she added.

I held up my hands, palms out. "I know."

"I'll do the shaping." She went to the shelves to assemble her materials. When I came up beside her, she glanced over her shoulder to where Miriv was making gulls again. "I've been thinking," she whispered. "Maybe Piret will loan us money."

I spun to look at her. So that was what had made her perk up. She looked straight ahead, a spot of pink blooming on her round cheek. "Don't do that, Gillis. You don't want to owe him. We'll find the coin somewhere."

Gillis looked at me slantwise. "You've never gone hungry, have you?" She turned away.

I picked up the blowpipe, gathered glass, and set to work, fretting all the while. If only I'd beaten Kedry to the Rhythian ship. If only I'd found the right question to ask Dain. By the day's end, I was as tired as I'd been in the week after my mother's death. I finally understood what people meant when they said they couldn't think straight. My thoughts kept chasing one another in tight little repetitious circles.

From the food bin, Miriv took out a crescent of dark bread and a fist-sized round of goat cheese. Moving slowly as a crone twice her age, she set it in front of me and Gillis. "Eat.

I'll have something later."

I'd be sick if I tried to force food into my squirming stomach. "Thank you, but I'm not hungry." I fled up the stairs to my room, stumbled to the window, and shoved my head out, gasping for air.

After a moment, I gripped the windowsill and laid my cheek on my hands. Tomorrow I'd enter the palace and seize any chance to ask about my mother. And Symond might order more glass which would help us financially. So that was good. Tomorrow's trip might help fix both of the problems weighing on me. What else could I do?

I put one hand to my throat and paused with my forefinger in the hollow between my collarbones where my mother's beads should have been. Then I crouched to open my clothes chest, snatched up my mother's work journal, and jumped onto the bed to sit cross-legged with it in my lap. I hadn't had the energy to do more than glance at it when Miriv gave it to me, but I knew that some of my mother's designs would be hard enough to make that they'd draw a high price. Tomorrow, I could offer them to Symond.

I sped through the pages. One showed a platter with layers of different colored glass that Renie might be able to make, assuming she could work. Another showed a footed cup with glass seashells trailed down the outside. Dolyans were fond of sea-inspired designs, so that one might be worth trying. Miriv maybe?

I wished I could trust myself to match my mother's designs, but I was far more likely to make something unsellable. Luckily my fellow glassmakers could do the work.

The journal suggested my mother had been interested in glass lore too, just as the Sage had said. On bottom of the next page there was a detailed drawing of the Dragonshard necklace used at the Flame Testing of every new Kuralian drake. Above it, my mother had sketched one of the legendary Dragonblades, knives of dragon glass that rendered all the drakes invincible against the blades of their enemies. I started to flip past that page, but my fingers tripped at its edge. I stared at the drawing of the knife. Stared at the hilt to be precise, because sketched on it was something I hadn't noticed in the quick look I'd taken before: a graceful letter L.

A chill slid down my back. All the Dragonblades had been made on Kural in this very glasshouse in the first years after the dragon riders found the islands. The dragon glass had come from the Heights. That and the inspiration the dragon had breathed into the crafters were what gave them their power. A drake wielding one could draw on the dragon's long experience with war to defeat an attacker. Why was the knife belonging to Lyz in my mother's journal? A horrible suspicion crept into my head.

The Sage had said my mother asked to see books about Kuralian history. But, he said, she'd been most interested in the dragon glass objects.

Night had slipped into the room, blurring my vision of the journal page. I slid off the bed and opened my door to find the stairs dark, but a lamp glimmering below. I tiptoed past Gillis's room and went down to where Miriv was keeping the night's watch on the furnace. She looked up from the book she'd been studying, her elbows propped on the marver table.

The account book. I winced. "Are you busy? Wait. That's a stupid question. I see you are. How badly off are we?"

She grimaced. "Pretty bad."

"But we have enough to go on?" I asked quickly.

Wearily, Miriv rubbed her temples. "I don't know. Did

you need something?"

Yes, money. And the identity of the killer. Also, maybe an explanation for the picture I just found. I laid the journal open in front of Miriv and pointed to the knife. "Why did my mother draw a Dragonblade with an L?"

Miriv stared, then whispered, "I can't believe she kept that drawing. Actually I can. That is just like Calea."

In the long silence that followed, my own rapid breathing nearly covered the rush of the fire. Until I'd seen Miriv's reaction, I hadn't fully believed it. "My mother made a false Dragonblade for the drake of Lyz. *That* was why Dain courted her."

Miriv ran a finger over the drawing. "He'd been sent to Kural to get a new Dragonblade. The one belonging to Lyz's old drake shattered when he dropped it. Apparently, he didn't want his enemies to know he'd lost that protection. A look-alike might not actually work, but if it kept his enemies from going after him in the first place, that would be good enough."

That certainly made it clear that Dain was first and foremost a user who only cared for his own needs.

"What was she thinking?" I asked. "When Kural's drake lost his knife three drakes back, he took it as a sign he should abdicate. Those knives are meant to ensure each island has a just ruler who needn't fear enemies. They supposedly only break when a drake is unworthy to use one." Here was an explanation for why my mother went to the bookhouse to read about Dolyan history. I thought of all the lectures she'd delivered on respecting our craft and felt a flare of anger. "How could my mother consider making a fake one for a cruel ruler like Lyz's?"

"I don't believe the drake's nature entered into her

85

thinking at all. She was so young." Pushing her chair back from the table and the shocking drawing, Miriv gave a bitter laugh. "Dain flattered her, and she reasoned herself into it. I watched her do it. She said they'd all been made here in the first place and there was still dragon glass on the Heights, so why couldn't we do what our ancestors did."

"Taking that glass is against the law. The dragon's power is in it. Handling it can corrupt people."

"I know. But she said she was one of the dragon's crafters, so she should be fine. And then, of course, Dain paid her a lot of money, and I think that matched her sense of her self-worth. She was your mother, Emlin, and I loved her, but she was arrogant about her dragon-given talents and that's the truth."

A shape in my mind that had seemed unchangeable cracked like Miriv's gull left on the marver table. Calea, the glassmaker whose work was treasured across the Dolyans, who'd spoken often of what we owed the dragon, had abused her gift. "Miriv," I choked out, "could someone from Lyz have killed her to keep that secret?"

"I've wondered that," Miriv said, "but it was so long ago. Why would Lyz wait? No, I think that in the end, the dragon finally turned his gaze on the offense and let her fall."

"The dragon didn't hold the knife," I said. "A man did. I told you I think her death was meant to hurt the glasshouse. I think someone from Lyz wants us gone. Maybe Dain, though he doesn't seem to be the kind to hold the knife himself."

Miriv shot a sharp look my way. Her jaw was tense, and the grooves from her nose to the corners of her mouth deepened. "I want you to forget you saw this, Emlin. I've lost your mother, and I don't want to lose you. I don't intend for you to wind up dead in the street too."

I swept my mother's journal off the table and slapped it shut. "I don't intend that either. Good night." I kissed Miriv's cheek, climbed the stairs, and closed the door to my room. I leaned back against it and found that my strongest feeling was anger at my feckless parents.

Thank you, Mother. Thank you for giving me a heritage that makes it wrong to do the thing I love. Between you and Dain, I've inherited a cartload of guilt.

I clutched the journal tightly to my chest. All right. The glasshouse needed money, and Kural needed protection from Lyz. I could help meet both those needs. With Kural's knife lost and Lyz's Drake Jaffen about to arrive, our Drake Haron must be concerned about his safety. I certainly would be if it were me. If a fake Dragonblade worked to protect Lyz's drake, it might work for Kural's. Haron could just say the knife, lost years ago, had been found. People would take it as a good sign. There was a rightness to repeating my mother's offense for better reasons than a man's request. It felt like undoing her actions rather than repeating them. And surely Haron would think it right to reward me, as Dain had rewarded my mother, so the glasshouse would have the money it needed.

Even beyond being Calea and Dain's child, it was right that I should be the one to gather the dragon glass. I might already be doomed as a glassmaker. If I failed the test on my birthday, Miriv would let me live here, but she'd have to stop me from making glass. So, the cost of any crime was unlikely to make things worse for me. Unless, as Miriv said, I wound up dead in the street, of course. I paused over that thought, then shrugged. Someone was already trying to kill me. The only thing that mattered was whether I could stop the glasshouse from also falling.

I returned the journal to the chest, washed, and pulled on my nightgown. Then I climbed into bed and fought for sleep against my own tense body and busy brain. I must have dozed at one point because I dreamed of being trapped in a hole, unable to move my arms or legs. Then the dream changed, and I was flying unafraid, stars overhead and sea below.

I WOKE TO the crow of a rooster from the dawn streets below and lay there for a moment trying to picture myself climbing the mountain to the Heights, gathering the glass, shaping it. My breath wobbled. Every woman in the glasshouse would reject me if she knew. They'd have to, no matter what they felt for me. I pulled the blanket up around my shoulders, thinking furiously.

Maybe I could put the decision off. Before I took the risk, I should make sure it would pay off. Today when I delivered the window to the palace, I'd find a way to speak to Drake Haron as well as Symond. Maybe Symond would even help me do that. And then, I'd carefully, carefully ask Drake Haron if he wanted a dragon glass knife.

Chapter 11

I CAT-FOOTED DOWN the stairs, checking to be sure Miriv wasn't in the workshop before I slipped out into the yard and hid my mother's journal under the stained-glass window in my cart. I'd considered telling Miriv that I'd use the journal only to entice Symond to order expensive objects, but I was afraid she wouldn't believe me. Justly so, as it happened, since it would have been a great big lie. I went inside as Miriv came downstairs, still buckling her belt. "I'm off to deliver my window." I called up my inner Gillis and concentrated on keeping my face relaxed and bland under Miriv's gaze.

She gave a crisp nod then crossed to the food bin. "Eat first."

"I'm not hungry." That was true, mostly because I still felt too sick to eat.

"Then wait for me to get Renie's money. You can take it to her." Miriv went back up to her office and returned with the coins.

I WHEELED THE cart from the yard and headed toward Renie's

house behind the palace. Halfway there, the space between my shoulder blades began to itch, but when I looked behind me, I saw only people heading for work and the shops. Guilty conscience, my mother would have pronounced. But my nerves were on edge over more than my guilt or the possibility someone wanted to kill me. In the night, it had occurred to me that Haron might already have bought a fake Dragonblade. That could have been the glass my mother took to the palace that night, which would explain why it wasn't in the order book. That was one more reason I'd have to be careful how I suggested Haron order one today.

I turned into Renie's street. The back of the palace wall rose smooth and pink on my left, facing houses inhabited by the tradesmen who served Drake Haron, including Renie's carpenter husband. A huge chestnut tree loomed inside the palace wall and cast shifting green shadows on the cobbles in front of Renie's house. Drake Haron's garden must be cool on the hottest summer days. Even from the street, I could smell damp earth and growing things.

Ahead of me, Renie's door opened, and a woman carrying a healer's bag came out and strode away down the street. Renie's husband slumped in the doorway, watching her go. My heart kicked against my ribs.

"What's happened, Tae?" I asked.

He straightened. "Renie fell down the stairs."

"No! The baby?"

He shook his head, then rubbed his hand across his trembling mouth.

I parked the cart next to Tai's carpenter's ladder lying crookedly across their hallway as if he'd flung it down in haste, then ran up the stairs to Renie and Tae's bedroom. Face pale, Renie lay on her back in a bed whose shapely posts and carved headboard Tae had crafted before they were married. Renie, Gillis, and I had gone to watch him work on it one day. Tae had answered Gillis and me when we spoke to him, but he kept turning toward Renie like a flower following the sun. I'd been angry with him for taking Renie away from the glasshouse. After that day, I let my anger go.

I grabbed the hand Renie reached out to me and dropped to my knees next to her. "I'm so sorry," I gabbled, stupidly helpless to say anything that mattered.

"I know," she said wearily. With her free hand, she stroked my hair.

"Don't," I said. "Don't comfort me. I should be comforting you." I tried to swallow my grief for her and Tae. "Tae says you fell."

She turned her head to look out the window where the branches of the chestnut tree in the palace garden swayed. "I did, though I don't actually remember that part. I was making the bed, and I thought I heard a step in the hallway. I thought maybe Tae had come home sick from work, so I started down. And then I woke up, lying in a heap at the bottom of the stairs."

My grip on her hand tightened. She'd heard a noise. What if someone had come into the house and pushed her?

"Luckily, a neighbor heard me call." Renie turned back to me. "She sent for the healer and Tae."

She was starting to slur her words. Her eyelids drifted shut. The healer must have given her something. I let go of her hand, kissed her brow, and went downstairs to find Tae, leaning against the wall as if it were the only thing holding him up.

I drew the coins out of my pocket and handed them to him. "That's some of Renie's back wages. We should have more soon."

He didn't even look at them, just set them on the hall table, and opened the front door for me.

I hesitated before saying, "Tae, I don't know if Renie told you, but I think someone is attacking all us glassworkers."

He hissed out a breath. "She told me. Don't make this worse than it already is, Emlin."

"Just be careful, all right?" I backed my cart out onto the street and pushed it the way I'd come, thinking sad thoughts for Renie.

At the corner, I turned to follow the palace wall toward the square. A tall, dark-haired figure in gray was bent over the jaffel bird shrine carved into the wall. Addy. A jolt of pleasure surprised me. He was so unfailingly cheerful, as if something good had happened to him, and he still wasn't over it. After Renie, I needed someone who was joyful.

Addy straightened, smiling broadly. "I thought I saw you just now."

I jammed to a halt. "Were you following me?" He'd turned up as I left Dain's house too. That seemed like an awfully big coincidence.

He frowned. "I was heading toward the palace and saw you. I'm still hoping to get a glimpse of the palace library."

I weighed his explanation and decided I was seeing threats everywhere. What possible reason could this boy have for harming a glassmaker? My shoulders relaxed. "Have you found any books to buy?"

"No, but I've seen lots of dragon work." He waved toward the shrine, an egg-shaped hollow in the wall, housing a small bird so deep a pink it was almost the red of my tunic. The jaffel swiveled its head to blink at us.

I'd never seen the little birds anywhere but around the

palace, so I guessed they liked the spaces the old dragon riders had made for them. Addy scrounged a small coin from his purse and flipped it into the dish below the shrine. The clatter left the bird unruffled. It was probably used to coins raining down on it. I wished I could say the same.

"I suppose it's not surprising there's so much of the old civilization here," Addy said. "This palace was the home of Drake Kural, after all, and the old writings say his dragon was the most powerful of the weyr." Lips pursed, he looked toward the mountain where Kural's dragon slept. "Do you know if there are any remnants of the dragon's lair still there?"

Alarm pulsed through me. I didn't want Addy poking around on the Heights if I went to gather dragon glass. "I've never heard of any. You can't go there anyway. It's against the law. The Watch sends patrols up there to keep people away."

He frowned. "That shouldn't be. You can go to the mountain tops on all other islands."

"The other islands don't have dragon glass."

He nodded. "That's true. Kural is the only one with the right kind of soil to mix with lava and make it."

"Yes, and some past drake decided he preferred people not getting entranced by the power in it." As I heard myself say the words, I felt a twinge of doubt about my plans. I stamped it out. If my mother could do this without triggering a longing for power, I could. We were different. We were glassmakers.

He shrugged and then grinned at me. "Are you taking your window to the palace? Allow me."

Over my better judgment, I let him take the cart. One thing you could say for Addy, he had good manners.

As usual, he talked nonstop, this time about how all the dragon riders had built their palaces on the same sacred pattern. Since he kept up the conversation on his own, I didn't have to pay close attention, which was good because I was still grieving for Renie and Tae.

At the gate, the guard lowered his pike to bar our way. "Not you again," he said to Addy. "The steward's not going to let you into the library no matter how often you ask."

"I'm delivering a window Symond bought from me yesterday," I cut in. "Symond also suggested I see Drake Haron about glassware he might want." I half expected the word "lie" to pop out on the pink palace wall. I ignored the drop of sweat tickling down my back.

"Wait." The guard stepped through the small gate set into the big one, spoke to someone I couldn't see, and returned. "I've sent word."

"Thank you." I waited, letting Addy's pleasant voice wash over my head and blot out Renie's devastating loss. At last, a page came out and spoke to the guard.

"You can go in. Follow the boy." The guard held the gate open. I seized the cart handles and walked through, my mind full to my scalp with the patter I meant to use on the drake. Only after I was in the yard did I realize Addy was still with me.

"What are you doing?" I said.

"I'll just keep you company and buck you up."

"I'm conducting business. I don't want company."

My prickly tone must have penetrated his normal distracted daze because he snapped his eyes from the palace tower to me. "Please let me stay." He bent close. "I want to see if I can worm my way into the library. I'll never have another chance." His breath on my ear unexpectedly made my spine tingle.

I pulled away. "Is that why you're helping me?"

He flushed. "A little. I like seeing you too, of course. Please, Emlin."

I wasn't keen on men who were users, especially now, but at least Addy was an honest one. "Don't blame me if you end up in a cell." I looked around for the boy we were supposed to follow.

He'd halted a few yards in front to wait for us and now started walking again. I hurried to catch up. "Were you working the night the glasshouse mistress was killed? Did you see her?"

His eyes widened. "No, but that was terrible. Murder almost on our doorstep."

I dropped back next to Addy.

"I've never seen anything to beat this." Addy scanned the palace, the tower, the courtyard and the walls as if he intended to set up an easel and paint a picture.

I swept my gaze around the courtyard and across the face of the palace. Color shimmered everywhere. Red, yellow, and purple flowers clung to the walls, filling the air with a scent that made me think of silk. No wonder I'd been able to smell them all the way from Renie's street. More chestnuts, like the one across from Renie's, rustled over the walkway. A jaffel swooped across the path. I'd seen it all before, and I was still impressed.

The boy strode toward the palace's arched entryway. Trailing Addy in my wake, I followed into a wide hall leading straight ahead. At the end of more corridors stretching right and left, doors gleamed with gold. "Lots of dragon work here," Addy observed. "Of course, that's true of all the palaces in the islands, but the work here seems to have been covered with gilt."

I was impressed by how cool he managed to sound. "You don't approve?"

He shrugged. "Dragon work doesn't need decorating."

To my surprise, I found I agreed.

The page had evidently been hoping for a more dazzled reaction. "Symond had that done this year. Kural's the best of the Dolyans, and its palace should show that." He tilted his head toward a waiting servant. "He'll take the window and leave your cart by the gate." I snatched my mother's journal from the cart, and the boy beckoned us on.

We entered a hall running between woven hangings from Frydar Island's crafthouse. The boy halted and pointed to a bench tucked into an alcove across from a narrow servants' hallway dead-ending in the one we were in. "Sit there. Symond will see you when he's finished his breakfast."

"And Drake Haron?"

"Symond says he'll take care of everything." The boy started to move away.

"But I will get to see the drake?"

The boy shook off the hand I'd laid on his arm. "The drake wouldn't see his ministers yesterday, so he's not likely to see you." He scuttled away.

I sank onto the bench. How was I supposed to find out what Drake Heron might want if I couldn't see him?

"Problems?" Addy perched beside me.

"I need to see Drake Haron. The well-being of the glasshouse depends on it." I ran my hands over the cracked leather cover of my mother's journal. When I saw how they trembled, I locked them around the edge.

One finger tapping his knee, Addy studied the floor. "Maybe the rumors are true, and the drake's health really is failing."

"I hope not. With Lyz on the march, Kural needs a strong ruler."

Addy frowned, but before he could say anything, footsteps sounded. I looked up to see a serving man coming straight toward us down the servants' hall, carrying a silver tray covered with a cloud-white napkin. He stopped outside a door in the narrow hallway and juggled the tray to fumble one-handed at the latch. After a moment or two, he cursed, gave up, and came toward us again. He turned into the wider hall, passed Addy and me in our alcove, and went along to where a bored looking guard stood outside a door which I knew opened to the drake's sitting room. The smell of fried bread drifted behind the tray.

"No one's there to help the old boy eat," the guard said.

The servant shrugged. "I'm not hauling this tray back to the kitchen. The woman who cares for him will be along eventually." The guard opened the door, and the servant vanished. A moment or two later, he came out again and went back the way he'd come, scanning us without much interest. The guard resumed his post next to the door.

Like me, Addy had leaned out of the alcove to watch. Now he drew back on the bench. "If you need to see Drake Haron, then you shall. Hang on a bit." He peeked around the edge of the alcove at the guard again, then darted soundlessly across into the servants' hall. By the time I clapped a hand over my mouth to cut off my squeak, he'd stopped at the door the servant had tried. He grasped the handle, his back briefly blocking my view. With a twist of his body, he slipped through the doorway.

Every muscle in my legs twitched with the urge to kick him.

He popped back out and crooked his finger at me. When I shook my head, he tiptoed toward me, scouted for the guard, and swooped down to grab my arm and lift me from the bench. "It's the drake's room," he whispered. "You want to see him? Now's your chance."

"You picked a lock! Is that what they do in Vinan?"

He grimaced and looked away. "I learned how as a boy. Does it matter? Come on."

Against all good sense, I realized that he was crack-brained, but he was right. This was my chance. With him timing our movements, we darted across the corridor, down the hall, and through the door, which he shut silently behind us. I struggled to quiet my breathing in a tiny, lamp-lit entryway facing a leather curtain. Folded linen sat on a shelf against which leaned a broom. From the other side of the curtain came the sound of something metallic clattering to the stone floor. Someone gave a sad mew.

Addy spoke into my ear. "It's his bedroom. He's there all right, but another door opens on the room from the other side, from his sitting room probably. You should be ready to move if you hear someone coming."

"No joke," I muttered breathlessly.

He grinned and lifted the edge of the curtain.

Clasping the journal to my chest, I stepped through, ridiculously grateful when I felt the brush of Addy's hand against my back and knew he'd come in too. A huge bed lay directly in front of us, its head against the wall to our left and its occupant screened by the bed's half-drawn silk curtains.

Heart galloping, I took a tentative step. "Sir? Drake Haron?"

"My knife," a thin voice quavered.

My shaking legs nearly gave way. He already knew about

98

the Dragonblade. It really was what my mother delivered. I started to back away.

"I dropped it," the old man murmured. "How will I eat?"

I stopped. Not that kind of knife then. "Sir?" I forced myself to move around the bed curtain.

A thin old man with wispy white hair sat propped up against embroidered pillows, a bed-table set across his legs. He blinked when he saw me but seemed unalarmed. "My knife?" he asked.

I swallowed. "Where did it fall?"

He pointed near where I stood, then dropped his bony hand to the cover and waited with a hopeful smile, looking frail as a newborn chick.

I saw nothing on the floor, so I shifted my mother's journal to the crook of one elbow and stooped to search under the bedside table. Was this the same powerful ruler I'd seen at public ceremonies all my life? Surely the night-shirted man in the bed was smaller. The only thing under the table was a dustball, but when I groped under the bed, my fingers brushed something hard. I felt cautiously for a handle and fished out a silver knife. When I rose and showed it to him, he beamed.

"Now the jam." He nodded at the food on his bed-table.

I set my mother's book on the bed and hesitated an instant before wiping the drake's knife on the napkin tucked under his chin. I spread strawberry jam on his fried bread and stepped back so he could eat. Instead, he opened his mouth and waited. Hastily, I cut a strip of bread and fed the end into his mouth. He hummed as he chewed it and opened his mouth for more. I gave him more bread, then offered a sip of wine. He seemed happy. Maybe he'd still be interested in buying a Dragonblade. He was vulnerable enough to need one.

I glanced over my shoulder at Addy, lingering out of the drake's sight but certainly not out of hearing. "Go," I said. "I want to talk business."

His mouth pinched, but he nodded and slid behind the curtain. I waited for the sound of the hallway door shutting.

"Sir, I'm from the glasshouse. I'm Calea's daughter. You remember her?" I cut another strip of bread.

He smiled vaguely. "Calea?"

"The craftmistress." I fed him the bread. "She made beautiful glass."

Drake Haron brightened. "She made something for me? What?" A bit of bread escaped from the corner of his mouth, leaving a trail of jam. I dabbed at it with the napkin.

He obviously wasn't going to be able to tell me anything about my mother. He sounded as if he didn't even know she was dead. "I'd like to make something for you if you'll let me." I drew a deep breath. "If you'd like, I could make you a copy of the Dragonblade. But only if you'd like."

"A knife?" He frowned. "My knife fell on the floor."

I moaned. Desperate to make him understand, I grabbed my mother's book and leafed through it until I found the right page. I thrust the picture of the knife under his nose. "See it? Kural's blade is lost but if you want a copy, I'll make it for you. It might scare off enemies like Drake Jaffen."

Drake Haron examined the drawing, then dropped a shaky finger on the page. "They burn the false ruler, like fire from the Dragon's mouth." He cackled and looked at me, as if inviting me to share some joke.

I craned my neck and saw he was pointing not at the knife but at the Dragonshard necklace sketched below it. "Not that! The knife!"

His mouth trembled. "No need to be angry. It was only a jest."

I looked into his crinkled, anxious face and felt a flash of guilt. Poor old duck. Impulsively, I bent to kiss his cheek. "I'm sorry." I forced a chuckle. "Very funny."

Looking surprised but pleased, he touched the spot I'd kissed. "And clever, too."

At that moment, I heard a woman's voice in the next room, growing louder as if she were coming our way. I snatched my mother's book out from under the drake's hand. His startled look was the last thing I saw as I fled back behind the leather curtain. As it dropped behind me, footsteps entered the bedroom. I froze, scared I might make a noise.

"How are you today, Lord Drake?" a woman asked. "Let's get you fed, shall we?"

"Can I go for a ride today?"

"No. I've told you before. You have to stay in your room."

"But I want to ride my horse."

"No. If you try to leave again, I'll tell the cook not to send you any dinner."

To my horror, the drake began to cry.

"Stop that noise," the woman said. The muffled sound of a slap came through the curtain.

Unable to listen to any more, I cracked the door open to be sure the hallway was empty before I scampered back toward the alcove.

"Here, you!" I whirled to find the drake's door guard frowning and walking toward me. "You were to stay on that bench," he said. "Where have you been?"

"I went to find a privy," I said.

"What about the man with you?"

"Same thing," I said.

"I told Symond you were here, and he said you were to wait while he decides if he has time to see you. Sit down and don't get up again."

My knees shook. Sitting was a good idea.

Chapter 12

I COLLAPSED ONTO the bench, and the guard stomped back to his post. Addy must have seized his chance to go off and search for the library. Just as well. What kind of childhood had the boy had if it taught him to pick locks? I didn't want him breathing in my ear anymore. It clouded my judgment.

My pulse still raced to the memory of how cruel the serving woman had been. Symond must not know. The drake's son would never allow his father to be treated so badly.

I tried to remember the last time I'd seen Drake Haron looking powerful. It had been at least a year, I decided, and rumors his health was failing were all over Kural. In my hearing, no one had suggested he'd gone grey-witted, but sure as storms in autumn, that's what he was. Symond must be ruling in his place. Did Dain know Haron was so weak? If so, and he'd told his Drake Jaffen, no wonder my father expected trouble. Jaffen would want to get what he could before the younger Symond became drake.

That could be why my mother had to die now, before she saw what was happening and told anyone the Dragonblade

Jaffen carried was fake.

Caressing the book in my lap, I tried to figure out what to do. The drake wasn't going to be buying a Dragonblade; that was certain, but it seemed to me that Kural's ruler needed protection more than ever. Maybe Symond would want a blade for him.

Someone came hastening down the hall, and I leaned out of the alcove to see Dain. I knew the instant he recognized me because he stumbled to a halt. Then his gaze shot toward the guard, his face went smooth, and he started walking again as if he meant to go past without acknowledging me, just as he'd spent the last seventeen years not acknowledging me. My body flamed with the righteous anger I'd felt the night before when I realized why he'd romanced my mother.

I jumped to my feet. "Don't you dare ignore me."

He looked past me and sidled into the alcove, his hands on my shoulders to move me in there too. "Keep your voice down," he whispered.

"You were sent to Kural to get something, were you? You needed a fake Dragonblade, and you went straight after a glassmaker to get it. You used her to serve Lyz. You are despicable."

His face was pale. "We are not having this conversation here. Can't you see the danger you're putting me in?"

"Excuse me? You're in danger? And yet you're still walking around. My mother's not. Why is that, Dain?"

He tightened his grip on my shoulders. "Come and see me tomorrow."

"Why should I? Is there something you want from me too?"

He flapped his hands at me and retreated rapidly back the way he'd come.

"What really happened that night, Dain?" I called after him.

A door opened and closed behind me, and I turned to see Symond frowning after Dain. My heart still pounding with fury, I bowed. Symond beckoned, and I followed him through a door across from the drake's and into a small sitting room.

Symond settled into a silk-cushioned chair. "You're acquainted with the Lyzian trade representative?"

"He knew my mother," I said.

"Did he? He didn't tell me that." He ran his hand over his mouth.

My tongue trembled with the urge to tell him what the serving woman had done to his father. But how could I explain knowing that?

For the sake of the glasshouse, I drew a calming breath and opened my mother's journal. I'd start by offering him beautiful glass. "Yesterday, you said you might want to buy something beyond the window. These vases are unusual. No one else would have anything like them." I showed him the picture. He put out his hand, and I gave him the book.

He examined the vases. "You're right. If I had my way, every piece of glass in the palace would have come from Calea. I can see these are her designs. I'll take two of them."

"Sir," I asked, "do you know what glassware she delivered here the night she was killed? Do you know who she saw?"

He cocked his head. "No. She wouldn't have brought anything straight to me, of course." He turned a page and stopped. I craned my neck to see what had caught his interest and realized he was staring at the pictures of the Dragonblade and the Dragonshard necklace. His head lowered over the page. "A Dragonblade." His eyes rose to meet mine. "I've often wished my father had the one that used to be Kural's."

I licked my lips. "Me too. He'd be safer if he had it."

Symond drummed his fingers on the arm of his chair. "Suppose you tried to make a knife of dragon glass. It would be fake, obviously, but his enemies wouldn't know that. Could you do it before Drake Jaffen gets here in two days?"

As easily as that, I had what I'd come for. I couldn't believe it. "I think so."

He snapped the book shut. "Then I want you to do it. I don't trust Jaffen. I want my father protected."

My body felt light enough to float out of my chair. Still, best to be sure Symond and I both understood what I'd be doing. "I'd have to break the law to get the glass."

He shrugged. "I'll see that you come to no harm for it." He leaned toward me. "But my father is an old man, and surely the dragon would approve of protecting him."

Given my mother's fate, I didn't think there was anything sure about it. At least I now knew she hadn't delivered a Dragonblade the night she died. If she had, Symond wouldn't be ordering one. It seemed most likely the secret of her death lay with the Lyzians.

"I'm sure you're right, sir," I said.

He handed the journal back. "Two days. I'll send word on when to deliver it. After what happened to your mother, I'm going to send a guard to escort you home now too."

"Sir," I ventured as I rose to leave, "I hope Drake Haron is being well served."

He raised an eyebrow. "A hope we all share."

I fled the room.

I SCARCELY WAITED to shed my guard and plunge through the glasshouse doorway before giving my news – at least the part of it I could share without Miriv blowing up. "Symond wants two filigree vases from my mother's journal. He'll pay a draco for the pair."

Miriv blinked at the journal tucked under my arm. "You took that to the palace?" Her eyes narrowed.

"When I saw him at the docks, he said he might buy more than the window. I'd have told you, but I thought you might not approve."

Gillis frowned from me to Miriv. "Why not? We need the money." She used the tongs to move the beaker she'd just finished from the marver table to the annealer.

"It's just vases, Miriv." I concentrated on keeping my voice even.

Miriv's mouth tightened, but she went to the shelves to gather what she needed. "Set the drawing on the table, Emlin," she said over her shoulder. "Gillis, will you help me?"

She was angry that I hadn't simply locked up the journal with the incriminating drawings. Since she was trying to protect the glasshouse, I could hardly take offense.

"I also have to tell you that Renie fell down the stairs and lost her baby."

"No!" Gillis cried. "She'll be so unhappy."

Miriv rubbed her hand over her face. "How many more things can go wrong?"

I flipped my mother's journal open to the vases so Gillis and Miriv could see them. "Do you need me to keep making those beakers you were working on?"

"I do," Miriv said. "The ship from Lyz is due any day, and we need to finish that order." More sharply than usual, she added, "Keep your mind on what you're doing now."

I picked up the pipe Gillis had put down and went to gather glass. Sweat slicked my face the moment I neared the furnace, but I welcomed it. Heat meant I was home.

THE THREE OF us worked steadily. I tried to focus on my task, but I was still distracted by laying my plans. Symond had given me two days to make the knife, which meant I'd have to slip out tonight to get the dragon glass from the Heights. That would be the hardest part. It was Gillis's turn to watch the furnace tonight, which was one piece of luck. If it had been mine, I couldn't have left, and if it had been Miriv's, she was worried enough about me that she'd have asked where I was going, whereas Gillis would just assume I had a man, Addy probably.

"What are you smiling about?" Gillis asked.

To my surprise, I realized I'd been picturing meeting up with Addy, and it had felt like it would be entertaining. Not in the way Gillis would expect, of course. Addy would tromp on my toes if he came near enough to, say, breathe in my ear. "Nothing." I turned my face away from her and Miriv. I needed to keep my mind on what I was doing or I was likely to make beakers shaped like strange flowers or insects. In my opinion, those pieces would be interesting, but our customers were unlikely to agree.

AFTER LUNCH, MIRIV went out to give our suppliers their share of what my window had brought in. The shadows in the yard lay long by the time she returned, her step heavier than usual.

"Something wrong?" I asked.

"Probably." Miriv twisted her crafter ring.

"The suppliers made trouble?" Gillis asked.

"No, that went as expected. They aren't happy and let me know it, but I paid what we'd agreed to, so they accepted it. But I heard rumors that the drake might close the port."

Symond, not the drake, I thought. The poor old thing was lucky if he could decide to close his fly. Then I woke to the implications of a port closure. "We won't be able to sell to the merchant ships if they can't dock. We'll be destitute within a week."

"Why would Drake Haron do that?" Gillis asked. She was cleaning up from our day's work. The swish of her broom hushed as she waited for Miriv's answer.

"I don't know." Miriv sank onto a stool, pulled one foot from its shoe, and bent to rub it. "But the Watch was everywhere, stopping people they didn't know and going in and out of inns, asking for strangers. Also, a curfew's been set. No one's to be out after dark."

"Doo. Sounds like a manhunt," Gillis said, then giggled, which was oddly reassuring. Gillis would never stop being Gillis.

"Maybe they decided my mother's murder wasn't random, and they're searching for her killer," I said.

"I hope so," Miriv said grimly.

I tried to decide what the curfew and a hunt by the Watch meant for my plans. *Nothing*, I concluded. I'd just have to be careful.

WITH THE CURFEW in effect that night, I doubted even Gillis

would let me leave through the workshop. Hands on the window sill in my room, I heaved myself up. The glasshouse yard yawned a long way below me. I gulped ocean-scented air and looked up instead of down. The stars of the Dragon constellation pricked the sky. The one that was Kural winked at me.

All right. I take that as approval.

I passed the strap of my leather bag over my head, tucked it against my side, and turned around to back through the window and onto the slanting roof. Instantly, my feet shot out from under me, and I bounced to lie flat on my stomach. I grabbed the window sill, waited until I stopped breathing like a bellows, then managed to turn over and sit so I could at least see the death I was sliding to. If I could worm my way to the chimney, I could use its sloping shoulder to work my way lower while clinging to the iron rod bolted to its side. The rod was supposed to fly the glasshouse banner, but the banner had blown away during a storm the previous year and Kedry hadn't got round to replacing it. At the chimney, I clutched the iron rod and pulled myself up.

There was a soft *crack*, and my right hand sagged as the end of the rod tore away from the bricks. My feet skipped, and I dangled from the rod like a fish on a line. For an instant, the night held still. Then my hands slipped away and I was falling, rolling off the chimney. Inky sky rushed away from me. I landed on my back on the shed roof, all the breath driven out.

"You there," a man said. "Thief! Come down off that roof."

I rolled toward the voice and raised my head. A Watchman stood in the yard looking up with his club pointed at me.

"You make me come after you, and you'll be sorry."

I climbed off the shed onto the handcart and then to firm ground. My teeth hurt from banging together when I fell. "I'm not a thief. I live here."

He spat on the cobbles. "Just routine to use the window, I suppose. What's in the bag?"

I opened it and showed him it was empty.

He scowled, a cat afraid the mouse was escaping its claws. Then he brightened. "You're out after curfew. Come along with me. You can spend the night in a cell thinking up a tale for the Watch captain." He grabbed my arm and hauled me toward the gate.

"Wait!" My tongue tripped trying to get the words out. "Wait! I'm not out after curfew because I'm not out. I'm in our yard."

He stopped, swearing under his breath as his head swiveled from the glasshouse door to the yard gate. He gave my arm a hard shake. "All right," he said. "Let's see what they have to say inside about you crawling out a window." He shoved me to the door and rapped it with his club.

I searched my head for what to say to Miriv if his pounding woke her.

The man raised his club, but before he could knock again, the door opened a handspan, and Gillis peeked through the crack, clutching the open neck of her white nightgown. "What is it?" Her gaze caught on me, and her eyes widened. She opened the door all the way. "Emlin! How did you get out there?"

"She was sneaking out a window," the Watchman said. "Off to see her man, no doubt, and shame on her for that."

Gillis's jaw sagged. "Yes, indeed," she finally managed. "You are so right. You can let her go now. Get in here, Emlin.

What is wrong with you?"

I was torn between wanting to smack Gillis and wanting to hug her. The Watchman pushed me through the doorway, unable to resist a last show of being in charge. The workshop glowed with the heat of the furnace, or maybe my face was hot all on its own.

"Good night," Gillis said and shut the door in the Watchman's face.

"I wasn't—" I began, but Gillis raised her hand.

"Shh." She waited, ear to the door. "He's gone." She looked toward my workroom. Its door opened, and Piret, the boy who'd been hanging around Gillis, came through. His shirt hung outside his trousers, and he clutched an armful of jacket and shoes.

He smiled sheepishly. "Good evening, Emlin."

Gillis glanced at me, read my face, and said, "You should go, Piret." She pecked him on the mouth and shooed him out the door, still barefooted.

I whirled on her. "Are you mad? Think of the risk." We both knew I wasn't just talking about the risk of Miriv stumbling on Gillis and Piret together, though Miriv wouldn't be happy about that. It was the possible consequences of Piret's visit that Miriv would be more worried about. By Dolyan tradition, the glasshouse had cared for me as a crafthouse child. Given our money situation, though, this wasn't the time for us to take one on. And I thought Miriv was right about Piret. His parents would never let him marry Gillis.

"You're hardly one to talk," Gillis said. "I *knew* that bookhouse boy liked you from the way he talked when he brought the jajas."

"I'm not—" I stopped. What could I say? I was going to

the Heights to steal glass from Kural's dragon?

"I won't tell if you won't." Smiling smugly, Gillis eased the door back an inch, peeked out, and opened it the rest of the way. "All clear."

I settled the leather bag on my shoulder and stepped into the doorway. I looked back. "Be careful, Gillis."

"You, too," Gillis said.

I went out into the night and started for the Heights.

Chapter 13

I FOLLOWED THE street until it gave way to a dirt lane. At that point, I began watching for the path leading to the Heights. I went slowly because once I was out of town, the only light came from the newly risen moon, and I was afraid I'd miss it in the shrubs and grass along the edge of the lane. Then through a gap in the undergrowth, I spotted it. Clutching the strap of my bag, I started my climb. Night birds called and small creatures rustled through the scrubby grass, hurrying away from me. After a while, the path turned toward the grassy spots where goats grazed. I kept going straight up, but now I scanned for the Watch patrol charged with keeping people away.

A light flashed three times from somewhere ahead.

I froze, but the light didn't appear again. The patrol must have moved on. I lowered my head and kept climbing. If my mother could do this for Dain, I could do it for my glasshouse family.

Beneath me, the ground rumbled. I smothered a yip. Could that be Kural's dragon stirring? Black rock spread ahead of me, and I realized I'd reached the Heights. In Drake Kural's time, his dragon had spewed fire here. It had melted rock like a glasshouse furnace and sent it rolling down the hillside, burning and then covering everything in its path and, in the process, making dragon glass. Tufts of grass brushed my trouser legs, leaving them damp against my ankles. To my left rose a cliff too steep to be climbed any farther, but I was already on ground that was forbidden, not only because the dragon slept here but also because of the power he'd left in the glass. Drakes had learned early that when people touched the glass, they felt that power and often couldn't stop longing for it. It was longing for dragon inspiration, the Sage said, but people wound up seeking other kinds of power instead. Trouble always followed.

The night had fallen quiet. I heard only the warble of a jaffel. So the little birds were here as well as at the palace. Given that they nested in dragon work and the dragon's lair had been here, that made sense. Ahead of me, the ground sloped to a drop-off where the starry sky plunged down to the ocean. Behind me lay the town, small in the distance and quiet under the curfew, with the Watchmen's lights darting here and there like fireflies.

I took another step and felt a flush of gratitude when the earth held still. It would be wonderful if Kural's dragon awoke in answer to the one on Lyz, but not now. As I walked, I scanned the ground, looking for the shine of glass. My mother had once told me that loose cobbles of dragon glass lay all over the field, and in some places spread in flat layers. It had never occurred to me to wonder how she knew that, but now I realized she must have seen it when she gathered glass to make the Dragonblade. When I reached the drop off, I found a shelf skirting the cliff's edge. I was turning to follow it when a light once again flashed three times, this time clearly out on the water. Frowning, I tiptoed toward the drop off.

"Emlin."

I would have skittered over the edge if a hand hadn't grabbed my arm and dragged me back. I clutched a fistful of shirt and found myself clinging to Addy.

"Sorry," he said. "I didn't mean to scare you."

"You startled me. That's all." I released his shirt and tried to shake his hand off my arm, but he kept his grip until he'd backed two more yards away from the edge.

"Then I was the only one scared," he said. "I'm not good with heights."

I glanced back toward the water. "Did you just see lights flash out there?"

His gaze flicked seaward. "I saw. From a ship maybe."

"Probably the one from Lyz. It's due in tomorrow. I hope the harbor is open. They've ordered some of our glass. What are you doing here?"

Even distorted by the lantern light below his chin, his face instantly sprang alive with enthusiasm. "I'm camping. You told me there was dragon work here, and you were right. You won't believe what I've found."

"Camping? But it's forbidden ground."

"It's blessed." He nodded, sounding like a kid who'd found an unclaimed toy chest.

"But being here is illegal."

"Kural's dragon sleeps here, and the remnants of its knowledge are thick on the ground. All knowledge is precious, and it should never be banned," he added with bookhouse logic. He shone the lantern into my face, making me hold up a hand to shield my night-blind eyes. "And if it's illegal, what are *you* doing here?"

The unexpectedly sharp question surprised me. "Looking

for dragon glass." I meant to sound defiant, but his face didn't change, so he evidently didn't understand how much I was tampering with powerful things. Or didn't care. That made me hesitate. If he didn't know what to be scared of, maybe I should be scared of him. He'd picked a lock and then left to sneak around the palace. I needed to collect my glass and get out of his company and off the Heights.

"What does dragon glass look like?" Addy asked.

"Shiny surface, usually black, though sometimes a sheen of color depending on the light. The stones in the drake's necklace have rainbows in them, but that's rare."

"Could it be sharp-edged, sticking out of the roof of a cave?"

"Yes. Where is it?"

He grinned. "Come with me. I'll show you not only dragon glass but dragon work like you've never seen." He gestured toward the flat ground running along the edge of the drop off.

I went where he pointed, still wondering how much I should trust this slippery, charming boy. "Did you get into the drake's library this morning?"

He made a face. "No. The moment the guards spotted me without you, they threw me out."

I slammed to a stop. "Did you make trouble? Is it you the Watch is looking for?"

"I went quietly," he protested. "What do you mean about the Watch?"

"They're searching for someone. They've set a curfew and might close the port."

He resumed walking, eyes straight ahead. "Well, that's not my fault. Did you get what you needed from the drake?"

"No, but I did from Symond." I followed him around a

clump of spindly bushes. He'd better show me glass soon.

"Here we are." As he ducked into a cleft in the rising ground to our left, the ground once again shimmied under my feet.

I halted, waiting for it to stop.

Seemingly unfazed, he looked over his shoulder. "What I think is dragon glass is a bit farther in." He held up the lantern so I could see better, and his excited face came into view again. The tension in my stomach eased. He was much too absorbed in seeing something new to be thinking about harming me. Silently begging the dragon not to collapse the mountain on our heads, I followed him into a narrow cave, inhaling the scent of moldy air and damp earth.

A bed roll and pack lay tidily just inside the entrance. To one side were huge tumbled stones, to the other lay sturdier looking rock. "Is this safe?"

"I think so, though the ground seems to have shifted pretty recently." He glanced back. "I'm guessing that's what uncovered the dragon work I'll show you. Careful now. I nearly sliced my head open the first time I came through here." He slowed, walked a few more yards, and lifted the lantern. "There." Dragon glass gleamed in great chunks, like black icicles thrusting down from the cave's ceiling. "Is that it?"

Awe stopped my tongue. All I could do was nod.

"Can you reach? Shall I get it for you?"

"If you would. You should be able to knock some loose with a rock. But be careful. It really is glass, so it's not only sharp, it's fragile, and it'll break if you drop it. And you shouldn't touch it. I was going to wrap my hand in this." I offered him the leather bag. If he'd already touched it, there was nothing I could do.

He searched for a likely rock to use as a hammer, grasped a chunk of dragon glass in a leather-wrapped hand, and whacked it loose.

I cringed, but I needed this glass. The glasshouse needed it. Drake Haron needed it.

I remembered Miriv saying my mother had reasoned herself into making the knife.

Addy set the glass carefully on the ground and went back for a second piece and a third. "Is that enough?"

"More than enough probably, but I need extra in case I make a mistake." A low murmur rose from below us and grew until it made the ground shiver. Unable to suppress a yelp, I had to grab at Addy to keep my balance. I imagined the dragon stirring, a red-gold eye cracking open. Slowly the earth steadied again. Embarrassed, I let go of Addy's arm.

"It's been doing that," he said. "I should have warned you."

"You're afraid of heights, but not of dragons?" I sounded like I was choking.

"Dragons love scholars," he said blithely and scooped up the pieces he'd knocked loose with the mouth of the bag. But when I reached for it, he slung it over his shoulder and took a step away from the cave's entrance, deeper into the earth. "Now let me show you what I found."

That was not the direction I wanted to go. I licked my lips. How certain of him was I? It was odd that he kept turning up in my path. Also, wasn't he the one who'd tipped over that cart of jajas in the market and started the riot? "Addy, give me my bag. I have to go."

"Oh, come on. You won't be sorry, I promise." He walked deeper into the cave.

I followed him, sweat trickling between my breasts,

hands twitching to grab the bag of glass. Finally, I halted. "Addy, you may be happy in here, but I want out."

He lifted the lantern in front of us. I thought for a moment that there might be a faint answering light. Then I realized I was seeing our own lantern reflected in pink stone through a narrow opening in the cave. Addy led me through and halted. Smiling like a host showing a guest through the front door, he turned in a slow circle, lantern held high.

My mouth fell open. We were in a wide hallway, its walls, ceiling, and floor all made of the same smooth pink stone.

Dragon work.

Chapter 14

I WANTED TO say something but managed only an embarrassing squeak.

Addy held the lantern closer to one wall, and a man loomed into view. I jumped, then saw I was looking at a mural. I inched closer, only just coherent enough to shut my gaping mouth. The life-sized painting showed a dark-skinned young man in a blue and gold tunic, a gold circlet holding back his dark hair. Behind him rose what was unmistakably the palace tower, and next to him, in a half-finished wall, was a jaffel shrine holding a sleepy looking bird. What caught and kept my gaze, though, was the man's Dragonshard necklace.

I shot Addy a glance. "Our dragon rider? Kural himself?"

"Looks like it to me. Whoever did the murals sure treated him like a lord. He's in almost every picture along here."

"There's more?"

"Oh, yes." He lowered the lantern and smiled at the jaffel who had been shown fluffing itself out in indignation at the dragon rider's presence.

The bird blinked at me.

I was surprised into a laugh. What I'd taken to be part of the mural was a real jaffel shrine with a real bird, unhappy over being disturbed but not frightened into flying off.

Addy grinned, and I smacked his chest. I felt silly for suspecting him of luring me to harm. He was just happy at the chance to show off his find.

"Come and see the other pictures." He led me along, pausing every few yards to hold up his lantern and let me look. As he'd said, Drake Kural appeared over and over: reading a book to a little girl with her hand on his knee, crouching to feed pottage to a ragged old man, examining a melon vine heavy with fruit. My admiration and awe grew.

"What a ruler he must have been," I said.

"The muralist thought so anyway." Addy stopped by the second-to-last picture before the passageway ended in a jumble of stones. I hurried forward to look, but when he held up his light, I scrambled until my back hit the opposite wall. Glittering with blue and gold scales, Kural's dragon wheeled toward me on spread wings, its head thrown back, clouds trailing from its open mouth.

"I had that same reaction the first time I saw it." Addy joined me, then slid down the wall to sit cross-legged on the floor. He patted the spot beside him. "Rest a little, and get used to it. The riders used to link minds with those things. I keep thinking if I look at it long enough, I'll figure out how they did it and who first had the nerve to try it."

I let my shaky legs fold and collapsed beside him. "It's a terrifying notion. The dragon inspires my best designs, and when that happens, I know I'm doing the work but it feels like someone else is helping me, nudging me to do things I didn't deliberately think of." I found I was whispering and cleared my throat. "It's... agitating, I guess is the word. I can't rest until I feel like I've done it justice, and then it's deeply satisfying. But what must it be like for a drake who shares minds with a dragon? Do they forget entirely where they stop and the dragon starts?"

Addy's forehead wrinkled. He chewed his lip, gaze running over the painted dragon.

"Why is this here?" I asked. "I thought only the palace had these dragon work walls."

"I think it was the dragon's lair," he said casually.

I puffed out my breath. "If you think that, why did you bring me through that crack? There's a dragon here!" I frowned. "How much dragon glass did you touch?"

He grinned. "You mean am I longing for power? I kept away from the glass." He unhooked a leather flask from his belt, uncorked it, and handed it to me. "I saw the jaffel flying this way and wondered where it was going." He smiled lopsidedly. "I never could resist snooping after answers. My father always said I had the longest nose of anyone he knew."

I took a swallow of water and handed the flask back to him. "Is that why he sent you to a bookhouse?"

"He didn't exactly send me." He took a drink, wiped the mouth of the flask with his shirt, and offered it to me again.

I shook my head. "What do you mean?"

Addy picked at a scratch on the leather around the flask's opening. He was silent so long I thought he might not answer. Then he spoke, eyes still on the flask. "My father had a cabinet in his study. Usually he kept maps in there, and I liked to look at them. One day, I found the cabinet locked. When I asked him why, he told me to keep out of the cabinet and his study too." Addy sighed. "As I said, I never could resist snooping. I like a challenge." He gave me an unreadable look.

I ignored the resulting shiver in my belly. "You must have been a real pest."

He jammed the cork back into the water flask. "My father was the magistrate for our part of the world, so there were cells in the lower level of our house. And as luck – or something – would have it, one of the cells held a man who'd picked the lock on a silver seller's door and helped himself to a tea set."

"A lockpick? You didn't."

He gave a short laugh. "I did. I told him I'd give him two gulls if he showed me how to pick locks. Actually, I offered him one, but he bargained his way to two. I handed over the coins, and he was honest enough to teach me to do it – practicing on his cell door, of course – before he locked me in the cell, scooped up the dagger I'd brought to work with, and escaped."

That explained what he'd done in the palace. I rolled my eyes. "Your father must have been livid."

Sobering, he contemplated the dragon. "You could say that. He hauled me before his court, and then turned me over to his guard captain to be flogged in front of the whole household. I ran away as soon as I could move again."

The pain in his voice made my throat close. I looked away to give him some privacy. On the edge of my hearing came a long sigh. I glanced at Addy, but his chest rose and fell evenly, though his mouth drooped. "How old were you?"

"Thirteen." He shrugged a little too broadly. "Old enough to manage on my own."

Not nearly old enough. "It's lucky you went to the bookhouse."

He studied the water flask. "I traveled some too, even went to the Westlands for a while. I like seeing other places."

That was impressive. I knew no one else who'd dared the sea stretching endlessly west from Lyz Island. "But you never got to see what was in the cabinet," I said lightly.

He grinned sideways at me. "Well, as it happens…"

I gave an answering grin. "What was it?"

He looked back at the dragon, then shifted so his knee was a bit farther from mine. "Pictures of things a thirteen-year-old boy is dying to know and wishes he had use for."

"Oh." My face grew warm, and I had a terrible urge to ask if he ever found use for what he learned. The dragon on the opposite wall watched us with what seemed to me to be an ironic tilt of its head. "So all knowledge is precious?"

He laughed, then waved at the line of paintings. "This knowledge is anyway. People should see these pictures. The Dolyans have a history of wiser, more humane rule than what we have now. Kural's bad enough. The money gets funneled into far too few hands here, but Drake Haron isn't the worst ruler in the islands by far."

"Drake Jaffen from Lyz would be worse. He'd start a war over who ruled the Dolyans. That's the kind of thing the original dragon riders left the Westlands to escape. Dragons shouldn't be weapons of war. They're brilliant dreamers who ask us to make the world better." Once again, I heard what sounded like the breathing of someone deeply asleep. I knew we should get out of this tunnel, but it was hard to leave these wonderful pictures.

Addy hesitated and then spoke slowly. "At the bookhouse, they say Jaffen's building schools for poor children. And that Lyzian medicine crafter's presence in the market means Jaffen is letting them travel. That's as it should be."

"That can't be true."

"I saw the manuscripts." He sounded offended by my slight on his scholarship. "Both book and craft knowledge should be able to travel. Let me show you something else." He hooked the flask to his belt and rose, putting out his hand to pull me to my feet. His palm was warm and dry, and he kept hold of me long enough to draw me the few yards down the hall to the last picture. He held up the lantern.

I felt a moment's disappointment. Instead of dazzling me with a rider or his dragon, the mural showed a map of the twelve Dolyan Islands that looked a lot like the window I'd just sold to Symond. As in my window, a dragon's image had been laid over the islands, with Basur at the east tip of its tail near the mainland, Kural as its open-mouthed head, and Lyz as the tongue of flame shooting westward. A shiver ran through me at the possibility that the dragon had inspired both me and this ancient Kuralian artist the same way. A string of words in a language I didn't know was inscribed along the picture's top.

I found Addy looking at me expectantly. "What?" I asked.

"The inscription is in Westish."

He was bouncing up and down on the balls of his feet in such a frenzy for me to ask, that I had to oblige "Can you read them?"

"I can! They say, *The dragons sleep, but when the fire comes, they will rise to the aid of their people.*"

I frowned. "I'm not certain I know what that means even in my own language."

"Sure you do. What do you think of when you hear the word *fire*?"

"The dragon." How could I think of anything else in this hallway?

"And?"

"Light, I guess."

"Good. And?"

"Glassmaking."

"Yes! And in the language you see here, the words for *fire*, *light*, and *knowledge*, both book and craft knowledge, are the same. When people know something, they're said to be *enlightened*."

"Uh, interesting. But we should go, Addy. And you shouldn't camp in here."

"It's *jaff*," he said.

"What's *jaff*?"

"The word for all those things. I think it's where jaffels get their name too because they're fire-red. But think, Emlin. Who else has a name like *jaff*?"

I stiffened. "You don't mean Drake Jaffen?"

"I *do* mean him. I saw these words in archives in the Westlands. I can't believe I found them here. Maybe they're on all the islands. I think this is a prediction that Jaffen will lead the Dolyans to a better life. What's more, I think the dragons may fly again. The fire's on Lyz now. There's melted rock running down the hillside. And as you've felt, Kural's dragon is restless."

I glared first at the words on the wall and then at Addy's flushed face. "I don't believe it. You can make all you want of old words, but I'll never believe a Lyzian should take over Kural. Our dragon would burrow even deeper underground!"

He nearly thumped the side of his fist against the painting but drew back at the last instant. "Have you been to Lyz? No. You're judging it without knowing it. Try to be a little more broadminded."

"I know all I want to of Lyz. My father came from there and seduced my mother because he wanted her to make a fake Dragonblade for the old Drake of Lyz. As soon as he had it, he left her, left us as it happened, though he says he didn't know I was on the way."

His mouth opened and closed, as if I'd said too much for him to sort through. When he did speak, he was kind enough to settle on the least humiliating thing. "The Dragonblade Jaffen carries is fake?"

"If it's the one his father carried, it is. My mother made it."

"She told you?"

"I found the plan for it in her journal. My father, the lying and maybe murdering Lyzian, talked her into it."

"You think he killed her?"

"I don't know, but I mean to find out." I yanked the strap of the bag of dragon glass off his shoulder and strode back along the hallway.

Addy trotted after me, caught the bag's strap, and spun me to face him. When I couldn't hide that I was blinking away tears, he wrapped his arms around me so I was between the warmth of his body and the warmth of the lantern in his hand. "Emlin, I'm so sorry."

I closed my eyes and rested my head on his chest. For a moment, I stayed there, listening to his heart and drawing deep breaths that echoed the long sigh on the edge of my hearing. "I keep trying to work out who the killer was or why he did it, but I can't make the pieces fit."

"You know, Emlin, it's probably best if you don't tell anyone your mother made a fake Dragonblade for Lyz." When he spoke, his chest vibrated against my ear.

"You think I *want* anyone to know?" I pulled free, fumbled a handkerchief out of my pocket, and swiped at my nose. "I have to go."

"I'll walk you home." He steered me toward the narrow

opening to the cave. "With the killer still loose, you shouldn't be out alone."

Despite our argument, all my wariness of him had gone. His love of learning was so unmistakably earnest. And in the story he'd told me of his father, he'd let himself be vulnerable in front of me, trusting me not to hurt him. I found I'd somehow decided to trust him back. We emerged onto the Heights.

"Is Dain after your work now?" Addy asked.

I shook my head. "I'm not really sure what he's after."

To our right, the lights of a Watch patrol pierced the night, so Addy lowered his lantern's shutter nearly all the way. We picked our path through the dark. At the edge of town, Addy tripped over a loose cobble, caught himself with an arm braced against a wall, muttering something savage under his breath. He leaned there a moment, staring down the dark street.

"It's all right," I said. "You don't have to come farther. No sense both of us risking being caught out after curfew."

Without answering, he pushed himself erect and started walking again. At last, we approached the glasshouse. Addy stopped at the end of the street with the gate in sight. "Go on. I'll wait."

I paused at our gate to glance back and see his shadowy form still waiting. I waved and went into our yard. The moment I passed through the gate, I felt safe, though I still had to get inside. Spilled sand and ash crunched under my feet as I crossed the yard to the door. To my mixed relief and annoyance, Gillis had left it unbarred. I eased the door open, slipped through, and barred it behind me.

Someone let out a loud, ragged snore.

I crept toward the pallet and was happy to find Gillis

alone. She must be deep asleep to make that noise though. It occurred to me that the workshop wasn't as warm as it should be. Gillis must have slept through the need to add wood to the fire. Miriv would be furious if she knew.

I went to the furnace, opened it as quietly as I could on its lame hinge, and fed the fire from the wood Gillis had waiting. Then I tiptoed up the stairs to my room. Why should I wake Gillis? There was enough large and small grief in this world already.

Night Flights 3

Addy is dreaming of dancing. His feet effortlessly go where he wants them to go. He is graceful as a bird.

Kedry is dreaming of a creditor breaking into his house and beating him. He wakes up sweating but comforts himself by rubbing his silk sheet between his forefinger and thumb.

The Sage of Kural's Great Bookhouse is dreaming of a manuscript from the Westlands that they have begun deciphering. They are equal parts puzzled and entranced.

Dain is dreaming of his daughter. He sees her at his kitchen table on Lyz. She is smiling.

Drake Jaffen is dreaming of flying.

Chapter 15

I N THE MORNING, the face in my mirror glimmered pale as the mist drifting through my open window. My body ached from lack of sleep, but even so, I'd make the knife tonight so I could deliver it to Symond tomorrow. During the few hours I'd spent tangling myself up in the blankets, I'd at least thought of a way to explain the extra money to Miriv: I'd say Symond had decided my window was worth more than he paid me and made up the difference.

A rap sounded on the door. I opened it to find Addy, bright as a gleam of gold and smelling of damp wool. Drops of mist clung to his dark hair like bits of glass.

"The girl downstairs told me to come on up," he said happily. "I wanted to be sure you got home all right and also to give you this." He thrust something at me.

I grabbed his wrist and dragged him into the room. With a glance down the stairs, I eased the door shut and whirled to face him. His back to me, Addy stretched on tiptoe to peer across the bed and out the window.

"You're very high up," he said faintly.

"Addy!"

He turned at my sharp call, eyebrows raised.

"Who was downstairs? A girl, you say? Not the craftmistress?"

"A girl." He sounded certain. "The one I gave the jajas to the last time I was here. She, uh, was still in her nightgown."

Gillis. I might have known. "You have to get out of here before Miriv gets up. I don't want her asking questions about what we might have been up to together."

He glanced at the bed.

"Not that," I snapped. "On the Heights or in the palace. Do *not* talk about those. Or the bed either for that matter." I reached for the door.

"Wait. This is for you." He held out a small, triangular stone with a hole in one corner. "I looked around some more and found it last night. It's not dragon glass or special or anything, just a stone." He laid it in my palm, eyes avoiding my face. "I noticed that you had beads on the first time I met you, and you seemed to miss touching them. I thought you could put this on a chain or something and wear it."

Warmth flushed through me. "Thank you." I closed my fingers around the stone. "I will." I sidled around him, opened the chest, and tucked the stone inside. "But I still need you out of here."

I went ahead of him, checking the stairs from every landing and beckoning him along when they were blessedly empty. Even Gillis had vanished, though she'd left the yard door standing open. Relief rising, I was leading him across the workshop when a dark shape loomed out of the fog in the yard – Miriv, carrying an armload of wood.

She halted on the doorsill, eyes flicking from Addy to me and back again. "Who's this, Emlin?"

"We met before, Craftmistress Miriv, albeit briefly." Addy surged toward her, arms extended to lift the wood from her grasp. "I brought the jajas, remember? I'm Addy, from the Vinanian bookhouse. Emlin and I met in the market the other day, and I was hoping she'd let me see some of the older books you have here, but she says that's not possible." He added the wood to the few sticks in the basket near the furnace.

Dragon fire, the man was a smooth liar.

As he straightened to beam at the stiff-faced Miriv, Gillis clattered down the stairs, still tying a leather thong around the end of her braid. She took in the scene and had the good sense to slide out of harm's way into the corner by the food bin. I shot her a dagger-edged glare.

"All our books are craft-closed," Miriv said evenly. "So Emlin's right. It's not possible." She stepped to one side of the door. "That being the case, you'll want to be on your way."

"Sorry to have bothered you. Good day to you all." Looking sheepish, Addy bowed, then hastened out the door, his gray clothes fading quickly into the fog.

"How long has he been here?" Miriv asked.

"I let him in just a few moments ago," Gillis said, softening my annoyance with her.

"Why didn't I see him?" Miriv asked.

"I sent him upstairs. I probably shouldn't have, but I was rattled because I wasn't dressed." Gillis waved toward the table by the food bin, where for the first time, I noticed a basket of food. "He brought eggs and fresh bread."

The tightness around Miriv's mouth eased a little. "That was thoughtful of him, but no visitors in the bedrooms, either one of you. Not unless the rest of us agree. It's too disruptive to everyone's privacy."

"Of course not," I said.

"Right." Gillis nodded rapidly. "Never in the bedrooms."

As usual, Gillis's eyes were wide, her face innocent. How did she do that? Avoiding Miriv's gaze, I went out to use the privy. I was starting back inside, wondering what to use to turn the triangular stone into a necklace, when I heard a man's raised voice. The sound of it was muffled by the fog but I recognized Dain.

"Keep away from my daughter!"

"Just what is it you think I'm doing here?"

Dragon save me, that was Addy. I moved to the gate. The two of them were just outside, standing toe to toe and glaring at one another.

"I don't know what you're doing here. I'm not even sure I believe you're—" Dain spotted me and snapped his mouth shut.

I looked from him to Addy, who was opening and closing his fists. It was the first time I'd seen him look other than eager to meet whatever came next. Then, right in front of me, his face smoothed out the way Gillis's had. The change happened so quickly, I wasn't sure he hadn't always looked the way he did now.

"Something the matter?" I asked.

Dain took a step toward me. "Of course there is. The Watch is stirred up about something, and the drake has ordered a curfew. Plus one of the night fishermen spotted a Lyzian ship. It'll be in the harbor as soon as the fog lifts. I want you to take shelter in my house in case their presence makes things worse."

"The ship is heading for the harbor?" Addy asked, his tone disbelieving.

"I'm fine right here." Even apart from not wanting to be near Dain, I couldn't leave the glasshouse. I needed to craft a Dragonblade. If the Lyzian merchant ship was here, Jaffen's ship was sure to follow.

Dain reached a hand toward me, but Addy stepped between us. "You heard her. She doesn't want to go with you."

"You planning on protecting her?" Dain asked.

"I don't need either one of you to protect me," I said before Addy could answer. "As a matter of fact, right now, having either one of you around strikes me as dangerous."

What kind of danger Addy posed I wasn't sure, but the image of his shifting face flickered in my head.

A long moment passed during which Addy looked away. He turned back, face blank. "She's right. I'll stay away from her if you will."

Pain pinched in my throat. I'd just told them I didn't need them. But it turned out I was a hard person to please, because I'd sometimes fantasized about what it would be like to have a father, and smooth-faced liar that Addy was, I liked the way he raced to embrace new knowledge. And he'd brought me the triangular stone. Now it looked as if, like my father, he could decide to walk away. When it came to sticking by someone, the two of them had a lot in common, I thought bitterly.

"Go." I turned my back on them and strode inside.

"Who was that I heard?" Miriv asked.

"The baker. I told him we already had bread. Are we ready for the Lyzian ship? The baker told me it was waiting offshore."

"Good." Miriv kept slicing bread, apparently believing me without question. If I counted her hiding the truth about Dain for seventeen years, which I did, we were a crafthouse full of champion women liars who drew men liars as visitors. How did anyone ever come to know what someone else was really like? Miriv nodded toward three crates stacked near the door. "That's the Lyzian order. I only wish it were more."

Gillis was shoveling glowing coals from the furnace into the brazier, getting ready to cook some of the eggs. "Will the money they owe be enough to make up the difference in our pay?"

"No," Miriv said.

I wished I could tell them I'd be getting money from Symond tomorrow.

In silence, we ate breakfast and then set about making glass, but all the while I kept hearing Addy in my head. He'd been quarreling with Dain about me. He had sounded as if he cared about me, a thought that left a sweet pang in my chest. And yet, he'd said he'd leave me alone. And I couldn't shake the vision of his face going blank.

By mid-morning, the fog had burned away. I put thoughts of Addy and my father aside, hung up my apron, and set off to deliver glass to the Lyzian ship. It was a market day, so I stopped there first to buy something for Gillis. Then I started for the docks. When I finished, I should have time to go to the Watch headquarters to ask if they'd learned anything new.

Bees buzzed in the weeds flowering in dirt patches at the road's ragged edge as I rattled the glasshouse cart down to the harbor, rushing a little when I passed Dain's door. Fishing boats crowded against the far docks, their catch already sent to market, their nets drying in the sun. The sleek merchant ship from Lyz resembled them only in that it was floating in water.

More sailors than I'd expected swarmed around it. A handful of fisherfolk leaned against the pilings, gossiping and squirting thoi-leaf juice between their stained teeth. Sailors were going up and down the gangplank, unloading the goods Kural imported from Lyz. Merchants' carts waited on the dock, along with half-a-dozen horses, their reins held by men and women in an unfamiliar black uniform. *Not sailors*, I realized with a speeding up of my heart. Lyzian soldiers. What were they doing here?

I maneuvered the cart around the horses and approached the sailor at the bottom of the Lyzian gangplank. "Excuse me, but may I see the mate? I have the glass goods you ordered."

Without so much as glancing at me, she pointed to a spot some yards away. "You'll have to wait. Not that wagon," she shouted to a sailor lowering a crate onto a cart bed. "The second one."

I halted my cart near a group of gawkers. "What are the horses for?" I asked a shrunken old fisherman in a tattered sweater.

"Not what," he said. "Who. Drake Jaffen himself's on that ship, come to see our Drake Haron."

Sweet baby dragon. Jaffen was a day early. Symond would be frantic for his father.

At that moment, a stray breeze caught the second flag on the ship's mast – a banner with a spread-winged dragon, breathing not clouds, but fire. So that was how Drake Jaffen saw himself now – a dragon ready to attack, meaning he didn't care dragons weren't supposed to be weapons of war. "What does Jaffen want?"

"Now, girly, no need to worry." He pointed toward the soldiers with the horses, a wave of fishy smell wafting off his sweater. "They say he's come to talk about an alliance between Lyz and Kural. Drake Haron will know what to do with him."

So Dain had spoken the truth. About *that*, anyway. I

found it hard to believe Jaffen was offering an honest alliance, not with that threatening dragon flag flying. Maybe Dain had even told him Drake Haron's health was failing so Kural was without a ruler to lead it. A war wouldn't even be necessary if Jaffen got rid of Haron and Symond. In that glowing hallway the previous night, Addy had sounded so convinced that Jaffen was the kind of ruler a dragon would awaken for. It just went to show how naïve you became when you lived between the covers of books.

A horse sidestepped toward me. My eyes on it, I wrestled the cart to a safer distance away.

"Send to the palace if you need me," a deep voice barked. "I'll be back tomorrow."

All the Lyzians were bowing to a grim-mouthed young man with a nose like a hawk's beak. He made his way to the horse that had crowded in on me. With a foot in the stirrup, he spoke quietly to one of his soldiers. "Remember my orders. A soft hand until we know where everyone is."

The soldier had been frowning at me, one fist resting on his sword hilt. He grimaced but let go of his weapon. "Yes, sir."

With a jolt, I realized that this soberly dressed young man had to be Drake Jaffen. I glanced at the knife sheathed on his hip. I could see only the hilt, so I couldn't be certain it was the Dragonblade my mother made, but it must be. He wouldn't come to a rival island without all the protection he could carry. Not that this one would do him much good. It occurred to me that Symond might like to know the knife was fake. I'd tell him when I saw him.

Jaffen swung into the saddle, nudged his horse into motion, and trotted up the winding road to the palace. The soldiers scrambled to mount and ride after him.

The old sailor next to me spat thoi-leaf juice over the edge of the dock and into the water. "Saw his father once. This one looks like him."

Maybe Dain was right. Trouble was brewing. Dain could have told Jaffen the knife was fake, and Jaffen might have wanted to silence the woman who made it. I had to do something but, against Jaffen, I'd need Symond's help.

A man wearing a mate's kerchief and carrying a fistful of papers came down the Lyzian gangway, spoke to the woman at the end, and beckoned to me.

I wheeled my cart over to him. "I have the glass goods you ordered."

He frowned. "Where's the man who usually brings them?"

"Probably still sleeping." I met his skeptical gaze.

He lifted the cover on of each crate and poked in the straw, evidently satisfying himself that I really did have the glass he was expecting. "It looks all right." He opened the fat pouch hanging from his belt, handed me coins, and waved a sailor over to take the cart. As the sailor wheeled the cart onto the ship, a hand grabbed my elbow, and I spun to see Kedry, his face purple.

"What are you doing? Did you take my money?" He glared at the Lyzian mate. "Did you give her my money?"

"The money's not yours." I struggled in his bruising grip. "It belongs to the glasshouse."

Kedry shook me hard enough that my head snapped back.

"Here. Let her go." The mate's voice rippled with such authority that Kedry released me, looking startled by his own obedience.

I slipped away from Kedry. "We own the glasshouse

now, Kedry. You gave it to us, remember? If it belongs to you, why are we the ones paying off its debts?"

Eyes wild, Kedry took a step toward me, making me slide halfway behind the mate.

Hand raised to halt Kedry, the mate flicked shrewd eyes from Kedry to me and back. "This sounds like a legal dispute you'll have to take up at Drake Haron's court. In the meantime, it's not my business, so I ask you to move away from this ship, sir."

Kedry gave an incredulous laugh. "You're siding with her? I'm the one who signed the contract for the goods you just took aboard."

"Take it up in court," the mate said.

"That's exactly what I'll do." Kedry mounted the horse waiting behind him and galloped up the road, knocking aside an old woman who didn't get out of his way in time.

"Thank you," I told the mate.

His eyes still followed Kedry. "I'd watch out for him if I were you."

I turned to watch Kedry's retreating form. Was it possible *he* was the source of the danger to us glassmakers? He was spiteful enough, and he had talked about closing the glasshouse anyway. It was hard to believe though. He was too lazy to climb Renie's stairs much less the glasshouse roof.

The sailor returned with my cart and handed it off to me. With the departure of Drake Jaffen, the crowd was dwindling. I started up the hill. As my alarm over Kedry faded, it left room for worry over Jaffen. I told myself that Jaffen was expecting to deal with poor old Haron, but was about to run directly into Symond, and Symond wouldn't trust Jaffen to dust his furniture.

Chapter 16

WHEN I REACHED Dain's door, I slowed. On the way up the hill, I'd mulled over the notion that my father probably knew what Jaffen was planning. He'd warned me there might be trouble. If I told him I was worried about the glasshouse and asked him what kind of trouble, it was possible he'd offer some bit of the truth I could tell Symond when I delivered the Dragonblade tomorrow.

When I knocked, the door surprised me by swinging ajar. I stared at it. Cautiously, I pushed it open. "Dain?" No answer.

He must have left it unlatched by accident when he went out. I started to turn away, but an image popped into my head of Dain hastily hiding a note. Maybe it would give me some hint of what was going on. I hesitated. Sneaking into his house and reading his correspondence felt dishonest, but Dain had been as dishonest as a man could be with my mother.

I left my cart where it was and stepped into the empty front room. A single mug sat on the table in a scatter of dried ale rings. A sharp smell lingered in the air. The door to the back room was ajar, and I ventured toward it. "Dain?" Still no answer.

I opened the top drawer of the sideboard. The note rested atop a litter of pens, paper, and what looked like an account book. It read: "I'll be there at the time you named." It was signed with a tiny drawing of a gull with jagged wings. I looked more closely. Not a gull. A dragon.

I frowned. Given the flag on the Lyzian ship and the fact that Lyz's dragon was the only one awake, his promised visitor was probably Lyzian. Jaffen must have sent spies ahead of his visit. If Symond didn't already know that, he was a fool.

Disappointed, I laid the note back in the drawer and slid it shut. I was turning away when I glimpsed the tip of a finger on the back room's floor. "Dain?" I whispered and pushed the door open. My father lay sprawled flat out.

I dropped to my knees and pressed my fingers to the side of his neck. His pulse was thread thin. I rolled him over. His face was battered. One eye was beginning to swell. In the corner of my vision, a shadow moved.

A dark-haired man brought his clasped fists down on the side of my head, toppling me over, across my father's body – solid between me and the floor. The man charged through the front room and out the door, nearly tripping over the empty cart standing outside.

The image of him swirled in my head and settled on one detail. He'd worn an earring with a red jewel in the top of his right ear.

I staggered to my feet, for a moment too stunned to know what to do. Then I lurched to the doorway and looked up and down the street, seeing no one. "Watch!" I shouted. "Help!"

"Sit." The Watchman pulled out a chair from Dain's table. "Talk to me while the healer does her work with him."

I collapsed, reaching to touch the empty place on my chest. I clasped my hands in my lap, my gaze catching on the ale rings on the table top. Someone should clean them away, my brain busily distracted itself by thinking.

"What happened?" the Watchman asked. I'd recognized him as the one who'd come to the glasshouse.

"Someone was here when I arrived. I think it was the man who killed my mother." He raised an eyebrow. I didn't blame him. I could scarcely believe it myself. "He wore the same red earring," I added.

Without comment, he wrote on his wax tablet. "Would you know him again?"

"Maybe. I just got a glimpse of him." I cursed myself for not getting a better look.

"And why are *you* here?" the Watchman asked.

I tilted my head toward the bedroom doorway. "He's my father."

"Huh. You didn't tell us that before. I'm disappointed in you."

I thought, but did not say, that I hadn't been impressed by him either.

He assessed me with a shrewd look. "Judging from the state of his face and ribs, whoever it was wanted something, information maybe. Could he have valuables concealed somewhere?"

I lifted my hands. "I don't know."

The Watchman rubbed his beard stubble, making a faint, sandpapery sound. "Did he have enemies? Someone he'd quarreled with maybe?"

I squelched the thought of Addy and Dain arguing outside the glasshouse only a few hours earlier. I couldn't imagine Addy beating someone, much less clubbing me on the head. Besides, I'd have recognized him. "My father has obviously been working for Drake Jaffen, and I wondered if they'd fallen out. Jaffen just arrived. Maybe that timing isn't a coincidence."

This time, the Watchman didn't even write my answer down. I could see he thought I was just overwrought. And I thought he was still a fool.

The healer came out of Dain's bedroom, buckling the carry bag banging against her lean hip. She smelled comfortingly of an herb mixture my mother used to brew into tea for me when I'd hurt myself.

I stood. "How is he?"

She smiled. "You must be the daughter he's been asking about. He has two broken ribs. I don't think they've pierced his lungs though. He should heal. I'll come by again in a couple of days." She nodded to the Watchman and let herself out.

"You still live in the glasshouse?" the Watchman asked me. When I nodded, he said, "I'll take you home."

"Wait. I want to say goodbye." I should at least tell my father who attacked him, assuming he didn't already know.

I went to the bedroom doorway. Dain lay under the covers, reminding me oddly of Renie yesterday. The bruises on his face were already beginning to darken. A small puddle of blood had dried on the floor, its edges smeared where one of us had walked through it. "Dain," I said. He cracked his eyes. "I have to go now. The healer says you'll be all right. You should know though that the man who beat you was the one who killed my mother."

His eyes popped fully open. "Are you sure?" I nodded. "Curse the bastard," he said.

"The man who beat you?" I demanded. "Or Jaffen?"

"No." He dragged his hand over his mouth.

I glimpsed the Watchman writing on his tablet.

"I have to go," I repeated.

"Wait." Dain struggled as if to sit up, then grimaced and flopped flat, breathing hard. I shifted from foot to foot, waiting until at last he crooked his finger at me. I drew closer and bent over him. He glanced past me to where the Watchman lurked in the doorway. "I have to get out of here," he whispered.

"The Lyzian ship docked this morning. Maybe they'll take you home. Get the Watchman to ask them."

"No!" He grabbed his side and sucked in air. "Can you find another boat? A fisherman maybe? Someone to take us both?"

He was obviously afraid of my mother's murderer – and whoever sent him – and he didn't want to go to Lyz. To me, that suggested that despite his denials, Jaffen had betrayed him. I eyed his battered face and reluctantly said, "If I can, I'll ask around tomorrow for someone to take you wherever you like."

"Where's your key, sir?" the Watchman asked.

"On the mantle," Dain said.

"I'll lock up on the way out and slide the key in under the door. You should keep it locked. You want me to send someone to check on you?"

"No." Dain didn't hesitate. I imagined a Watchman constantly looking in on him was the last thing he wanted.

We took our leave. The Watchman stayed at my side as

we walked back to the glasshouse, me pushing the empty cart. When we entered the overheated workroom, Miriv and Gillis looked up from their work, faces eager. I was so disoriented that it took me a moment to remember I'd sold glass to the Lyzian ship only an hour ago, and they wanted to know how things went. When they saw the Watchman, both of them stiffened. "What happened?" Miriv asked.

To my great gratitude, the Watchman explained. I leaned against the marver table and tried not to think about finding both my father in the middle of a savage attack and my mother with her throat cut. Something must be wrong with me. The Watchman stopped talking.

"Thank you." Miriv steered him out the door and came back to embrace me. She smelled like my mother always had of sweat and melted glass. "Are you all right?"

I laid my head on her shoulder. "I'm fine. Dain will heal." Assuming whoever went after him didn't try again. "And anyway, I don't even know him really. He means nothing to me." *My father would admire this window*, I heard my 10-year-old self say. *My father would want to know how I did it.* My voice would have been small and charged with longing. I pulled free of Miriv's grasp and held out the Lyzian payment. "Drake Jaffen was on that ship, by the way."

"Drake Jaffen is here? Did you see him?" Gillis asked. "Was he good looking?"

"Gillis, sometimes you make me want to shake some sense into you," Miriv said. "Come up to my office, Emlin." Miriv took the money and steered me by the elbow toward the stairs. Upstairs, she pressed me into a chair at the table, then took a bottle and a tin box out of her desk. She poured a finger's width of what smelled like rum into a scarlet glasshouse goblet and set it in front of me along with a honey cake from the tin. Gillis would whine like a two-year-old if she knew. The rum burned all the way down to my stomach. I couldn't have forced the cake around the lump in my throat, so I crumbled it while I leaked tears. Miriv handed me a handkerchief, then ignored me as she spread the coins out on the desk and sorted them into piles, small ones for the glasshouse's suppliers and even smaller ones for its workers. I wiped my face and drew a long breath. She looked up.

"Do you want to talk about the attack?" she asked gently. "It has to shake you, having been on a scene like that again."

I sat up straight. "I'll be fine." I frowned at the coins for a moment. Then I thought about the dragon glass hidden in my room, waiting to be shaped into a knife for Symond and felt better.

Miriv leaned back in her chair and brushed a stray hair from her face. "If you're really all right, I want to talk to you about something else, too."

The reluctance in her tone made me cautious. "What?"

"That scholar Gillis sent up to your room this morning—"

"I told you I was sorry about him, and nothing happened for me even to be sorry about."

"You said that. But seeing him worried me because—"

"Miriv, if you need to worry, worry about Gillis, not me."

"I do worry about Gillis, and I've told her so. Piret is a boy, and it'll take a strong whack to knock him out of the cradle. Young as he is, though, that scholar strikes me as a man who goes after what he wants. Harmless enough when he's hunting down some manuscript, but not so trifling when he steps out into the real world. He's just the sort Calea would have liked, and you're far too much like your mother for me not to be concerned."

I leapt to my feet. "I'm nothing like my mother." The ferocity of my denial surprised me. I hadn't realized until now how much my view of my mother had been changed by her cheating the dragon and then lying about both that and my father.

"You're *exactly* like her. Even apart from your dragon gift, you act like you can manage anything on your own as if asking for help was a sign of weakness. As if you were alone."

I dug my nails into my palms. "In case you haven't noticed, Miriv, I *am* alone." I swallowed guilt when Miriv flinched. She'd been a second mother to me for years, but the hole in my heart was too big for me to take back what I'd said. "And nothing is going to happen between me and Addy because he said it'd be better if *he* left me alone, too. But beyond that, I'd never lie to my child the way my mother did to me. I *trusted* her."

Miriv made a helpless gesture. "Calea didn't want you to think badly of her or your father. She didn't want you to think you'd been abandoned."

"*She* was abandoned, not me. Dain didn't even know about me."

"Don't judge her so cruelly, Emlin. All our hearts are fragile sometimes. And don't act as if you were wrong to trust her. She lied to spare you, but her care for you was true."

"She lied about being faithful to our craft, too. One of the last things she told me was that trifling with the dragon's inspiration could lead him to abandon me, and yet she made a fake Dragonblade."

We stared at one another. I realized I'd argued full circle. I was like my mother after all. Or more accurately, I was trapped in what she had done. And like her, I was lost. But Kural and the glasshouse didn't have to be. While it was my turn to watch the furnace that night, I'd make the dragon glass knife.

Tomorrow, I'd deliver it.

Chapter 17

I STOOD AT the foot of the stairs, head cocked. Over the hum of the furnace, I heard only Miriv's faint snores. I crept up the stairs, stepping over the fourth one that squeaked. Not that either Miriv or Gillis would question my climbing to my room. They'd assume I was going to change into my nightgown. Still it would be better not to disturb them because a sack full of dragon glass would be hard to explain.

When I lifted the leather sack from my chest and picked up my mother's journal, the triangular stone slid off into a corner. I hadn't touched it again since seeing Dain and Addy together outside the glasshouse gate. I flicked my eyes away and lowered the chest's lid.

I tiptoed back to my workroom. I could keep track of the furnace from there, and Miriv or Gillis would assume I was restless and had decided to work. Which was true, though 'restless' didn't come near to matching what I felt.

Everything was as ready as I could make it. I slid the dragon glass onto the table. My mother's book gave dimensions and not much else, but no one who saw my copy would know any better. I picked out the least likely looking chunk of glass. I'd flaked the edges of normal glass to fit it into a lead strip, so I wasn't a beginner to this kind of work, but if I made mistakes, I wanted to ruin the least useful piece.

The dragon glass tingled against my fingers as I touched it for the first time, making the hair rise on the back of my neck. The power of it made me momentarily freeze. Maybe I shouldn't do this.

But I'd already told Symond I would. I wrapped the hand holding the glass in a leather scrap. The hesitation had come too late. I was committed.

I sat down, rested the glass on a thick pad spread across my thigh, and studied it to see what it needed. Then I took up my small chisel and struck. Accompanied by a shatter of fine shards, a long flake fell away and landed on the apron spread on the floor. The inside of the dragon glass shone like a live thing. I stared at it. The furnace's roar blurred into a whisper I couldn't make out.

Footfalls on the stairs made me jerk upright. To my relief, it was Gillis rather than Miriv who appeared in the doorway, but I still groped for an explanation before I realized she was shuffling toward the far corner of the room.

"Do you need something?" I asked cautiously.

"Don't mind me." Her face was puffy with sleep, but it settled into a smile when she spotted a scrap of cloth peeking out from under the shelves. She scooped it up and I recognized a man's stocking. She waved it at me. "Don't tell Miriv," she said and left without giving me a second look.

The night wore on. At first, I struggled to stay alert against the drowsiness brought on by this night's work on top of the previous one's trip to the Heights, but every time I accidentally touched the glass, I felt a surge of energy. My first effort had taken on the shape of a blade before a careless blow from my chisel broke it. I gritted my teeth and started over. Again a blade took shape. I set it down and went to feed more wood into the furnace before I tackled the more delicate part of the job. My hands were flecked with tiny drops of blood where powdered glass had made painless cuts.

When I was done this time, I held a four-inch blade in my leather-wrapped hand. I set it on the table, regarded it critically, and decided it would do. I fetched a glasshouse knife and pried the blade loose with the thin metal piece I used to score glass. Then it was just a matter of pouring glue into the handle, inserting the end of the glass blade, and wrapping the handle with a strip of leather I'd cut from the inside of my apron hem.

I wiggled my stiff shoulders and moved to open the window to blow away the smell of the glue. The stars had wheeled far enough across the sky that the Dragon constellation was directly overhead, waiting to peer in at me. Feeling as if the glue had spilled to stick my feet to the floor, I swallowed and pivoted to eye the knife on the table.

Then I hid the knife in my carry bag and cleaned up. Done was done. If I had acted wrongly, it would be on my own head. Drake Haron needed protection from the man who probably had my mother killed, and the glasshouse needed money.

SOMETHING BANGED, AND I awoke with my heart galloping. I stared at the ceiling, far higher than it should have been. My muzzy brain worked sluggishly to offer the news that I was on the pallet in the workshop, not in my attic bedroom. The image of myself shaping dragon glass burst into my memory.

I shot up to sit, then clutched the blanket around my shoulders as a cool breeze swept through the room.

"Sorry I woke you." Miriv smiled from the open doorway. The bang must have been the bar swinging up out of its brackets and hitting the wall. It occurred to me that we should use the key now that we owned it. We'd wait until Kedry gave up on claiming the glasshouse though. Hanging it next to the door would put it within a sneaky man's reach.

Gillis was near the food bin, glaring accusingly at whatever was in there. "I wish your man would bring us more eggs, Emlin."

"He's not my man." My chilly body recalled Addy's warmth when he held me on the Heights. I pulled the blanket across my chest.

"Why not?" Gillis frowned.

"He's not interested."

She shrugged. "He looked interested to me. You're bad at judging men, Emlin."

It was hard to argue with that.

"Did you have a good night?" Miriv asked, clearly changing the subject. "No problems?"

"No problems." I sounded thick-tongued. Still wrapped in the blanket, I shuffled toward the stairs, pausing when I heard a quick tread in the yard that turned out to be Renie's husband, Tae. He stopped in the doorway, flushed from his hurry.

"Are you looking for Renie's share of the Lyzian money, Tae?" Miriv asked. "I meant to send it to her today. How is she?"

"Better," Tae said, "but I came because Renie sent me to warn you all. The drake is dead!"

I nearly tripped over the blanket tail.

"He died?" Miriv's brow puckered. "They said he was ailing, but I didn't know he was that sick."

"He didn't die of illness," Tae said, and it dawned on me that his voice shook with something other than breathlessness. "Drake Jaffen murdered him."

"Murdered?" Gillis clutched her throat. "By Jaffen?" She spun to face Miriv. "Do you think he killed Calea too? Or rather had her killed?"

Good question, Gillis.

"Don't be silly." Miriv tipped her head toward me, as if warning Gillis to watch her words. Then to Tae, "What happened?"

"I don't know for sure," Tae said. "The drake is dead all right. Mourning ribbons are tied to every branch, pole, and mast in town. And Symond has arrested Jaffen. They say Symond will wait until after the Flame Testing makes him drake and then put Jaffen on trial."

I pictured the grim young man I'd seen on the docks. That poor old man wouldn't have been able to put up any fight at all. Too bad Jaffen hadn't arrived a day later. If Haron had had my knife, Jaffen might not have gone after him.

Gillis laughed scornfully. "Do they think Symond is making things up?"

"The Lyzian captain and some of his crew stormed up to the palace and demanded Jaffen be handed over," Tae said, "but of course the guards wouldn't let them through the gate. Now they've taken the ship out of the harbor but are anchored still in sight. Symond better keep a good eye on them. I have to get home. The Watch has given everyone an hour to get off the streets unless they're involved in the funeral preparations." He glanced at me. "Renie says she'll try to come for the ceremony though."

Miriv nodded. "Good. We'll do it as soon after the funeral as she's ready."

Ceremony? It dawned on me that the day after tomorrow was my seventeenth birthday. In all the turmoil, I'd lost track. I was supposed to display some of my best work, swear the oath, and be given a crafter's ring. In my mother's desk, I'd seen the oversized rings from the silver crafthouse on Salep Island. If the dragon accepted me as a crafter, the ring would shrink to fit my finger and stay there until I died. I nearly threw up. I'd spent the last two nights crafting a fine piece of sacrilege. If I mouthed the oath, lightning would probably strike me.

Twisting my fists in the blanket, I pulled it taut across my shoulders and started upstairs to dress. Symond would become drake now. It was too late to do his father any good, but with enemies like the Lyzians around, surely he'd want my knife even more for himself. He'd said he'd send for me to deliver it today. I had to be ready if – when – the summons came.

Behind me, Miriv spoke reassuringly. "Symond is undoubtedly on guard. And what can one ship's crew do? To summon help, they'll have to sail home. And when they get there, who'll decide what action to take?"

I rounded the second landing. The voices dwindled but I could still hear Gillis, talking dreamily as if of some romantic adventure. "Maybe some gallant captain? Or the criminal brother? Idyriel, is that his name? Edyriel?"

I slammed my door. If Lyz and Kural went to war, the one thing it would not be was an adventure.

Chapter 18

I SPRINKLED WATER over the chalk coating my pattern board, then took up a rag to rub in the chalk and water mixture. I couldn't mark the board with a window design until I knew the dimensions, but I might as well have everything ready. From the workshop came the sound of the furnace, muted to a hum by my closed door. Gillis's excited chatter had quieted when Tae left with Renie's money and the day's work started. For the hundredth time, I glanced out the window, trying to gauge how much of the morning had passed. I hadn't heard the bell at the bookhouse ring the hour for quite a while.

The workroom door opened. "Emlin," Gillis said, "a palace messenger is here for you."

I laid the rag aside and hung up my apron, using the familiar actions to prove I was fine, just fine, with delivering a fake sacred object. "Are the vases out of the annealer?"

"Miriv took them out a little while ago," Gillis said. "They're beautiful."

I had my carry bag in my workroom with me, the Dragonblade tucked safely inside. I slung the strap over my shoulder and followed Gillis. A bored looking messenger in blue and gold livery leaned against the door jamb. He straightened when he saw me.

"Ready?" he asked.

Looking as pleased as I'd seen her in days, Gillis handed Miriv a bag that presumably held the vases. "I'll take those," I said.

"I'll carry them." Miriv shouldered the bag and joined the messenger in the doorway.

My heart tripped. "You're going? You don't have to, Miriv. You have work to do, and I can carry everything."

"Symond wants you both." The messenger strode across the yard, leaving me and Miriv hurrying to catch up.

I spoke to his back. "Why both?"

He shrugged without turning around. "You think he explains himself to me?"

"Perhaps he means to order more glass," Miriv said, "though it's strange timing."

Maybe Symond had added Miriv's name to the summons because orders usually went to the craftmistress. But how was I going to hand over the Dragonblade with Miriv there?

The messenger led us along streets eerily empty of anyone except Watchmen and palace guards. Nearly every house and shop had a white ribbon rippling from the front, but their doors were tightly closed. Even if the Watch hadn't ordered them off the street, I suspected folks would huddle inside. Someone had murdered our drake, making it feel like the earth might collapse from under us.

As the messenger led me and Miriv along the palace's side wall toward the square, the sound of shouts and hammering came from ahead. When we rounded the corner, men and women swarmed in the square, building some sort of huge wooden frame. A funeral dragon, I realized. I'd never seen one, but that was the traditional pyre for a drake. Those wooden spars like spread fingers must be the framework for the wings. I glimpsed Tae among the carpenters.

The messenger led us around the barriers at the square's edge and toward the gates, where a platform was also being built so Symond could watch the funeral and be seen during the Flame Testing. White silk hung in swoops on the palace doors. I felt a pang for the old man who'd been Kural's drake all my life.

"What happened to the drake?" I asked the messenger. "What did Jaffen do?"

He threw a look over his shoulder that said he thought I was a nosy thrill-seeker. "Smothered him in his bed. Used the drake's own pillow."

I grimaced. Jaffen must have no good in him to do that to a helpless old man. I was doing the right thing to help Symond any way I could.

Inside the palace doors, the messenger led us to the bench where I had waited with Addy two days earlier. "Someone will fetch you," he said, and left us on our own.

I sat down beside Miriv, resting my bag on my lap. I had a ridiculous fear that the knife might have cut its way out and be lying exposed for Miriv to see, but a quick look told me I was letting my brain breed bogeymen. Maybe Symond would send Miriv off to talk to the steward about ordering glass.

A door opened and closed farther down the hall. I leaned out to see it was the door to the drake's sitting room, rather than Symond's. Drake Haron's body was almost certainly laid out in the bedroom beyond that sitting room. The servant who came out stopped in front of me and Miriv and crooked a finger.

I rose hesitantly. "Me? Or Miriv?"

"Both." The man went back the way he'd come, knocked once on the drake's door, and waved me and Miriv through without him. Feet sinking into thick carpet, I crept after Miriv. Were we being asked to make some reverence to the dead drake's body? At least his throat would be intact, I thought wildly. Miriv stopped and bowed, revealing Symond seated in a padded chair.

I let out my breath. Of course it was Symond, though I wouldn't have expected him to move into his father's rooms before the end of the mourning month, let alone before the funeral. I moved to Miriv's side. "I think the servant may have misunderstood, sir. Perhaps you meant to see me about another window while Miriv delivers the vases you ordered to the steward." I pointed to the bag Miriv held.

"On the contrary, I want to talk to you both." He flicked a finger toward two chairs. "Sit."

Miriv settled uneasily, putting the vases carefully on the floor next to her. I perched on the edge of my seat. The cushion was soft enough that I nearly slid off.

"We're sorry about your father," Miriv said.

"Thank you," Symond said. "Emlin, since I saw you last, I learned Dain is your father. I understand he's been injured. Is it serious?"

"The healer says he'll recover in time."

"Good to know." Symond clapped his hands once. "You have it?"

Miriv offered the bag of vases, but he ignored her.

I wanted to cry. There went any hope I had of hiding what I was doing from Miriv. I pulled the wrapped knife out of my bag and passed it across to Symond. "Be careful. It's sharp."

Symond rested the packet on his knee and pulled the

wrapping away. A flash of blue flickered over the knife's polished surface.

Miriv gaped at it, then shrank back in her chair. Her face went white, then red. "Emlin, what did you do?"

Symond picked up the knife to turn it this way and that, smiling. "A Dragonblade."

"It's only a copy," I felt compelled to remind him. "It might not really protect you. And you shouldn't touch the blade."

"If people think it's real, it might as well be." Symond set the knife on the table next to him. "I'll put out the story that I found it, though sadly too late to save my father."

"Sir, perhaps you already guessed this, but the blade Jaffen carries is also a copy," I said.

"Is it now? It's true it didn't do him much good."

I looked steadily at him rather than Miriv. Maybe when she saw the money he'd pay, she'd feel better. And Drake Haron had been murdered. She'd understand that Symond needed the blade. At least I didn't have to worry about taking part in a sham ceremony on my birthday. If only for my own safety, she'd never let me swear a false oath. I blinked away the wetness in my eyes. I'd done what was needed to save Kural and the glasshouse. I would take what happiness I could from that.

Symond looked back and forth between us. "I wanted you both here because I need to speak to you about something else. Kedry has been to see me. He says you've stolen the glasshouse from him."

I stiffened. "That's not true. He told us to run it ourselves, and he gave us the key."

"Nonetheless, if Kedry voices his complaint in court, it would make problems for you. As it happens, since the last time we talked, a problem has presented itself for me too. Perhaps we can help one another."

I licked lips that had gone dry and opened my mouth to speak, but Miriv got there first. "Be quiet, Emlin."

Symond turned his head toward her.

"What is it you want, sir?" Miriv asked.

He rested his hands on the arms of the chair. "The funeral and Flame Testing will be the day after tomorrow." His hands tightened around the jaffel birds carved into the chair arms. "Unfortunately, the Dragonshards are missing."

I gasped. The Dragonshard necklace identified the true ruler of Kural during the Flame Testing, and had done so since the time of the dragon riders. Symond couldn't become drake without it. No one could. Without the necklace, Kural would have no ruler, a disaster any time, but a true horror with Lyz infuriated over Jaffen's arrest and ready to attack.

Symond's gaze was still on Miriv, whose face, I saw, had gone gray.

"We're uncertain when they disappeared," Symond said, "but we suspect the theft happened two days ago when a strange man was spotted in the palace. Since then, the Watch has been searching for him, but they've found no sign of him or the necklace. We believe the necklace may be on the Lyzian ship."

My hands spasmed around the strap of my bag. Two days ago, I entered the palace to offer to make the knife. And I didn't enter alone.

Addy.

It had to be him. He'd used me to get past the guards. Then he'd slipped away, but not to the library. As certain as if I'd seen him do it, I knew he'd picked the lock to the treasure room in the palace tower and taken the necklace.

"No," Miriv said as if answering a question. "We won't do it."

I tore my thoughts away from Addy. A moment later, I caught up to what she'd already understood. "You want us to make a copy of the Dragonshards? We can't."

"I hate to do this," Symond said. "But it's for the good of Kural. Guard!"

The door opened, and a guard came into the room.

"The craftmistress is ready to go with you now," Symond said.

The guard gripped Miriv's upper arm, drawing her to her feet.

"Remember what you owe to your craft, Emlin," Miriv said as the guard pulled her toward the door. "It's not too late for you."

I stood, ready to run after her.

"Sit down," Symond ordered in an iron voice.

I swayed. Then, still twisted to see Miriv, I sank into the chair. The door snapped shut behind Miriv and the guard. I turned to Symond, who smiled, sending ice sliding down my spine. Miriv was wrong. It was very much too late for me.

"Don't worry about Miriv," he said. "As long as you help me, no harm will come to her."

And if I didn't? What a fool I'd been to trust this man.

"I saw the drawing in your mother's journal," Symond said. "It tells you everything you need to know to do it."

"But... but making that would be beyond irreverent. Besides, the knife is one thing, but the Dragonshards are much more complicated. Every piece of glass in them is a different shape and color. And a fake knife might scare off your enemies, but the Dragonshards have to create fire at the testing and then protect you from it."

"I expect I can get around that." He held up the knife. "And I think we've already settled the question of how irreverent you're willing to be."

I felt trapped like a fly in a web. Was this my punishment? To be forever made to repeat my sin?

Symond leaned forward. "Emlin, I'm sorry to force you, but given Jaffen's murder of my father, the Lyzians are surely behind the necklace theft. You don't want them to prevent me from taking my rightful place as drake, do you?"

"No." I bit my lip. Symond might be the rightful heir, but everything about this felt wrong. Addy's name felt ready to fall out of my mouth, but I hesitated. "What if it wasn't the Lyzians?"

"I don't see that it matters," Symond said. "I still need a necklace. I'll keep Miriv safe until you bring me one. Then she can go home, each of you carrying a fistful of gold. The Flame Testing will be in two days. I'll send someone to fetch you and the necklace late tomorrow afternoon. Guard!"

I struggled to my feet as a guard entered the room. I didn't want to make that necklace, and in the thin slice of time I'd sat there trying not to slip off my chair, I'd thought of something that might mean I wouldn't have to. As soon as I was out of here, I was heading for the Heights.

"Show our guest out," Symond said.

As I skirted my chair to go with the guard, I saw the bag of vases on the floor. "Do you still want those?" I asked, pointing to them.

Symond laughed. "Take that to the steward," he told the guard, "and see that she's paid for the vases before she goes."

The guard gestured me from the room. I followed him, struggling to make sense of what had just happened. When Symond talked about acting for the good of Kural, I could only agree with him. I knew rulers had to make hard choices. But his threat to hurt Miriv made my heart freeze. The more I thought about him, the more uneasy I became. He wasn't the one who'd slapped his father while I lurked behind the curtain in the drake's bedroom. But he'd hired the woman who did.

And why hadn't I told him about Addy? *You're bad at judging men, Emlin*, Gillis had said. She was right. And at the moment, bad judgment about Symond or Addy might get Miriv killed. But which man was I judging badly?

I needed a clear-headed moment to work through my growing suspicion of the one who wanted my help to become Kural's drake. But right now, I didn't have it. My thoughts swirled, and the one that came out on top was that I needed to get Miriv to safety.

Chapter 19

I DODGED AROUND the end of the board a carpenter was hoisting onto the platform by the gates. As I fled along the edge of the square and up the empty street to the glasshouse, my thoughts focused on Addy. He had stolen the Dragonshards, sure as winter rains. He'd lied to me, used me. No wonder he'd found it necessary to rearrange his face when he saw me.

And why? Why would he steal the necklace? I could understand scholarly desire to see them, stupidly dangerous as it was to sneak around to do it. But I'd never dreamed he'd steal a sacred object. What was he going to do with it? I couldn't help fearing he meant to act on his belief that Jaffen was the true Drake of Kural, and give Jaffen the necklace. When Addy stole it two days ago, Jaffen hadn't yet killed Drake Haron –assuming that Jaffen had, of course – so Addy wouldn't have thought of him as a murderer.

Only as I passed through the gates to the glasshouse yard did I realize that the steward had paid for the vases, but Symond hadn't paid me for the knife. My fury widened to send tongues of imaginary flame over him. Trivial as it might be compared to everything else, it bothered me that Symond had moved into his father's rooms during the mourning period. When I mourned my mother, I'd left all her things exactly where they'd been the night she died. Miriv didn't move them either. That was right. That was respectful. You shouldn't hurry the dead away as if you were glad to be rid of them.

I strode into the workshop, already fumbling with the steward's purse tied to my belt. I tossed it to Gillis, over near the annealer.

"That's for the vases. Pay yourself the portion we agreed on and leave the rest on Miriv's desk."

Gillis blinked. "Where's Miriv?"

I started up the steps. "She's staying in the palace for a day or two to consult with the steward about new glassware for Symond."

"She'll be back the day after tomorrow, right? Your oath taking is then. I want to see the ceremony before I take mine."

"I don't know. I'm not counting on it." Not counting on it at all.

I shoved open the door to my room, went straight to my chest, and pulled out the dragon glass I hadn't used in making the knife, including the packet of fragments I'd chipped away. I was lowering the lid when I glimpsed the triangular stone Addy had given me. Teeth clenched, I scooped it up and shoved everything in my carry bag before stomping back down the stairs.

Gillis was bent over the coins she'd spread on the marver table. She looked up as I crossed to the door. "Where are you going?"

"To see if the apothecary will sell us what we need to make our special blue dye." Dragon fire. That lie came out without my even having to dream it up.

"Does Miriv know you're doing that?"

"She thinks it's a wonderful idea." I hustled out the door, across the yard, and through the gate.

With reckless indifference to whether Gillis was watching, I headed away from town rather than toward it. I didn't have time to waste worrying about anything other than having a necklace to give Symond so he could wear it at the Flame Testing. His willingness, or rather eagerness, to wear the one that had been stolen counted in his favor. He believed the dragon would approve of him becoming drake. Surely that meant he hadn't killed his father. He'd use a fake if he had to, but that wasn't what he'd planned on.

ON THE HEIGHTS, I skirted the rise and found Addy's cave behind the second clump of brush I searched. I halted just inside the entry where enough light seeped in for me to see. I knew at once that no one was there. The space echoed with emptiness. I had trouble thinking of Addy as dangerous, but given his cracked scholar brain, someone such as Jaffen could be using him. Even my father could, I supposed. It was better not to take the chance.

To my relief, Addy's gear was still piled on one side. I'd been half afraid he'd moved since he showed me his hiding place. So he either trusted me or thought I was stupid.

I grabbed his pack and pawed through it, tossing out a comb, a packet of dried fruit, and a balled-up gray tunic. The tunic hit the rocky ground with a faint tinkle that sounded way too much like breaking glass. Fighting a wave of panicked dizziness, I crouched to pull the cloth open. The glass gull Addy had bought from us when he brought the jajas lay shattered into pieces.

I searched the rest of the pack more gently. No necklace. I flung his bedroll open and felt among the blankets, ignoring the spicy smell it had picked up from his skin. Nothing. Where could he have hidden it? Still crouched on my heels, I looked toward the dark end of the cave.

A lantern and tinder box lay next to the mess I'd made of Addy's belongings. How helpful of him to leave them. It would just be rude to ignore the gift. I lit the lantern and picked my way deeper into the cave until the light reflected off dragon glass shards in the ceiling, and I recognized the place where Addy helped me gather what I needed to make the knife. There I set the lantern down so I could shake the leftover glass from my bag, scattering it more or less where I'd found it.

"Thank you," I murmured. "I truly am sorry." I picked up the lantern and went on until I saw the glow of pink stone.

Something moved.

A flash of red darted past me, brushing my cheek with a breeze. I didn't quite muffle a shriek before I realized it was the jaffel. I squeezed through the opening the bird had just come out of and paused to let my heart settle down.

Swinging the lantern from side to side, I made my way down the hall, looking for any possible hiding place. Pictures of Drake Kural flashed into sight and then receded into darkness. Leaving the necklace in the jaffel shrine would suit Addy's odd sense of humor, but it was empty. I got all the way to the end where the map of the Dolyans glimmered on my left without finding a hiding place. Now what? If he hadn't left it here, I didn't know where to look for it. Maybe he'd hidden it somewhere in the outer cave. I had started to turn away when my eye caught on the tumble of rocks closing off the corridor.

I set the lantern down and sifted through the rock pile. When I lifted a flat stone that had been balanced across two others, a small, leather-wrapped package lay as if waiting for me. I stretched out my hand, thought a prayer, and lifted the thing from its hiding place. Holding it carefully, I peeled back a flap of leather.

The lantern was on the floor so the light was bad, but irregular pieces of black glass streaked with every color of the rainbow gleamed in its glow. I pulled the wrapping into place and breathed again. As I laid the necklace carefully in my bag, my fingers brushed something else. I smiled grimly.

Let's trade

I pulled the triangular stone from my bag, set it in the gap in the rock pile, and balanced the flat stone back where I'd found it. I wouldn't have his gift in my house if it was covered in gold.

MY EYES FLEW open. Heart pounding, I stared into my dark bedroom, knowing something had awakened me but unsure what it was. What sounded like a boot scraped over the roof tiles outside my window, and a voice whispered, "Don't look, don't look, don't look."

I shot up to sit. *Surely not.* Clawing my way to the end of the bed, I rose to my knees and shoved my head out the window. Addy sprawled against one of my open shutters, fingers wedged around its top edge, his face no more than an arm's length away.

He was breathing hard. The whites of his eyes showed all around the gray irises. "I have to talk—"

I grabbed the shutter he wasn't on and yanked it shut.

"No!" He lunged to grip the sill.

I seized the shutter he'd been clinging to and swung it inward, banging him on the head. "Get away. You used me to sneak into the palace!"

In answer, he elbowed the closed shutter open and heaved himself through. I had to scramble out of the way as he dove inside head first. He crashed off the end of the bed, whacked some thieving part of his thieving self on the chest, and came to rest, huddled over, clutching his knee, and moaning with each panted breath. Thank the dragon's rare mercy that Gillis was the only other person in the glasshouse, and she was all the way down in the workshop, taking Miriv's turn at tending the furnace.

Hands planted on my hips, I said, "Let me guess. You want the necklace."

From the floor, he looked up at me. "I do." His gaze drifted over my nightgown, pausing for a moment.

I kicked him with my regrettably bare foot. "Then you can go on wanting it and anything else you thought you might be collecting."

He had the good grace to blush as he shoved to his feet, banging his head on the slanting ceiling. He yelped, then said, "Where is it?" He spun, head ducked to inspect the room.

Before I could tell myself not to, I glanced at the chest behind him.

Holding me off with one hand, he flung the lid open. The necklace lay on top, still wrapped as he'd left it in the painted hallway on the Heights. He swooped down on it.

"Leave it alone!" I tried to grab it from him, but he thrust it overhead and fended me off. "I have to have that, Addy. Symond's holding Miriv until I make him a replacement for it, but that would take too long, even if I could do it, which I'm not sure I can. I need this one."

"I'm sorry, but I need it more than you do."

"Not possible." I jumped and swung from the arm holding the necklace. "Give it to me!"

When he tried to shake me off, I grabbed at his hand and bent the thumb back until he squealed. With agonizing slowness, the wrapped necklace slid from his palm. I tried to snatch it from the air. The tip of my longest finger brushed leather, but necklace and wrapping hit the floor, and I heard the unmistakable ping of breaking glass.

For an instant, I stared at the part of the necklace peeking out of the wrap. Addy, too, froze. Then I dropped to my knees and pulled away the rest of the leather. One of the pieces had split in half. Addy's hand convulsed on my shoulder. He spat a single, savage word in a language I didn't know.

"Look what you've done!" I cried.

"What *I've* done? You dislocated my thumb! Don't blame me for the results."

If I'd been able to look fire, he'd have been charred head to toe. "Symond threatened to hurt Miriv if I don't bring him a necklace."

Addy eyed my face, drew a deep breath, and sank onto the bed. "You've seen Symond? What's he doing with Jaffen?"

I picked up the bit that had broken off the necklace and ran my fingers over both its sides. A burr of glass slid under my fingertips. Frowning, I turned the piece over. "Holding him until the Flame Testing is through and there can be a proper trial."

Addy rubbed his hand over his face, then focused on the necklace. "Can you mend it? You have to fix it and then let me have it."

"Why?" Drawn by his intense tone, I looked up. He was breathing hard, and his hands were opening and closing in his lap.

He looked away. The straw mattress rustled as he shifted.

I narrowed my eyes. "And why the concern about Jaffen?"

"I told you what I found in the western archives about *jaff*. As sure as sunrise, Jaffen's not only the rightful Drake of Kural; he's meant to be the Great Drake of all the Dolyans."

"You can't give him the Dragonshards." I fell sideways from my crouch to sit on the floor. "He's not someone out of a book, Addy. He's not Kuralian, and he might even be a murderer." I was less and less certain of that last point, but now wasn't the time.

Addy shook his head. "I don't believe it. Jaffen's ready for a fight, but he'd never kill that old man."

"You sound like you know him." I rubbed my finger over the dragon glass piece and saw again the way he'd smoothed out his face outside the glasshouse yard. Gillis's voice echoed in my memory, asking *Idyriel? Edyriel?*

"Adyriel," I said.

He looked up. "What?"

"Dragon fire. *You're* the criminal brother." I pushed my bare feet into the floor and scooted away from him, dragging the necklace with me.

"I'm not a criminal." He sat up straight, his face as severe as I'd ever seen it. "The closest I've come to crime was letting that thief out."

"And stealing this necklace and for all I know killing my mother. That's why you're here on Kural. That's why you befriended me. You thought I might know about a glass piece like this, know exactly where it was maybe."

"Killing your mother? Never! You can't think I'd do that."

I didn't. I'd just enjoyed saying it. "I guess not," I said grudgingly, "but you did the rest."

He held out his hands, palms up. "Jaffen sent me to find out why Dain hadn't yet sent word about the state Drake Haron was in. He'd heard rumors that Haron was ill and was worried because he'd much rather deal with Haron than Symond. Dain was supposed to find out if that was possible. He was slow, and Jaffen thought Dain might need an ally."

I snorted. "You weren't working together the day I met you. You didn't know one another. Unless you were lying about that too."

"As I told you, I'd lived away from Lyz since I was thirteen, so I'd never met Dain, but he sounded worrisome enough that I was following him before I spoke to him and I saw him approach you. I didn't mean to use you. I just wanted to know more about him before he and I joined forces."

"And the Dragonshards?"

"Oh. Well, Jaffen did send me to steal them, and for good reason. Emlin, think. Symond is holding Miriv hostage. You surely don't believe he'd be a better drake for Kural than Jaffen."

"The only thing I know about Jaffen is what you tell me, and you're a liar. A liar and a user. Like Dain. Like all Lyzians for all I know." My anger drove me to my feet, pulling the wrapping back around the necklace, including the broken piece. "All along you've been plotting for your brother."

Addy stood and shuffled to where the ceiling was high enough for him to stand straight. "It's not *plotting*."

I clicked my tongue scornfully.

"Emlin, listen. Six months ago, my father died." Addy's face was shadowed, but I didn't need to see him to recognize the pain in his voice. Had he loved the father who treated both the people of Lyz and his own son cruelly? Had Addy somehow hoped a connection could eventually be forged between them and lost all possibilities to death? A pang closed my throat.

"For the first time since I'd left, I could go home," Addy went on. "When I told Jaffen what I'd found about *jaff*, he put it together with the fire pouring out of Lyz's mountain and decided Lyz's dragon was trying to tell him something. He'd been hearing whispers in his head and dreaming of flying for some time." Addy looked off into the room's darkest corner, one side of his mouth curving in a faint smile. "I think it was the first time he ever saw use in my studies."

"So you think he's entitled to rule Kural because you read some book?" I let my scorn show.

ADDY FIXED ME with an earnest look. "Jaffen's a good man. He'd be a good drake, much better than Symond, and I swear to you, he'd never kill Drake Haron."

For a moment, I wavered. Then I thought of Miriv and even of Symond's promise to keep Kedry from taking back the glasshouse. How much difference was there between Symond and Jaffen? They could quarrel over being in charge as much as they wanted. All I wanted was to make glass and protect the people I loved. "Jaffen has soldiers to fight for him. All Miriv has is me." I braced my back against the room's door. "I have to do what's best for me and mine." I jerked my head toward the window. "Get out, or I'll call the

Watch."

His eyes lowered to the wrapped necklace in my hand. Hastily, I dropped it down the neck of my nightgown, curling my other arm around my waist to keep it from falling straight through. I could only hope the leather would prevent the broken glass from cutting anything. I readied myself to shout the skies down if he grabbed for it.

He stayed where he was, chewing on his lower lip.

"I'll mend it and tell Symond I made it," I said. "I won't tell him that I got it from you or where you are."

"You can fix it?"

I nodded.

Addy stared at the place where the weight of the necklace made my nightgown droop over my arm. He spoke slowly. "If you say you made it, Symond will think it's fake. But it's the real one. At the ceremony, it'll burn him."

"If you believe that, you don't need to take the necklace. It'll do its work no matter who has it, but Miriv will be safe and so will the glasshouse."

"Jaffen thinks Symond is slippery enough to get around whatever the necklace does, and he's a good judge of these things."

I shook my head. "It doesn't matter what Jaffen thinks. He's in a cell in the palace."

"For now."

Surely he wouldn't be so stupid. Well, yes, he would, but I didn't have to be roped into his craziness. "Leave. Go back the way you came."

He looked at the window and shuddered. "You'd have to throw me out there."

I could see he meant it. "Come on then, but be quiet." Still clutching my middle, I jerked the door open and crept down the stairs, with Addy behind me. He caught his foot on the edge of a step and had to grab the handrail, but only once. From the last landing, I heard Gillis snoring. I tiptoed into the workshop and across it to the door, where I fumbled one-armed with the bar.

Addy waited a moment, then reached around me and lifted it quietly to one side.

I didn't wait to see him leave the yard. As soon as I had the door shut, I crouched and let the necklace slip into my grasp. I set it down, barred the door, and fled back upstairs, necklace in hand.

In my room, I hurried to the window, unwrapped the necklace, and held the broken piece up to the moonlight until I found what I was looking for. My eyes confirmed what my fingertips had told me – the letter C swirled in glass across the back of the piece.

This necklace would never burn anyone. No doubt about it. It was a copy, and my mother had made it. My mother, who'd apparently lied about more than who my father was. I finally knew what glass she'd delivered to the palace that night. I knew why it was worth killing her, and maybe the rest of us, to keep her secret. And who was at the heart of all this evil? Symond, who now held Miriv prisoner. No wonder he hadn't been afraid of what this necklace would show.

Night Flights 4

Symond is not dreaming. He hasn't since he was a boy.

Chapter 20

I SLID THE lamp globe into the annealer and stood for a moment, resting my arms. I wished I could escape into my workroom so I could fret over my worries alone, but with Miriv and Renie gone, Gillis needed my help if we were to have goods for the merchant ship from Salep Island that was due in three days, assuming the harbor was open.

Gillis glanced at me from where she was poking through the jars on the shelf. "Do you think we'll go to war with Lyz?"

"I don't know," I said absently. I was listening for a step in the yard because whoever Symond sent to fetch me was due soon.

"Miriv didn't stay at the palace the other times we sold them glass. What's different this time?"

As I repaired the Dragonshards early that morning, I'd decided it would be foolish to trust Symond to keep his end of the bargain. That meant I'd have to be clever. I'd made a plan, but my palms itched with sweat when I thought about facing Symond and making my demand. And I still had one more thing to do before I let myself be dragged to the palace.

"It's hard to explain, Gillis, but there's something I need you to do."

She waited, finger tapping on a dye jar.

"I want you to leave the glasshouse and hide out until you're sure it's safe to come back."

"What?" She gripped the edge of the shelf.

"You're right when you think there's something odd about Miriv staying in the palace. Someone really is trying to hurt glassmakers." I realized the attacks on us had stopped in the last few days. Of course they had. Symond needed fake sacred objects he could get me to make here.

"Who?" She frowned.

"If I tell you, you won't believe me."

"Try me."

"Symond."

She barked a laugh. "Oh, stop. You scared me." When I stayed sober-faced, she blinked. "You're not joking."

"No, I'm not. He wants me to make something for him and says he'll hurt Miriv if I don't. I'm going to cross him in how I do it, so someone dangerous may come here. Things may settle down after Symond has what he wants, or they may not. I'm not sure you'll be safe here."

She braced her back against the shelves. "This has to do with what happened to Calea, doesn't it?"

I nodded.

"Where would I go?"

"I don't know. Maybe Renie's house?"

Gillis's eyes darted from side to side, as if looking for a way out. "I'm going to send the boy next door with a message to Piret. We've been talking about marrying someday, but now I think we should do it sooner rather than later."

I was startled enough to forget my own troubles for a moment. I tried not to sour Gillis's fantasies, but this one could hurt her. "Gillis, you must know Piret isn't likely to marry you. His parents have money. They'll object."

"He doesn't care." She straightened suddenly enough to rattle the jars on the shelves. "Besides, I'm a Dolyan crafter which makes me any man's equal." She strode out the door.

Helpless to fix anything at all, I watched her go, feeling a surprising stab of envy. For Gillis, life seemed so simple. She decided what she wanted to do and then did it. My life had become so confusing I couldn't even figure out the wanting part. Symond as drake? He'd ordered my mother's death and probably smothered his father. Jaffen conquering Kural? That plunge into the unknown and foreign frightened me as Gillis never seemed to be frightened. With a Kuralian mother and Lyzian father, was I now condemned to be forever torn?

I went up to my room. From the chest, I took the gift I'd bought for Gillis at the market. As I descended the steps and saw the workshop spread out below, I realized that with Gillis leaving, no one would be here to tend the furnace. It would finally go out. A fist squeezed my heart. It felt like the breaking of something central to my life. I couldn't bear thinking about it.

I began putting pipes and other tools away. By the time I had finished cleaning the workshop, Gillis marched in, crossed it without speaking, and started up to her room.

"Wait, Gillis." When she turned, I held out the packet of breath berries I'd bought from the Lyzian medicine crafter. It was the first chance I'd had to give it to her. She peered into the envelope. "They're—"

"Doo. I know what they are." One corner of her mouth lifted in a thin smile. "I bought some two days ago. I know you think I'm half-witted sometimes but I do understand how babies are made." She curled my fingers around the packet and pushed it toward me. "You keep it." She went up the stairs.

"I don't need it," I called after her.

"You never know," she called back.

Fat chance. I shoved the berries in my pocket, sat next to the marver table, and cradled my head in my hands. Yes, this had to do with Calea. I thought again about my mother's mark on that broken piece of glass, glass that no doubt had come from the furnace in this room. I marveled at her ability to make that necklace. Modesty aside, I knew I made wonderful windows, but I couldn't have copied the Dragonshards to save my life. It was typical of my mother that she couldn't resist signing the piece, claiming work whose beauty she was proud of. Every certainty I'd ever had about her was crumbling except for the fact that she'd been dragon-gifted to an astonishing degree.

And my certainties about myself and my future? They were gone too.

"Emlin?"

I jumped.

Piret stood in the doorway, regarding me with a worried look. "Are you all right?"

I nearly laughed. "No, I don't think I am."

Gillis must have been listening for him because she came down the stairs carrying a large satchel, which Piret took from her, smiling down into her determined face.

I stood. "Where will you go? You can't walk around town today. No one is supposed to be out."

"We'll take my boat to Praltown," Piret said.

"And then?" I looked at him steadily, and he had the decency to flush.

"Then we'll be married," he said.

I hugged Gillis, whispering in her ear. "Come home if it

doesn't happen, Gillis."

Scowling, Piret put his arm around Gillis and guided her out the door, taking what felt like the last piece of my girlhood with him.

For the first time in my memory, I was alone in the glasshouse. The truth was I was more alone than I'd ever been in my life.

"Miss?" A knock sounded on the frame of the open door.

I looked up to find a palace guard waiting. I rose. "I'm ready." I fervently hoped that was true.

SYMOND WAITED FOR me in the drake's sitting room. The instant the door shut behind the guard, he leaned forward, face tense. "You have it?"

I licked my dry lips. "I made it, but I don't have it with me."

His head jerked back. "What?"

"I hid it. Arrange for me and Miriv to be taken aboard the Lyzian ship, and when we're there, I'll tell you where it is."

His lip curled. "Guard!"

The guard who'd escorted me there opened the door. "Sir?"

"Send for Rolan. Have him escort the craftmistress here."

The guard withdrew, face impassive. I could hardly believe it. Was Symond actually setting us free so easily? I realized I was twisting my hands together and forced myself to stop. Some part of me was already crying for the loss of my craft and my island, but I hadn't been able to think of any other way for Miriv and me to escape.

Symond watched me with hooded eyes, fingers drumming on the arm of his chair. I lowered my gaze so he wouldn't see my elation.

Someone knocked. At Symond's invitation, a broad-shouldered man shoved Miriv into the room. She cried out when she saw me, and I flung myself into her waiting arms. She smelled of sweat, and her hair was frowsy from sleeping on it and having no brush to smooth it. "Are you all right?"

"Emlin, you shouldn't have come," she said.

"Rolan," Symond said, "break one of the craftmistress's fingers."

"What?" I tightened my arms around Miriv.

Rolan shoved me aside, seized Miriv's left hand, and snapped her little finger.

A cry escaped between her clenched teeth. Even clutched in his grip, she bent over in pain.

I spun toward Symond. "What are you doing?"

"Tell Rolan where you hid it," Symond said.

I hesitated.

"Rolan." Symond gestured toward Miriv who cradled her hurt hand, her face growing pale.

"Wait! I'll tell him." I faced Rolan. Until now, I'd barely looked at him. At that terrible moment, I saw a red jewel in the top of his right ear. "You," I choked out.

He raised an eyebrow. I felt sick.

"Tell him," Symond repeated.

I could see no other choice. "It's in the glasshouse. The fourth step is loose. It's in a box inside."

He nodded, then spoke to Symond. "Do you still want me to torch the place?"

I hadn't thought I had anything else to lose. I'd been wrong.

Symond pursed his lips. "I think not. There are other glassmakers there. The export tax revenues add up. Before you go, take these two back to where we've been keeping the craftmistress. We'll hang onto them until I'm sure Emlin hasn't lied to me."

Rolan grabbed one of my arms and one of Miriv's. I was so dazed, I didn't resist.

Chapter 21

ROLAN DRAGGED US up a flight of stairs and around a corner. He shouldered a door open and thrust us inside a small room. The key rattled in the lock. His footsteps faded away.

"Emlin, what happened?"

I pushed Miriv to sit on the bed and crouched at her feet. "Let me see your hand." She laid it on her lap. The little finger bent outward. I grimaced in sympathy. "We should at least straighten that and bind it to the next one."

I looked around for something to use as a bandage. The room was small but well-furnished with a carved bedstead, a padded chair, and an inlaid wood dressing table. A room for a lady's maid probably, I thought, seeing the connecting door. I rummaged in the dressing table's drawer and came up with a blue ribbon.

"What happened?" Miriv asked again.

I straightened the finger as gently as I could, though she sucked in her breath. A single tear trickled down her cheek. When I'd tied the finger straight, I sat back on my heels and met her sober gaze. "You heard him ask me make a copy of the Dragonshards." No need to say who 'he' was.

"Did you do it?" She sounded horrified.

"No! But my mother did." I told her the whole story.

Miriv closed and then opened her eyes. "I should have guessed when I saw the drawing in her journal."

I paced the room once, stopping to rattle the latch on the connecting door. Unfortunately, it was as firmly locked as the one to the hall. I leaned against it. "Why did she do it? I can understand the Dragonblade for Dain. When you're attracted to someone, sometimes you don't think straight." I blinked away a vision of Addy. "But the Dragonshards? For Symond? Why?"

"If I were to guess?" Miriv rubbed one temple. "Judging by what we've just seen, Symond threatened what she held most dear."

"The glasshouse?"

Miriv lowered her hand and smiled faintly. "No, Emlin. You. She once told me that of all the things she'd ever made, you were the finest."

I choked back the swelling in my throat. I didn't have time for grief. "Symond ordered her murder." I had to say it aloud to make it real.

"How could he let her live when she might tell someone the necklace was a fake? As it was, he was afraid she told the rest of us, so…" She waved her good hand, vaguely indicating falling tiles, rocks, and worst of all, Renie's lost baby.

Fury burned in my chest, my face, my hands. From the window high up on the wall came the sound of hammering, as work went on, readying the square for Symond to claim the role of drake. He deserved to be stabbed to death in the street as my mother had been – her plans, talent, joys, arrogance, love, future, all snatched from her by Symond. Instead, he was about to claim power, using a necklace *I* had put in his hands.

"Don't blame her too much," Miriv pleaded. "It's impossible to choose well when someone with power threatens someone you love." Her face hardened. "Symond killed the drake, seized his power, and abused it. If you want a betrayal of the dragon's law, that's the one to resent."

'Resent' was too soft a word for what I felt. But I couldn't look only at Symond. Symond had abused dragon-granted power, but so had I. And now here we were.

"The attack on my father." In my head, I heard Dain saying *Think of the danger you're putting me in.* I heard Symond say *You know the Lyzian representative?* "Symond was behind that because Dain is connected to me and I might tell him the truth about the necklace. He'll try again. He can't let Dain live." I drew a deep breath. "He can't let us live now either, can he?"

Miriv looked at me with pity. "No, he can't."

I PACED TO the connecting door, then turned and stalked to the one giving on the hallway. Huddled on the bed, Miriv dozed, occasionally stirring enough to moan and cradle her broken finger. Time crept like a snail when you were locked in a small room with nothing to do but wonder when someone was coming to kill you. Or more likely, take you somewhere else to kill you. Symond wouldn't want the mess of blood and bodies in his palace. So hard to explain, unless maybe he could blame Jaffen for that too.

I kept going over the things I'd done that landed me and Miriv here. No matter how much I tried to believe I couldn't have acted other than I did, I kept coming back to the fake

Dragonblade knife. I'd delivered the fake Dragonshards necklace but not made it, and I'd done it because Symond threatened Miriv. But I had no real excuse for making the Dragonblade. I'd gone to the palace *wanting* to do it, meaning to plead for a commission to do it. I'd taken the dragon glass from the Heights. And I'd done it not for love, but for money. I could have tried to sell more of the objects in my mother's journal even if I couldn't make them. I could have put up with the boredom of making gulls that someone else designed. I could have lived in poverty and let Kedry take the glasshouse back. Maybe none of that would have mattered, but maybe it would. I'd done this. I'd killed myself and Miriv. I wanted to weep for us and for everyone on Kural who'd now be subject to a man like Symond.

A door creaked. I was so worried about Rolan reappearing that it took me a moment to realize the sound had come from the connecting door, not the one to the hallway. Two guards moved otherwise soundlessly into the room, swords in hand.

Darting between them and the bed, I said, "Miriv knows nothing. I'm the one you want."

"We should probably take her anyway," a familiar voice said.

I tore my gaze from the swords to look into the guard's face – Addy, wearing not scholar gray, but a blue and gold palace guard uniform. He all but quivered with excitement. At that moment, I wanted nothing so much as to fling my arms around him. Of all the people in the world, he was the perfect one to be here.

Behind me, Miriv stirred.

"It would be dangerous for her to stay." Addy grinned. "Don't you think?"

"Whatever you're going to do, do it quickly," the other guard said from near the still open connecting door. An officer, by the look of him, despite the bruise darkening the left side of his face.

No. Wait. Not an officer.

Drake Jaffen.

With a strangled moan, Miriv jumped up.

"Don't worry," I said hastily. "They're friends." I glanced at Jaffen, who was peering into the other room. "At least, I think they are."

"Move," Jaffen said sharply. He beckoned and vanished; a man used to snapping commands and having them followed without question.

I pulled myself tall and obeyed, following Miriv, who was rubbing her eyes and shedding her grogginess. The attached room was large and elegantly furnished with ruffles and a lingering scent of roses. Addy came right behind us.

"How did you get into the palace?" I asked over my shoulder.

"I borrowed a carpenter's apron and just walked right through the courtyard like I knew where I was going."

"*Borrowed*?"

"I'd have given it back."

"And you knew I was here because...?"

He flushed faintly. "I followed you here from the glasshouse today. I thought maybe I might be able to, uh, *borrow* the necklace, but the man escorting you never left you alone."

"Have you followed me before?" I asked sharply.

"Just once," he protested. "The day you brought me inside the palace."

"You mean the day you forced your way in!"

"Hush." Jaffen cracked open the room's door and peeked into the hallway.

When I took a step toward him, I glimpsed two unconscious guards, tied and gagged, tucked between the wall and the big bed, and wearing only their underclothes. My heart clawed its way into my throat. True to his ruthless reputation, Jaffen must have knocked the guards out. Miriv and I would have to take care with him.

Hand on my elbow, Addy steered me toward Jaffen. "The guards will be well enough," he whispered. "I didn't hit them that hard."

"*You're* the one who hit them?" I said.

Jaffen eased the door shut. "Oh, yes. This part of the expedition is all Addy's. I'm just here to make sure he toddles home to bed on time."

I looked over my shoulder at the unconscious guards. I hadn't expected Addy to be that single-minded in getting what he wanted. Miriv had seen it and warned me, but I'd missed it entirely. It was a side of him I didn't know what to do with.

"Now pay attention," Jaffen said. "Addy and I are going to be your guards. We're taking you to an undisclosed place to do unspeakable things to you. So your job is to be scared-witless prisoners. Understand?"

I couldn't help myself. "I think I can grasp it."

Miriv squeezed my fingers. "We understand." She drew my hand firmly through the crook of her arm.

Jaffen shot Addy a look. "This one? You're sure?"

Addy scowled at him. "Shut up, Jaff."

With something that might have been a smile, Jaffen said, "The palace is laid out more or less like Father's?"

"From what I've seen, yes," Addy said.

"So there's a west stairway. All right. We'll take it. Move quickly. Don't talk to anyone." Hand on the door latch, Jaffen turned to Addy one more time. "Try to look threatening." Cracking the door an inch, he checked the hallway, then flung the door open and walked through, as bold as if he ran the place. Miriv hastened after him, head ducked, while I hunched my shoulders and tried to look cowed. Addy marched along behind us, his boots thumping with guard-like weight. Jaffen led us through an empty hall, then into one in which two chatting maids hastily flattened themselves against the wall to let him and his 'prisoners' pass. Down some stairs. Along a hall lined on one side with windows that looked out into the torchlit but still busy courtyard.

With each step, my breath came faster. Freedom was so close. The door guards turned their heads as Jaffen strode between them out into the gathering dark. One of the guards immediately went back to watching the workers drape the platform in sweeps of blue and gold cloth, but the other frowned.

Jaffen quickened his pace until I was almost running, footsteps jarring against the courtyard cobblestones.

"Excuse me, sir," the door guard called after us. "Halt, please."

Jaffen swung around the corner of the platform. The moment he was out of the door guard's sight, he broke into a run. I tore after him, urging Miriv along with me. Eyes wide with alarm, a man with a bolt of blue silk dodged out of our way.

Somewhere behind us, the door guard shouted, "Grab them!" Two guards watching the crowd spun toward us.

Bold as a seagull, Jaffen ran up to them. "Trouble. You're needed over there." In an irresistible officer's voice, Jaffen pointed the guards toward the west side of the square. "Hurry."

They took a few running steps in the direction he'd sent them as he struck out the other way and ran into the tangle of wood, workers, and cloth being made into a dragon-shaped pyre for the drake. In the courtyard, a whistle shrilled. All the workers stopped what they were doing and turned toward the sound. Jaffen raced across the square, the rest of trailing.

"Addy!" Jaffen called. "Which way?"

Addy flew past me and Miriv, then backtracked and grabbed my hand. With a familiar clumsiness that might have been endearing at some other time, he tripped over a wooden barrier meant to hold back the next day's crowds, yanking me nearly off balance. He hopped to regain his footing, and plunged into the spider web of streets off the eastern edge of the square. A trio of gawking boys who should have been at home watched us, open-mouthed.

"Halt!" someone shouted behind us.

"Let go of me!" I cried. "I can run better on my own."

Addy released my hand but stayed at my side, infuriating me by shortening his longer strides to match mine. When he pointed to a sliver of dark space between two shops, I scrambled into it, glancing back to see Jaffen steering Miriv toward it too.

"Halt or we'll shoot!"

Twisted to look back, Miriv stumbled and fell to her hands and knees. Jaffen hauled her upright. Something twanged and hummed, and an arrow sailed past in a blur.

No, not quite past. A tear appeared in the shoulder of Miriv's tunic. It gaped around skin quickly turning red.

Chapter 22

"MIRIV!" I LUNGED back down the alley, but Addy grabbed my arm. He'd already opened a slanting door to someone's cellar. Now he dragged me down three steps, waited until Jaffen half-carried Miriv in after us, and slammed the door. He scooped a padlock out from behind a barrel, looped it through the hasps, and jammed it shut, closing us into darkness.

I flung myself down next to Miriv, groping blindly. "I'm so sorry. This is all my fault – your finger and now you're shot! How bad is it?" When I found her shoulder, my fingers came away wet with warm, sticky blood. The feel and smell carried me back to the side of my dying mother. I felt a hot surge of nausea.

A large palm pressed over my mouth. "Quiet," Jaffen whispered.

Gagging, I slapped at his hand. He slowly lifted and then removed it. I gulped air.

"I'm all right," Miriv murmured, but her head lolled against my chest.

Outside, men shouted. Running footsteps approached. Someone yanked on the door, rattling the latch. As if they might hear me, I held my breath. In the corner, the solid shadow that was Addy stood absolutely still, probably afraid he'd stumble or knock something over.

"Locked," a voice said.

The steps ran on.

After a moment, I heard the whisper of Jaffen and Addy sheathing their swords. Addy fumbled, and a short time later, a lantern blossomed into life.

"Where are we?" Jaffen asked.

"The Rat's Rest Alehouse," Addy said, bringing the lantern closer to Miriv.

Jaffen gave a short laugh. "I like an honest barkeep." He squatted on his heels on Miriv's other side and peeled her sleeve away from the wound. He grunted. Miriv shuddered.

"We can't stay here," Addy said. "The barkeep could come down here any time."

I looked away from Miriv to find him watching Jaffen anxiously. "You've been here before?" I asked.

"When Symond sicced the Watch on me. The padlock was on the outside then. The owner was just begging someone to pick it."

"It's too dark in here for me to be sure, Mistress," Jaffen said to Miriv, "but the wound seems deep. It would be better if we could get you someplace safe." He rose, lifting his hand as if to run it over his hair, but he glanced at it and instead rubbed Miriv's blood off on his palace guard shirt. "Addy, I don't suppose you know a place we can hide until I can signal the ship to get us?"

"Not my camp on the Heights?"

"Too far now." Jaffen shot Miriv a sideways glance.

I bit my lip and stroked Miriv's hair, the gray threads coarse beneath the pads of my fingers. "The glasshouse?"

"The first place they'll look," Jaffen said. "And it would be better if we could see the harbor. I need to be able to signal my ship."

A hollow opened in my chest. I'd planned for me and Miriv to flee to Lyz, but the glasshouse had always been my refuge. Telling myself not to be so whiny, I cast about for places where Miriv, at least, would be welcome.

Renie's house maybe? Reluctantly, I concluded that, while Renie was fond of Miriv, Tae would object to the trouble sheltering us would cause them. And that house didn't have a view of the harbor. That didn't leave many choices.

"I know a place," I said.

Jaffen studied me for a long, silent moment.

"I trust her," Addy said.

Jaffen transferred his assessing gaze to his brother.

Addy's mouth twisted. "Take your time. What do I know, after all? I'm just the one you ignored when I signaled you not to dock."

"I already said I was sorry about that," Jaffen said. "Dain was very convincing. We don't have time to waste though. It would be best to go before Mistress Miriv grows any weaker." He cut away the rest of Miriv's sleeve and bound it around her arm.

Addy bent over the padlock while I helped Miriv to her feet. The lock sprang open, and he tucked it back in its hiding place. Cautiously, he lifted the door. Then he beckoned to the rest of us and ghosted out into the night.

In the alley, Jaffen put his arm around Miriv and waved me forward. "Show us the way."

I ducked out from under Miriv's limp weight and led them down the hill, following not the road, but the narrow walkways and stairs cutting between streets. Lantern light poked through the shutters of the houses staggering down the hillside. In the distance, the Watch called and, once, sounded a whistle. I heard running feet and a cry of pain. Some poor night wanderer had been mistaken for us. I offered a silent apology.

Addy seemed almost as familiar with the twisting paths as I was. He'd certainly not spent all his time on the Heights digging for dragon work. I'd wager Jaffen had told him to learn the town, and Addy had done it with scholarly thoroughness. When I started down the final set of steps, he let out a soft exclamation, telling me he'd realized where I was going. He held his tongue though. I remembered that he was someone who understood the stew of feelings a child could have for a father.

I peeked around the last corner with Addy leaning out behind me, and Jaffen supporting Miriv a few paces behind. He'd had to carry her down some of the steeper stairways. The street was empty. I called softly to Jaffen, who was looking toward the water, visible over the roofs of the houses down the sharply descending hill. Scouting for the Lyzian ship, probably. He shuffled toward us, with Miriv leaning heavily on him now, her mouth pressed tightly closed.

"Where to?" he asked.

"Dain's house is maybe twenty yards along."

Jaffen's face went expressionless. "As it happens, I'd welcome the chance to see Dain again. I'd like to know how much Symond paid him to betray me."

Was I really going to put Dain in this man's hands? "He's my father," I said.

His eyelids drooped. "I'm sorry to hear that," he said evenly. Miriv lurched in his arms, and he caught her around the waist. "Now would be good. Unless you have somewhere else to take her? For her sake, somewhere close by."

Miriv, my mother's true partner, someone who had always cared for me in both senses of the word. It was time to decide, and I saw no good choices.

Something heavy settled in my chest. With the rest of them at my heels, I slid down the street to the house whose purple front looked black in the night. Light leaked around the edges of the window, so Dain was home. I tried the latch, but of course, it was locked. From somewhere much too close, a dog barked, setting off others. I looked up to find the Dragon stars stretched overhead. *Forgive me*, I thought, though I wasn't sure who I was asking. I drew a deep breath and knocked. "Dain? It's me." We waited for a long moment before the key clicked in the lock and the door opened. Swaying, Dain blinked at me. Then he looked behind me and tried to slam the door.

Jaffen shouldered it aside and shoved his way in with Miriv. "Get the door, Addy. Lock it."

Addy hustled me after them and closed the door. He turned the key that still rested in the lock, then faced Dain and drew his guard's sword. It occurred to me that he looked as if he knew how to wield it. I guessed his father had seen to that in the years before Addy ran away.

Dain rapidly shuffled back, then dropped to his knees. He looked terrible. His face was blue and purple with bruises. One eye was black and swollen shut. "My lord Jaffen," he said through puffy lips, "I beg for your mercy."

"Shut up," Jaffen said.

I swallowed but hurried into the back room. "Put her in here." Jaffen lifted Miriv onto the unmade bed. A satchel sat next to it with clothes untidily jumbled inside. I caught myself wishing Dain had been quicker at packing. I grabbed a towel from the washstand and filled the basin from the pitcher.

"Find me something to clean and bandage this," Jaffen ordered without looking up. Irritated, I shoved the towel and basin into his hands hard enough that water slopped out and darkened his guard shirt. He looked at me from under raised eyebrows and said, "You're too on edge. Go."

"I want to stay with Miriv." And I did. But I also didn't want to see my father's battered face or hear what he might say to me.

"Have you treated arrow wounds before?" Jaffen asked. When I pressed my lips together, he said, "Go keep Addy company. Between the two of you, surely you can prevent Dain from going anywhere. Not that he's in any shape to escape but desperate people do stupid things. Who beat him?"

"The man who murdered my mother. One of Symond's people. My guess is he wanted to know what Dain had told me."

He shrugged. "If you're thinking it's your fault, think again. Being turned on is a chance that double dealers take. Go on." He bent over Miriv's shoulder.

With one last look at Miriv, I went into the front room. Addy had bound Dain to the chair with Dain's own belt. Addy's sword was now sheathed, and he was poking at the fire. Dain straightened to a tense line when I came in.

"I'm sorry," I managed, voice croaking.

"Ask him to let me go," Dain said.

I glanced at Addy, who shook his head, put one hand on the mantelpiece, and kicked at the grate. Sparks crackled up the chimney.

My knees gave way, and I sank into one of the two chairs by the hearth. I clamped my hands between my legs to keep them still, then rose and moved closer to stretch them out to the flames. Dain let his head fall back against the chair while Addy snooped around the room, opening and closing cupboards and poking aimlessly at a dry hunk of bread abandoned on the sideboard. He slid the top drawer open and stared into it. When I pushed my way next to him, he started to close it but I hooked my fingers around the drawer's edge. The note lay folded where I'd left it. I held it up to Addy.

"This is from you, isn't it?"

Addy fiddled with the hilt of his sword. "I was on my way here when I met you just outside."

"You and Dain were working together against Symond?"

He sighed. "That was the plan."

I faced my father. "But you were really working *for* Symond, weren't you? That's why you signaled Jaffen to come. Jaffen's right. You betrayed him." Dain opened his one good eye and then closed it. I threw the note into the fire.

After an endless time, Jaffen came out of the bedroom and *thunked* a basin full of bloody toweling onto the table.

"How is she?" I asked.

"She'll be all right if the wound stays clean." Jaffen cocked his head and considered Dain.

"Show some mercy, my lord," Dain said. "I served your father for twenty years."

"What you'll get, Dain, is justice. Help me move him into the other room, Addy. I want him out of my sight." Between them, they carted Dain and his chair into the bedroom, and then came back, closing the door.

We all stood around the fire as if we couldn't quite shake

the cold. I couldn't stop thinking about my father. About Addy and Jaffen's father too. And about Symond's.

"I wish you'd listened to me," Addy murmured softly enough that he could have been talking to himself. In his brother's presence, his vowels had flattened, so, for the first time, he sounded Lyzian.

Jaffen shrugged. "I should have, but Dain came out on a boat to meet us, with a message about how much Haron wanted me to become Great Drake. *Come stay in the palace. Haron wants to talk.* Symond left me alive only because he wants a show trial." He started pacing again. "Addy, one of us should signal the ship. It can meet us in that little cove up the coast, assuming we can get there."

After an instant's silence, Addy said, "You'll leave?"

Jaffen's trip back and forth across the room had reached the front door. He raised his fist as if to punch it, then yanked his hand back. I had seen Addy do much the same thing in the tunnel on the Heights, and I wondered if Addy had copied his gestures from the brother he obviously idolized. Jaffen wheeled to walk toward the fire again. "For now anyway. I hate to see this come to battle, but things are at a state between Symond and me that it may."

"Battle in Kural's streets?" I said. "No!"

"Wait for the Flame Testing, Jaff," Addy pleaded. "The necklace will burn Symond, and then we can get hold of it and—"

Jaffen shooed the idea away like a fly. "Symond will get around it somehow."

"It won't burn him anyway," I said. "It's fake."

Jaffen halted where he stood. He and Addy both stared at me, Addy opening and closing his mouth like a fish.

"What do you mean?" Addy asked.

"It has my mother's mark on it. She made it. It's beautifully worked, but it's just glass from the glasshouse."

"The one I stole from the tower treasure room?" Addy clarified. He seemed to be having trouble taking it in.

I nodded.

Jaffen gave a short laugh. "That takes care of that then." He resumed pacing.

Addy's head turned back and forth, his gaze following his brother. "Maybe we could—"

"No." Jaffen chopped the air with his hand. "Be quiet and let me think, Addy. You know nothing about how these things are done outside of books."

Addy dropped into a chair, propped his elbows on his thighs, and rested his head in his hands.

I made a disgusted noise in the back of my throat. "Oh, right. Addy knows nothing. He just brought home the news about *jaff,* which he had the wits to interpret in your favor. And I suppose that didn't help you at all. What other things did he bring home? Knowledge about medicine? Is that how Lyz regained that in the past six months?"

Jaffen regarded me with hooded eyes.

I knotted my hands in front of me. "He told you not to come and you didn't listen. What's more, you were rotting in a cell until he came along."

"Actually, I was in a very comfortable room and hadn't had time to rot."

"But a room with a lock," I said.

Addy had lifted his head and was watching me with a half smile.

"I'm glad he got me out of *my* room," I said, "even if it was comfortable. Though to be fair, I suppose I owe you thanks for that as well."

"You owe me nothing. Addy insisted, and he's always been good at wheedling what he wanted out of me. Besides, you're right. I owed him." He resumed pacing.

My brain hummed like a furnace. We couldn't wait until morning to decide what to do. By midday tomorrow, Symond would be drake, and it would be too late. I didn't know if Jaffen would be a good ruler, but Symond had convinced me he would be a terrible one.

"Addy," Jaffen said after a while, "when we get out of here, you don't have to stay with me. You could go to the Westlands again."

"You're saying you don't need me?" Addy asked lightly. "I understand."

"It's not that," Jaffen said. "This could get very dangerous very fast, and it's not the kind of thing you're trained for."

"Whatever you want," Addy said tonelessly. "But will you do me a favor and take Emlin and Miriv to Lyz? Emlin, I know you think you can't make glass on Lyz, but I think you can. I found this manuscript—"

"If she wants to go, of course I'll take her," Jaffen interrupted. "Miriv too. It obviously won't be safe for them here."

Addy nodded his thanks and leaned on his thighs again, gaze on the red and blue rag rug between the two chairs.

I rubbed my palms on my trousers. "I suppose Miriv and I have no choice but to leave. Assuming Symond becomes drake, of course."

After a moment's silence, Addy lifted his head and gave me a quizzical look. "Are you suggesting there's a chance he won't?"

"Do you believe the real Dragonshards would show who the true ruler is?" I asked.

"Yes," Addy said immediately. More slowly, Jaffen nodded.

"My mother delivered the copy only a month ago, so the chances are the real necklace was there when Drake Haron was tested."

"Maybe," Addy said, "but Jaffen is right that there are probably ways to get around the necklace's absence."

"How?" I asked. "The Sage puts the necklace on the person claiming to be the next rightful drake. If the person is wrong, the stones burn them. You could just claim not to be burned, but how would you fake the look of the fire?"

Addy shrugged. "You saw all those torch stands on the platform and barriers to keep everyone except Symond's friends at a distance. I was thinking he might plan to dazzle people with light and let them assume they saw what they expected. People are surprisingly easy to fool, I've found."

"Hm, yes." I pursed my lips, and he gave me a sheepish smile. "Let's assume the Dragonshards were there for Haron. They'd have been kept in the palace tower, right? That's where you stole the fake ones?"

He nodded.

"So where are the real ones? Could someone else have slipped into the tower and taken them?"

Jaffen drew near to listen as Addy narrowed his eyes and considered. "Maybe," Addy said, "but very few people could have done it. The palaces of the Dolyan dragon lords are all built on the same sacred pattern, so I knew where the treasure room was and what the locks were like. But more important than that, the tower accepted me, helped me even."

I blinked. "What do you mean?"

"The whole palace is dragon work," Addy said. "The

more closely you're descended from one of the dragon riders, the more easily it will open doors or muffle your footsteps while making other people's louder. That's the main reason Jaff and I could find you and Miriv, sneak up on your guards, and get you out." He looked into the fire and smiled. "I could beat any of my friends at hide-and-hunt in the palace. They eventually caught on and moved the game outside after which I never won another game. Obviously."

"So what you're saying," I said, "is that the real Dragonshards are probably still in the palace." I held Addy's gaze. "We should go back and look for them."

Chapter 23

"GO BACK?" JAFFEN gave an incredulous laugh. "You couldn't find some nice, quiet scholar girl?" he asked Addy.

Addy grimaced. "He's right, Emlin. Between the Watch and palace guards, we'd be pincushions before we got through the gates."

"Forget that for a moment," I said. "Let's think. Could Symond have hidden the real necklace and commissioned the fake one because he was afraid the real one would burn him?"

"Oh, no," Jaffen said. "Symond thinks he's born to be drake. He's been trained to it from birth. Even if he wanted to dump the responsibility and sail away, he'd think it was wrong, and trust me, Symond *wants* to be drake. I've talked to him." He paced back toward the door, Addy frowning after him.

"What do you think, Addy?" I asked. "Would the real Dragonshards accept Symond as the true drake?"

"No," Addy said at once. "Not if he killed the current drake. Besides, all the signs say Jaffen should be drake on all the Dolyan Islands."

"That's a good theory," I said. "But wouldn't you like to

know for sure?" I dangled scholar bait in front of him. "How many chances will you have to learn something like that?"

Addy looked thoughtful.

"She's playing you like a harp." Jaffen sounded alarmed. "You'd never get through the palace gates. I won't allow it."

"You should send your ship out of sight," I told him. "That way Symond will think you left and let down his guard."

"I plan to send my ship out of sight," he said, "and I plan for Addy and me to be on it. You, too, if you're sane enough to want to."

I faced Addy again. "Can we climb the palace wall?"

"No," Addy said. "The dragon work walls won't let even me do that."

"He's tried," Jaffen said. "Why do you think he's so afraid of heights?"

"I'm no longer eight years old, Jaffen," Addy said sharply.

Jaffen halted in mid-stride and stood looking expressionlessly at Addy.

I seized the opportunity. "I have an idea for how we can get over the wall a different way."

Addy tore his gaze away from Jaffen and frowned at me. "*We?*"

"Well, yes. I need you to pick any locks and because of what you said about the tower helping if you're there."

Jaffen snorted. "Not so pleasant when someone else refuses to listen to reason and looks ready to risk his – or in this case her – neck, is it, Addy?"

Addy ignored him. "If you find me a way into the palace, I'll search on my own."

Jaffen groaned.

"I mended that necklace and gave it to Symond." I met Addy's eyes steadily. "I know in my bones that he ordered my mother's death. If I'm ever to live quietly again, I need to do what I can to repair the damage I caused *and* make him pay for what he did." I inclined my head toward the closed bedroom door. "I've led your brother to my father. I also have to do everything I can to make that worth the price Dain will pay. Besides," I added, "if you don't take me, I won't tell you how to get in."

Slowly, Addy nodded.

"No!" Jaffen said.

The brothers glared at one another in a silence so tense, the air quivered.

"I swear I can fix this," Addy finally said. "If the necklace is in the palace, I'll get it for you. You summon your crew and wait near the fountain."

"If I ordered you not to go?" Jaffen asked him.

A moment passed. "Please don't do that," Addy said, "because I'd do it anyway, so you'd have to hold court with me as the guilty accused. I've already been before a drake's court once, and I found the outcome painful."

Jaffen winced and paced to the door again.

I squirreled away the knowledge that even with Jaffen Addy didn't hesitate to fight dirty. Not when he was fighting to keep hold of Jaffen with one hand while grabbing his own life with the other.

Jaffen faced us, composure regained. He studied Addy with a faintly puzzled look, as if he didn't quite recognize the man in front of him as his little brother. He wiped a hand down his face, and dropped his arms to his sides. "Then I'll be waiting."

Addy's shoulders settled under the stolen uniform.

Jaffen maneuvered around Addy toward the back room. "Emlin, I'm going to check on Miriv. You should speak to her before you go."

Of course I should. He didn't need to tell me. I followed him into the bedroom. Voices from the front room must have been audible from there because both Dain and Miriv frowned at us as we came through the door.

Dain forgot his own danger to glare at Jaffen. "Shame on you for dragging her into this."

Jaffen snorted. "I'm not the one doing the dragging." He closed the bedroom door and braced his back against it.

"You have the nerve to blame Emlin?" Miriv asked.

Jaffen raised his hands, palms out. "If you heard, then you know."

"Emlin," Dain said, "Calea let me coax her into a mistake. She was already sorry the day she handed over the knife. I saw it in her face, felt it in the way her touch changed. Don't let these two talk you into something you'll be sorry for."

To my surprise, knowing my mother had been sorry for making the blade felt like a piece of a stained-glass window had slid into place and solved some design puzzle I'd been trying to work out. I felt intense pity for the eager, bold girl she'd been. She'd broken her oath, but I couldn't find it in my heart to condemn her. She'd acted for love.

And I'd finally decided the dragon hadn't faulted her too badly either. The quality of her work never faltered, so the dragon had breathed dreams into her until the end.

"The only one making me act is me." I crossed to the bed and kissed Miriv's forehead.

She caught my wrist in her good hand. I waited while she found what she wanted to say. Finally, she jerked her head toward Jaffen. "Go with him to Lyz. Leave Kural. It's too dangerous for you here." She put her finger over the mouth I'd opened to answer. "Don't wait for me. I'd only slow you down. Go."

Something caught in my throat. I knew what it must have cost her to say that. "I can't." I stroked her cheek, tears stinging my eyes. "Thank you. Thank you for everything." I straightened to leave, but found Jaffen blocking my way, his back against the door.

Speaking fast and low, he said, "The most shameful thing I ever did was stand by while Addy was beaten. I swore I'd never let something like that happen again. Get him hurt and you'll regret it."

I regarded him steadily. "I already knew that."

He yanked the door open.

Against my will, my gaze swung to my beaten father sunken in his chair. Grief rippled through me. I knew I'd see that image forever. On impulse, I darted close and kissed his forehead too. The last thing I saw of him was the wide surprise in his one good eye.

Addy waited, jiggling one knee. "Ready?" I nodded, but he paused and spoke to Jaffen. "Don't wait by the fountain too long."

Jaffen gripped the chair back so tightly his knuckles went white. "You mean leave you if I have to?"

"I do." Addy reached around me and opened the door to the dark street. I went through, ready to fix the most shameful thing *I'd* ever done.

Chapter 24

T HE NARROW STREET along the palace's back wall was empty, but it wouldn't stay that way long, not given the Watch patrols Addy and I had hidden from on our way to Renie's house. With Jaffen loose, Symond was taking no chances.

I knocked and, after a moment, the door opened, spilling light across the cobblestones. Renie stood there with a shawl thrown over her nightdress. "Did you forget—" She stopped. "Emlin. I thought Tae had forgotten his key." Eyeing Addy, she stepped aside. "Come in."

The fingers Addy pressed against my back quivered. His tension was contagious, and I didn't need his urging to hurry inside. He eased the door silently shut.

"What's the matter?" Renie's color was better than when I'd visited after her miscarriage, and her voice was steady.

Addy held up his hand for silence. A moment later, I heard the booted feet of the Watch. Renie, Addy, and I stayed where we were until the sound faded, Renie looking at Addy's hand on me with raised eyebrows. Face coloring, Addy took his fingers from my spine.

"Tae is still working?" I asked. The feel of Addy's touch

lingered on my back.

"Yes. What's this about, Emlin?"

"I don't have time to explain it all, but Symond is planning to use fake Dragonshards in tomorrow's Flame Testing."

A flush crept up Renie's face. "He's not going to use the real necklace? That's beyond appalling."

I flinched away from what Renie would say if she knew my mother and I had put that fake necklace in Symond's hands. "We have to get into the palace to find the real one. I hate to ask this of you, but can you help us?"

"Are you doing something dangerous, Emlin?" Renie frowned at Addy, as if holding him responsible.

"It's less dangerous than not doing anything," I said firmly.

"I sometimes take food to Tae when he's working. Do you want me to try to take you with me?"

"We might have been through the gates once too often already," Addy said.

It was not a funny moment, but I nearly laughed at the understatement.

"And you are?" Renie asked him.

"Addy." He gave her the beaming smile that meant the person on the receiving end should be suspicious as a dog confronting a man with a net. "Emlin has an idea she hasn't shared yet, but she's just about to tell me."

"He's the scholar I've been seeing," I put in. "Ignore the uniform. Is Tae's ladder here? He doesn't have it with him, does he?"

Addy's smile vanished. "That's it? You should have told me. We can't use a ladder to get over the wall. It will push the ladder away. What's more the Watch is patrolling so often, they'll see it."

"We won't put it against the wall." I smiled as reassuringly as I could. "Don't worry. It will be fine."

Addy's brow wrinkled. "Don't worry? How is that possible?"

"The ladder's in the yard," Renie said. "I'll show you."

Addy followed her out the back door and returned balancing Tae's long ladder on one shoulder. He whacked it against the doorframe coming through and almost lost his balance.

I already had my foot on the bottom step of the narrow staircase. "Upstairs is all right?" When worried-looking Renie nodded, I raced ahead. On the upper landing, I opened the door toward the house's front and entered Renie and Tae's bedroom. The bed covers were thrown aside. We must have awakened her.

I swung the window open. As I'd remembered, it was directly across from the chestnut tree looming over the palace wall. One of the solid branches stretched within three yards of the window. I went back to the door and found Addy wrestling the ladder around the tight turn at the top of the stairs.

"Watch out!" Renie cried.

The end of the ladder swept past a lamp globe, missing it by a hair. "It's all right," Addy wheezed. "I have it." He hefted the ladder more securely and brought it into the bedroom. "Now what?"

I checked the street for Watchmen, then pointed out the window. "Lay the ladder to make a bridge between the sill and the tree. See how you can do it without touching the wall?"

Addy's hands tightened on the ladder. "Yes," he said, not

moving. A moment passed, at the end of which, he rested one end on the sill, propped the other on the bed, and began feeding it out the window. The length outside grew until Addy had to lean back, pulling against the weight.

I leapt to the window and grabbed one side of the ladder. The wood had worn smooth and darkened under other people's grips and sweat. An instant later, Renie appeared at his other side. I struggled, even with muscles bred by handling long iron pipes tipped with heavy gathers of glass. The far end of the ladder dipped as it inched toward the chestnut. Addy leaned on the end we held to keep the far one aloft. That end vanished amid shaking leaves. Then it reappeared and slid into place.

For a moment, all three of us still clutched the end in the bedroom. I forced my fingers loose and shook my hands to ease the cramps. Renie stepped back too, but Addy leaned out and put his weight on the farthest rung he could reach. The ladder settled solidly on a branch.

Renie let out a shaky sigh.

"We'll get rid of the ladder as soon as we're inside," I told her. "I don't want to make more trouble for you than I have to. Go visit Tae so you can say you had nothing to do with this."

Renie never hesitated. "I won't be driven from my own house," she said, but she left the room.

Even in the gloom, I could see that Addy's face was pale.

"See?" I waved toward the ladder. "It's like a path. Plenty wide. Plenty strong."

Opening and closing his fists, he peered down at the cobblestones.

"You climbed the roof to my room. You can do this too. I'll go first." I braced my arms on the ladder, ready to heave myself onto it.

Still without speaking, Addy pushed me out of the way and swung up to rest his hands and knees on the ladder. Jaw clenched, he crawled out the window. One foot caught on the sill, and he lurched and froze in place, hands gripping as if he couldn't let go. Carefully, he drew the foot free and began to crawl.

It's all right, I silently told him. *You're fine.* I watched him cross. He never looked down, and he never paused. If I hadn't known he was terrified, I wouldn't have been able to tell until he tunneled through the leaves and slid off the ladder onto a waiting branch. Then he hugged the trunk, dropped the side of his head against it, and gulped air as if he'd had to swim across underwater.

I was reaching for my end of the ladder when it twitched. I shot an alarmed look toward the chestnut, but the tree hadn't caused the ladder's movement. Instead, Addy had left the safety of the trunk to grab the ladder's other end. Face set, he was trying out different grips.

For an instant, I thought he was trying to settle the ladder more surely. Then he tugged, and I realized that rather than trying to help me cross, he was trying to keep me from getting into the palace.

I threw myself onto the makeshift bridge. Addy muttered something I couldn't hear, but backed away. The rungs dug into my knees. I grunted, shifted as much weight as I could to my braced toes, and crawled out. Addy had changed the ladder's position just enough that it slanted more steeply over the cobblestones. Within a few rungs, my hip dangled off the lower side. I gripped the other side and dragged myself higher. A branch popped, and the ladder shifted again.

Addy was steadying the ladder's other end – as well the

fool should – when I heard the tramp of heavy boots, and the light of a Watch lantern bobbed around the corner into Renie's street. There were two of them, and neither one was happy.

"All of us on duty," the woman with the lantern said. "All day and all night too. I ask you, what kind of sense does that make? We'll be stupid with lack of sleep."

"I hear Symond's spitting fire over Jaffen getting away."

"That's not our fault. That's the palace boys' doing."

"Well, they're out walking their feet off too and probably glad to be away from Symond."

I felt an almost irresistible urge to rush across the ladder into the shelter of the chestnut, but I held still as stone. They were probably half night-blind from carrying the lantern, but if I twitched and made a sound they might look up. There'd be no explaining what I was doing halfway across the street to the palace. The muscles in my arms shivered at the strain of holding myself motionless. I risked turning my head to send Addy a warning look, but his gaze was on the man and woman below.

I heard a click and a scrape that I identified as a door opening only when Renie ran out into the street and raced up to the Watch.

"Why are there so many patrols tonight?" she asked in a high, anxious voice. "Is something the matter?" She pulled her shawl tight around her.

"Just routine," the woman said. "Go on in."

She and her partner resumed walking, steering Renie toward her door, but when they reached it, she wriggled away from them and kept trotting along at their side.

"Should I be worried?" she gabbled. "What's going on?"

I held my breath as they passed under me, the

Watchwoman saying reassuring things and Renie fretting aloud as she dogged them down the street. The longer she followed them, the faster the two of them walked.

With their backs to me, I scrambled the rest of the way across. Addy gripped my arms and drew me onto a branch. He pulled me to his chest, and when I pressed my head against him, I found myself looking at a jaffel's nest. The bird aimed one bright eye suspiciously my way.

"Sorry to intrude," I whispered.

"She's with me," Addy said.

The bird hunkered down, still watching us.

Inside the palace wall like this, I heard the muffled sound of construction still going on in the courtyard on the other side of the palace. I tried to block it out, the better to hear Renie. Finally, the Watchwoman gave Renie an exasperated command. "Go home."

"Of course," Renie said. "I'm so sorry to have bothered you." The lantern light faded as Renie's quick steps pattered along the street. The door to her house closed.

I sagged against Addy. His heart thudded in my ear. Or maybe it was my heart. Despite the emptiness of the street and the urgency of our mission, neither of us moved.

Then I lifted my head and punched him in the chest. He made a whooshing sound. "I have to mend the mistakes I've made. You have no right to stop me."

He let me go, his tongue for once stilled. He struggled for breath, but his eyes met mine, and suddenly I, too, was breathless. The jaffel sang its heart-piercing song.

I licked my lips. "We should hide the ladder."

He nodded, and I moved to a different branch, aware of night air chilling the places that had shared Addy's warmth. Pulling the ladder in proved harder than laying it out. The branches got in the way, and we had to swivel it so it would drop in a clear place inside the wall. I teetered on my perch, afraid the ladder was about to crash into the street. Then the near end tilted down and the ladder smashed into the bushes below. I put a hand on Addy's arm. His muscle jumped beneath my grip. We waited, but no guards appeared.

"I think we're all right," I murmured and crouched to climb down. When I'd clambered to the branch below, I looked up to find Addy staring wild-eyed at the ground with his arms wrapped around the tree's trunk. "Now you're afraid? *Now*?"

He cleared his throat. "Just go."

I shook my head and worked my way down. A swath of crushed bushes led me to the ladder. I dragged it into deeper hiding, ignoring the soft squeaks coming from overhead as Addy gradually came lower. When his boots hit the ground, I went toward the sound and found him sitting against the tree, hands spread in the dirt. I was surprised he wasn't kissing it.

My mind skittered off on its own at the thought of Addy kissing.

He glanced at where I'd stowed the ladder and spoke in an admirably steady voice. "Good job."

"I suppose the necklace could be anywhere in the palace," I said, "but we might as well start with the treasure room. What's the best way into it?"

"It's in the tower, and as you saw when we delivered your stained-glass window, the tower entrance is at one end of the front hall." Addy rose. "I'm asking, not telling, but won't you please wait here? I'll get the necklace." Again his eyes held mine, sober and concerned.

"I told you, I can't." I started toward the courtyard,

which would be busy and torchlit, but might be noisy enough to provide some distraction. "I put fake Dragonshards in the hands of the man who ordered my mother's death. And Kural deserves a true ruler."

Addy caught my sleeve. "There's only one way into the tower, but we'll try a different way into the palace."

"There's another way?"

"There is in the palace on Lyz. Let's see if there's one here too."

Keeping to the shadows, he led me out of the trees and through a gate into what my nose told me was an herb garden. The tang of rosemary hung in the air. We went through another gate and then Addy slowed, slipping along close to the palace wall, scanning the bushes for something behind them. He gave a soft crow and shoved through a gap in the bushes. When I came up next to him, he was crouching at a door no higher than the length of my arm and pulled it wide open to show a narrow ramp slanting down into the dark. He lay on his belly and wriggled his legs and hips back through the opening.

"Is this safe? What is it?" I asked.

He shot me a grin. "You'll see. Wait until I tell you to come." He slid backward, but stuck when his chest reached the opening. "Haven't done this in a while," he puffed. He scrunched his shoulders and squirmed.

I put a hand on the top of his head and shoved.

He vanished down the chute. I heard what sounded like slithering and then a yelp. After a moment, he called, "All right."

I drew a breath, rich with the garden's green smell, eased my body through the opening, and shoved off. I whooshed down a slide, then skidded across a hard, flat surface, with what felt like straw bunching under my grasping fingers. My feet struck a wall and stopped me just as I discovered that the slippery surface was painfully cold even through the straw and my tunic. I jerked up to sit, but my trousers weren't all that thick either. I couldn't stop myself from squealing.

Somewhere in the dark, Addy laughed.

"What is this?" I asked. "It's cold as ice."

"It is ice," Addy said. "On Lyz, it's brought in on ships packed in straw, so it's probably the same here."

"I've seen that. I wondered how it was stored."

"Now you know." He sounded as if he might still be laughing.

"And the dragon loves knowledge," I said dryly. I rose to my knees. "Stop laughing and show me the way out."

My eyes were adjusting to the darkness, and I spotted him, still chuckling as he shuffled toward the other end of the room. I scrambled upright, slipped, and sat down hard. Surrendering my dignity, I scooted on my backside to follow him. Straw formed a dam under my trousers. Addy had the good sense not to laugh again. When I came to a halt near his boots, he climbed off the ice onto the floor a few feet below, then reached up to help me down.

He cracked open the door, peeked out, and then beckoned me after him into a narrow hallway lined with arches. Still shivering, I brushed at the seat of my trousers. At least it was warmer in the hall. Barrels of flour and bins of vegetables ranged along both walls.

Addy moved soundlessly toward a stairway, where he halted and bent to whisper in my ear, his warm breath tickling my neck. "These come up into a pantry. Stay close and move when I do." He climbed the steps, stopping when his head was high enough to see whatever was at the top.

I wriggled up to squeeze in next to him and looked along the floor of a room lined with shelves and sacks. A servant boy snored on a pallet nearby.

Addy darted up the steps and pressed himself against the shelves along one side. As he craned to look through the doorway into a hall, I scrambled up and flattened myself next to him. I felt him stiffen and leaned to see too. A guard was just emerging from a room.

My knees weakened, but the guard closed the door behind him and walked the other way, eventually vanishing around a corner.

Addy touched my arm and hustled me out into the hall, heading away from where the guard had gone. The hall was narrow and dimly lit. Servants' quarters, I guessed, with people who'd worked all day asleep behind the doors. They were unlikely to be disturbed by Addy, whose steps made no sound. I trod as softly as I could and still made more noise. The corridor's walls were plaster, but the floor glowed, a seamless expanse of pink stone that had to be helping him, just as he said it would.

When the hallway turned, it also widened and we moved into richer quarters. Addy shooed me to one side, and it took me a moment to realize that while the other side had no doors, this side had an indented doorway every few yards. He knew all the spots that would hide him from servants or guards. I guessed some of that knowledge came from exploring when he'd rescued Miriv, Jaffen, and me, but I was willing to wager he was also using a ripe harvest of skill he'd built up in the palace on Lyz. I pictured him as a slippery child with time on his hands and a craving to be places he wasn't supposed to be and learn things he wasn't supposed to know. I pitied any nurse or tutor who'd been responsible for keeping track of him.

Addy brought us to a halt at another corner and took a quick look around before pulling back. I felt the tension in his arm as he brushed against me. Head tilted, he seemed to be listening. I cocked an ear and heard it too: the rattle of a door latch being tested and then footsteps growing fainter. Addy stooped and spoke into my ear so softly I had to strain to hear him. "Be ready to move when I say." He fished a set of tools from a pocket and ducked around the corner.

I lunged to see him bent over the lock on what was unmistakably the gilded tower door, a door that was fully visible to the guards at the palace entrance. The footsteps were still fading. Sweat seeped into my armpits. If the guards from the palace's front door turned toward him, Addy was out in the open. He still wore his guard's uniform, but someone was sure to wonder what he was doing.

The tower door popped open. He glanced over his shoulder toward where the door guards were and beckoned to me, but I was already moving. He flung me through the doorway, stepped in behind me, and relocked the door, closing us into the palace tower.

Chapter 25

I FROZE JUST inside the doorway, listening for any sign we'd been spotted, though it would be hard to hear over the sound of my heart galloping around in my chest. Addy pressed his ear to the door. After a moment, he hissed out a breath and soft-footed through what turned out to be a short entryway.

I followed, scanning the room to see how hard a search we had in front of us. The round room was dim, lit only by the pink walls, but as my eyes grew used to the faint light, I took in shelves of chests and boxes, stretching from floor to ceiling and broken only by the door through which we'd entered and an archway on the room's opposite side. In the center of the room, a pink stone column rose a little higher than my waist, its top draped in silk embroidered with Kural's blue and gold dragon.

"The fake necklace was there." Addy nodded toward the empty silk. "I wonder where Symond is keeping it."

"Maybe he's taking no chance on someone stealing it again," I said. "After all, the thief could come back." Addy laughed. I gestured to my right. "I'll search the lower shelves. You go the other way and do the higher ones."

I lifted the lid of a chest and gaped at gold coins glittering in a messy heap. In my life, coins were valuable because they were rare. This chest held so many, they didn't seem real. On the room's other side, Addy was pawing through an equally full chest. Gingerly, I dug through the heavy coins, finding only more gold. Addy closed the chest he was searching and moved on to the next as easily as if he sifted heaps of coins on a daily basis.

"Is your father's treasure room like this?" I asked. "I suppose now it's Jaffen's."

Addy tossed a handful of coins aside. "I haven't been in there since Jaffen became drake. But my father had a hoard even bigger than this one."

He was at home in this setting. It could have been the surrounding dragon work affecting him, or the attitude he'd learned as a drake's son before he left. I became aware of how different his life had been from mine – how different it would be again if we succeeded in putting Jaffen on the throne of Kural as well as Lyz. As if he felt the brush of my attention, he glanced at me, one eyebrow lifted.

I dropped my gaze and lowered the chest's lid. Amid all this sign of wealth and rank, did he see me differently too?

I opened a box that turned out to hold an elaborate vase made of blue glass. I recognized not only the color but the vase itself. I didn't know how old I'd been when I watched my mother make it, but my chin had barely cleared the marver table, and my mother had more than once told me to move away before she dragged me to a bench and told me sharply to stay there until someone said I could get up. It felt strange to see the vase on a shelf below a chest of coins. It must be worth more than I'd thought back in the glasshouse. I had the irrelevant thought that it should be on display.

Otherwise, why had my mother bothered to make it beautiful? Symond did love beautiful things, apparently, but only to own them.

I heard the soft snap of Addy closing a chest, followed immediately by a rattle of metal handle from the doorway. Before my heart had time to resume beating, Addy bundled me through the archway on the room's far side. Stairs rose in a hallway winding upward between the tower's outer wall and the wall of the treasure room. We scrambled far enough up that the archway vanished around a turn.

Men's voices echoed from the treasure room.

"Symond wants a guard outside this door," said a voice I recognized as the palace steward's. "And until the Sage comes to fetch the necklace for the ceremony, he wants the room checked at every hour the Watchman cries."

"Does he think someone can walk right past a guard? What's the little weasel worried about now?" a second voice asked.

"Whatever it is, you'd do well to hold your tongue. A nervous ruler is a menace to anyone within reach."

I pressed against the comforting warmth of the pink wall behind me. Maybe Addy wasn't the only one drawing aid from those stones. Symond had descended from a dragon lord too. As a matter of fact, he'd descended from Kural's lord while Addy was an intruder. Maybe Symond's palace was warning him of trouble. Or maybe he'd made enough trouble that he had to expect it to come back on him.

In the warm stairway, I smelled again the faint odor of unfamiliar spices that I'd noticed when I first met Addy. I tried not to be obvious about inhaling, though all his attention was concentrated on the men in the treasure room anyway. At last, I heard footsteps and the sound of the door closing. Even then, Addy put out his hand to still me when I moved. When he lowered it, we tiptoed to the foot of the stairs, where I snuck a look around the archway before entering the room.

Atop the column in the room's center gleamed what looked like the Dragonshards. I knew which piece to check, but even before I turned it over to look for the C, I'd seen the nearly invisible scar marking the place where Addy and I had broken it. When I shook my head, he grimaced but wasted no time returning to the search. He'd probably had as little hope as I'd had that this was the real necklace.

Ear cocked toward the door, I went back to my own side of the room. I'd planned to start looking in the tower but move on to the drake's rooms if the necklace wasn't there. With a guard outside, though, we were trapped in here. From its box, I lifted a silk coat with embroidery so fine it had to come from the crafthouse on Eteald Island. I let the fabric slide like water over my fingers and folded it carefully away.

Sooner than I'd have thought possible, the key snicked in the lock again, and we had to flee to the stairway. The guard's footsteps made what sounded like a quick half circuit of the treasure room. Then he apparently decided to check the stairs because lantern light flared up the steps, and shadows shifted over the shining stones. I tried to melt into the wall behind me, afraid the guard would hear my breathing. When Addy groped for my hand, I gripped his warm palm.

The guard was less than thorough, which I suppose made sense, given his doubt that someone could walk past him into the tower. The light withdrew, the footsteps went away, the door thudded shut. We went back to our search. The guard interrupted us twice more before we finished. Our hours in the circular room showed me more treasure than I'd probably see in the rest of my life – even assuming that life extended beyond the next morning – but it hadn't yielded the one treasure that mattered.

We retreated into the stairwell and sat side by side on a hard step. I wriggled sideways to give him room, but his arm still brushed mine. A little shiver ran through me.

"Now what?" he asked.

I twisted to look up the stairs. "I don't suppose this takes us into the palace?"

"If it's like the one on Lyz, it just goes to the lookout tower."

"We could knock out the guard out the next time he comes."

"Someone would notice he was missing, and the guards would go straight to stand watch over Symond, which I assume is where we'd go to search too. Beyond his rooms, I have no idea where else to look." Addy's shoulders were hunched as if his stomach hurt.

He minded our failure even more than I did, I realized with a stab of pain. He'd wanted to help his brother, and even more to earn Jaffen's respect. "I'm sorry," I said.

His mouth twisted, but he said nothing.

Pushing to my feet, I said, "We might as well go up and wait for morning to watch the ceremony."

With Addy right behind me, I climbed the curling stairway. It fit seamlessly between the walls, all of them of a piece. True dragon work. But Kural's dragon had abandoned its people now. We'd let ourselves grow too small for the dragon to notice, I thought bitterly. We were led by men like Symond and let a man like Kedry take over our craft. Who could blame the creature for staying asleep on the Heights?

The stairs ended at a narrow door. I squeezed aside to let

Addy unlock it. In the shadows, his face was dark and opaque, like glass with no light behind it.

Picking the lock took him longer than usual, but eventually it yielded, and he waved me through. I mounted four more steps and emerged at the top of the palace tower with only a waist-high wall between me and a night sky that went on to the ends of the earth. Despite the weight in my chest, I caught my breath. The moon had slid low. We wouldn't have to wait long for morning, but in the meantime, surely the stars were close enough to touch.

I walked slowly along the wall, circling the tower top. The Heights sprawled in a black mass across the horizon that gave way to the sea, where moonlight silvered the water. Closer in, the town was dark, as people slept and dreamed their secret dreams. The window of the palace guardhouse glowed, but the hammering and shouts in the courtyard and square had fallen silent. The world lay as if in waiting, looking much as it must have done when the dragon riders still sailed overhead.

A thump made me turn around. The gold dragon statue loomed between me and the top of the stairs. When I rounded it, I found Addy sitting on the floor, his head thrown back against the low wall. I sat next to him.

"Do you mind being so high?"

"Does it matter?" he answered wearily. Beard stubble shadowed the hollows of his cheeks.

I leaned against him, trying to say without words that if he did mind, it mattered to me. That all his pain mattered. After an instant, he put his arm around me. My heart immediately beat faster.

"So why are you afraid of heights?" I asked. If we kept talking, we could stay the way we were. "Your brother said there was a reason."

He grimaced. "It's a long story."

"We don't appear to be going anywhere."

"When I was eight," he started, "I took it as a challenge to climb the wall around the palace on Lyz. You don't need to know all the things I tried, just that it all came down to a ladder I managed to drag out and prop against it. The wall let me climb the ladder and step onto its top, as thrilled with myself as ever a boy was thrilled. It was night, of course, because I had to sneak out to do it, and I looked up and grinned at the Dragon stars. That was when everything tilted."

"You fell?" I was horrified. The wall around Kural's palace was at least ten feet tall.

"The ladder fell, but not me, not yet. My feet lifted up off that wall so I was flying and spinning. Then I fell."

"How badly were you hurt?"

"Not as badly as I deserved to be. I woke up in my bed because my nanny had missed me and hunted me down. I was sore enough that I could barely move, but I didn't break anything. Except the ladder, of course. It was in splinters. It was only days later that I realized I was cursed to become clumsy enough to trip over anything within a yard of my feet at moments that mattered to me."

"Your mother must have been frantic."

"She lived in our country house, which is where I did too before that year. She and my father didn't get along. My father only brought me to the palace when she died. It was Jaffen who came and read to me so I'd stay in bed." He rubbed his chin over my hair. "I wish I could help him."

I pictured a hurt child, grieving his mother with only a big brother to show him affection, and felt a hopeless determination to help Addy get his wish for the person who'd loved him. "We could steal the fake necklace and try to get it to Jaffen," I said. "That's what you were going to do in the first place."

"Once they came in and saw it was gone, they'd know we were here somewhere. We'd never get out of this tower alive." He slid his hand up and down on my shoulder. "I hope Jaffen doesn't wait too long when we don't show up. We'll have to try to get away on our own, maybe during the ceremony while everyone is preoccupied. You'll come with me, won't you? I can take you and Miriv to the Westlands if you like. It's an odd country but beautiful nonetheless."

I thought about living among strangers and shivered, not entirely from the chilly night air. "You wouldn't go home to Lyz?"

"After this little fiasco? What use do you think Jaffen sees in me? He's been right all along. He needs someone tougher than a little brother with his nose in a book."

In my opinion, *use* didn't enter into it. Jaffen had looked far too fond of 'little brother' to want him flying the coop. "Tougher? You were on your own at thirteen."

"Not that kind of tough. More like him. Someone even our father would have seen as strong. So he could use me as his war leader or something like that." He contemplated the dragon statue. With the scales on its back lit by the last of the moonlight, it looked ready to soar. "Jaffen worried about me, you know. As soon as I ran away, he secretly sent people to search for me and bring me money. I can't tell you how good I felt the first time one of them showed up and I knew he was looking for me. When he summoned me home after our father died, I don't know what he thought he was getting, but even before I set foot on Lyz I wasn't sure I'd fit into his plans. The first day I met you, you said you didn't need scholarly secrets. Jaffen really doesn't. He spends all his time wrestling with power-hungry people in mind-numbing ways."

I thought of the few glimpses I'd had of Jaffen. "Isn't Jaffen power-hungry?"

His forehead wrinkled. "Maybe. I guess so. But he'd use it well. I know he would." He looked faintly unhappy.

"What?" I teased. "You're saying he'd be better than Symond?"

He rewarded me with a laugh. "Jaffen's smart, for one thing, and though he never saw much point to scholarly work, he believes in justice and all the other things the dragon riders practiced. But he doesn't need me around, really. You heard him say I could go on my way again."

I sat up straight and faced him. "Are you blind? He said that because he loves you enough to try to protect you whether he needs you or not. You're just feeling sorry for yourself because we didn't find the necklace for him." I leaned back against him. His shoulder was warm against mine. Once again, I thought of my father, now in Jaffen's hands. "If he's such a good ruler, Addy, why did Dain betray him?"

He sighed. "It's possible Symond paid him, I suppose. That's what Jaffen thinks. But really I think he didn't trust Jaffen, mostly because he knew Jaffen didn't trust him. Dain had worked for our father, and neither of them was what you'd call straightforward." He turned toward me. "I didn't know you were Dain's daughter until that day I met you outside his house, and then only because I demanded he tell me why you'd been there. I didn't even know he had a daughter. Well, obviously."

"What will happen to him now?"

He held my gaze steadily. "Dain is a traitor, Emlin. Jaff can't afford to let that go."

"Can't you ask Jaffen to, I don't know, exile him or something? Jaffen would give you anything."

"I can't," Addy said. "I'm sorry, but I can't. Jaffen is drake. This is part of what that means. It's not your fault, you know. Dain made his choices long before you knew him."

I leaned back against the low wall, my eyes stinging. "I know. It's just that it feels like there were possibilities there, and now they're gone."

Puckers appeared between his brows. "I understand."

I thought of his father. Maybe he did.

Addy slid a feather-soft stroke over my hair. At his caress, something in my stomach fluttered like a jaffel's wing. My breath quickened. *He's the brother of a drake, Emlin. Just what do you think could happen between you?*

"Would you rather go to Lyz than the Westlands?" he asked. "With Symond in power, you have to go somewhere, and you're half Lyzian."

I scrambled to my feet and went to lean against the dragon statue, facing the graying sky in the east. It was the morning of my birthday, I suddenly realized, the day on which I was to have sworn my oath and received a crafter's ring. Despair choked me. Everything I loved or wanted seemed to be slipping away.

I moved toward the dragon's mouth, open to roar toward the day just edging over the horizon. At that moment, the sun sent a wash of gold over the rooftops. It flooded over the dragon statue, bouncing so fire seemed to flare from the statue's open mouth.

Drake Haron's quivery, old man's voice echoed in my

head. He'd pointed to my mother's drawing of the Dragonshards and said, "They burn the false ruler, like fire hidden in the dragon's mouth." And he'd laughed as if at a joke.

My breath stopped. I leaned out over the low wall, trying to see into the statue's mouth.

"Careful!" Addy cried. He jumped to his feet and edged up next to me.

"Hang on to me." I leaned farther as he seized the back of my belt.

Inside the dragon's mouth, the sun glinted off something like dark ice. Light on glass, I thought dazedly. Truth and beauty in one. I stretched to reach inside the mouth and pulled out a necklace of rainbow-streaked dragon glass.

The Dragonshards.

Night Flights 5

The dragon of Kural is dreaming of a song that is not his.

Chapter 26

I HELD UP the necklace, spreading it so the sunlight shot through the glass, sending waves of color over the tower's pink stone. Something wild sprang to life in my heart. Power tingled against my fingertips. How could I ever have mistaken the fake for this reality?

"How did it get there?" Addy asked.

"Drake Haron, I think." The colors drew me in so that I had to force myself to answer. "Maybe because he was worried about the kind of drake Symond would be. Maybe just as a joke." At the edge of my vision, Addy stretched a finger, then curled it back without touching.

He gave a crow of laughter. "Bless the poor old duck. Now we have to get it to Jaffen."

When I moved the necklace, the colors on the floor danced into a new arrangement. An instant of dizziness buzzed inside my head, as if the tower were tilting in response to the shifting colors. I had to look away until everything steadied again, and when I did, the thing that filled my vision was the gold dragon behind Addy. "Do you truly believe Jaffen is the rightful drake of Kural?"

"I do. All the old texts show he's the rightful Great Drake

of the Dolyan Islands." Addy was still smiling at the necklace.

"And you trust the Dragonshards to prove that?"

Something in my voice must have penetrated his glee, because he looked up, his face settling into more guarded lines. "Of course."

"We need that true test of whoever claims the drake's role."

"Wait a moment, Emlin." He licked his lips, then leaned against the flank of the dragon statue and closed his eyes. "I *can't* risk Jaffen."

Merciless as a drake, I said, "A test would be an act of faith in the role you think belongs to him."

His face twisted as if some part of him were being torn in two.

"Jaffen should listen to you. If he's to govern the Dolyans, he needs wisdom at least as much as he needs a war leader."

From the courtyard below came the sound of booted feet. Someone shouted something about sweeping the cobblestones.

Addy opened his eyes and gazed off toward the horizon where smoke rose over Lyz. The corner of his mouth pinched. "Curse you, Emlin."

I STOOD ON the circular stairway, listening to the voices in the room below and smoothing my sweaty palms over the embroidered silk coat I'd filched from the treasure room. My wrists and fingers dragged with the unaccustomed weight of jewels. Addy had done something to my hair and assured me it looked elegant, but the way he bit his lip when he looked at my head made me uneasy. Still, if I stayed away from other women, I'd be fine. Addy adjusted the cuffs of his guard uniform.

In the treasure room below, a husky voice I recognized as that of the Sage began chanting:

Dragon
Maker. Shaper.
Dreamer. Destroyer.
Fire Breather. Flyer.
Cloud Climber.
Star.
Dragon.

The chant swelled as the other people in the treasure room took it up. Judging from how it echoed up the stairwell, the room must be crowded. I'd never seen a drake's funeral or Flame Testing, and obviously, Addy never had either. In all the Dolyans, only Kural had the Dragonshards and the custom of using them. Glass was our craft. But naturally Addy had read about what was supposed to happen. Symond would have invited witnesses from every district in Kural. He'd have chosen his friends and important people who'd be eager to please him. They'd be the ones inside the barriers in the square. They'd have brought their households too, so the hallway outside the treasure room was undoubtedly as jammed as the room itself.

The shuffling of feet smudged the sound of the music. The Sage's voice grew fainter, and then those of the others, until, abruptly, the sound was muffled. They must have left the tower, closing the door behind them.

I tiptoed down the stairs after Addy. He peeked into the treasure room, then beckoned me onward. As we crossed the room, I saw that the silk drapery atop the room's central column was empty. As Addy had predicted, the procession must be carrying the necklace out of the palace.

I swallowed and was embarrassed by how loud my gulp sounded. Addy glanced at me. "Don't worry," I said. "When I hold up the necklace, Symond will keep me near. So Kural will have its Flame Testing, and we'll still be able to get what we need."

Addy looked as if he wanted to say more, but he only nodded. He unlocked the door and pressed his ear against it.

My breath came fast. I felt ready to erupt like the fire on Lyz if I didn't move soon.

In one motion, Addy straightened and opened the door. Ahead of us were the last stragglers in the procession following Haron's body toward the elaborate funeral pyre and platform in the square. I glimpsed silk and velvet in all colors, but mostly Kural blue and gold. Addy seized my upper arm and, in as guard-like a way as he could muster, hurried me after the procession, the bruising force of his grip telling me how tense he was. The mourners had left a thick trail of perfume in their wake. My nose twitched, and before I could press a finger to my upper lip, I exploded in an unladylike sneeze.

Two men holding hands at the procession's end glanced back. I steered Addy toward the shorter one's side and rose to my toes to peer over the heads blocking my view. "I think I see my mother up there," I cried.

"You can join your parents once we get outside." Addy smiled brightly at the men. "Anybody else need to go to the privy?"

With indignant harrumphs, the men jerked their gazes ahead.

We passed between the door guards, whose eyes were on

Haron's bier as it left the courtyard on the shoulders of six guardsmen. Addy ducked his head anyway, pretending to speak to me. In the courtyard, the procession spread out as people waited to squeeze behind the platform built in front of the gates and go out into the market square.

Addy opened his fingers. "Go," he murmured and sidled away.

I darted into a group of men who looked so much alike they had to be related. They all sang off-key. Definitely related. They scowled at my intrusion, and one of them blinked at my hair, but they moved apart to give me room. When I glanced back, Addy had vanished. I patted a tuft of hair that seemed be standing straight up and concentrated on keeping out of sight. All I had to do was wait for the right moment. I fingered the necklace in my pocket, caressing my mother's mark.

Tucked among the flat-note singing brothers, I slid out into the square, the platform looming on my left. To my relief, the crowd ahead of me was so dense I couldn't have moved farther from it if I wanted to. I had been worried I wouldn't be able to get to the platform when I needed to.

I briefly glimpsed three people on the platform, their gazes aimed over the square where Drake Haron's body was probably being laid atop the wooden dragon pyre. One of the three was the Sage, clad in their scholar gray robes edged with glass bead embroidery and still leading the singing. Next to them stood Symond. His eyes flicked briefly away from his father's body to the third person – a page who stood just behind the Sage, holding the Dragonshard necklace on a silk cushion. Symond's mouth curved, then disciplined itself into a line as he turned back to the square.

Hot hatred flowed like molten glass through my veins.

Symond would never become drake if I had to fling myself onto a guard's sword to stop it. He'd ordered the death of my mother so he could stand where he was. He'd tried to hurt my friends and had hurt my father because he was afraid they'd talk. I was probably still alive only because he eventually realized the fake Dragonshards my mother made had gone missing, and he needed me. He'd sent me home with a guard the day he decided to buy the Dragonblade because he hadn't yet had a chance to call Rolan off.

The men around me closed ranks again, and my view of the platform and everything else vanished. I knew when the fire was lit under Haron's body, though, because everybody leaned forward. I heard crackling and then a growing roar, rather like the one I'd heard in the glasshouse furnace every day of my life. Smoke wisped, then billowed into the sky, pricking my nostrils with the scent of burning wood and Haron's fragile remains. With a pang of pity, I remembered the old man in the palace bedroom, crying because the servant caring for him had been cruel.

As the Sage raised both arms and intoned a new verse, flames shot up high enough for me to see. Heat washed over the crowd, and the people in front of me pressed backward. At last, I heard the pyre collapse in on itself. The Sage changed the song again, and the crowd shuffled, making way for a man in scholar gray who ran past where I stood, carrying a torch I knew he'd lit from the pyre. He ran up the steps to the platform and moved around its edge, lighting the waiting torches from the one he carried. The air around the flames shimmered.

My stomach shimmered too, and I slid my hand into my coat pocket again. Any moment now.

The Sage began a new song.

Dragon.
Truth teller.
Soul spyer.
Glass gazer.
Dragon.

They picked up the necklace from the cushion, and the page backed out of the way. Still singing, the Sage held the necklace up and walked toward Symond.

The servant with the torch scuttled down from the platform. When people made room for him, I managed to edge a yard closer to the steps.

"Emlin!" someone nearby exclaimed, and I recognized Kedry's voice. "Quick! Guards! She helped Jaffen escape."

Sweet dragon. I needed to get away from Kedry and onto that platform. I yanked the second necklace out of my pocket and charged toward the platform steps, holding it over my head. "Wait! That's not the Dragonshards. It's a fake. The true necklace is here."

The Sage's song cut off as they whirled toward me, the pieces of the necklace they held swaying and knocking together in a way that made me wince. Symond's face flushed with anger. He drew a knife from his belt, and to my fury, I recognized the Dragonblade I'd crafted for him.

I made it only halfway to the platform before guards grabbed my arms and yanked me off my feet so hard I thought my bones might pop loose from my shoulders. "I tell you that necklace is a fake!" I shouted. "I'm from the glasshouse. I know dragon glass when I see it. This is the true necklace. We just found it." I tried to show them the one dangling from my fingers.

"Keep her close," Symond snarled at the guards. "Put that necklace on me, Sage. Now." He waved the knife.

The crowd hushed to a low murmur.

I struggled in the guards' grip. Black dots swam in my vision at the pain in my shoulders.

The Sage looked down their nose at Symond's knife. Then, voice shaking, they resumed their song, though no one else sang with them. They laid the glass pieces of the necklace on Symond's chest and circled behind him to fasten the clasp. For a moment, their fingers worked at Symond's neck. Then they stepped away, arms at their sides.

"Let the dragon show us the rightful drake," the Sage declaimed.

Brandishing the knife, Symond threw back his shoulders and turned, letting the torches shine on the necklace. "It glows with dragon heat," he cried. "I feel the warmth."

In the torchlight, the necklace really did glow, the glass flushing deeper and deeper red. My breath caught.

Symond stopped, brows drawing together. Then he sucked in his breath and grabbed at the long pieces of glass on his breastbone. With a cry, he snatched his hand away, shaking it, then reached up again to fumble at the clasp. He worked one-handed, seemingly unable to let go of the knife he held in the other. "Help me!" he shrieked, turning toward the Sage. "Help me!"

The Sage gaped at him, eyes huge, mouth open but nothing coming out.

Symond screamed and clawed at the necklace. Smoke rose from his clothes. Where his dark hair touched the necklace, it turned ash white.

When the guards holding me loosened their grips and took simultaneous steps forward, I ripped myself free and ran up onto the platform just as Symond collapsed, still clawing at the necklace. Abruptly, his screams stopped, and I glimpsed his hand still gripping the Dragonblade knife hilt.

He'd fallen on the knife, the one that was as false as the Dragonshards in my hand, the one I'd made that shouldn't have fended off a true drake's enemies.

My stomach roiled. I swallowed hard, then flung aside the false necklace I'd taken from the column in the treasure room when I put the true one in its place. The Sage took a step toward it and halted, forehead wrinkling. I crouched, shoved aside Symond's burned hair, and touched the clasp below it. Pain blistered my fingertips. I smothered a cry, released the clasp, and dragged the necklace loose in a hand I quickly covered by my silk sleeve.

When I stood, I saw for the first time the overwhelming size of the crowd in the square, filling in the space around the smoldering dragon pyre. An even bigger crowd of watchers pressed against the barriers. *The east side of the fountain*, I thought desperately. Addy said he'd be on the east side of the fountain. Then I saw the tall figure in a guard's uniform balancing on the lip of the fountain, and my knees went weak with relief. But he was an eternity away. Why hadn't I realized how far it was to where he stretched up his hands?

In front of Addy, men and women formed a line, eyes scanning the crowd, hands tucked inside their jerkins. And behind them stood a hooded figure, his hand raised to steady Addy. Jaffen, I thought, with the crew he'd summoned, just as Addy told him to do.

Addy's lips moved, and I knew from the shape of them he said my name.

Then in one of those odd moments of silence that sometimes comes in a crowd, I heard a sweet, three-note song. I looked up to see a jaffel bird perched on a crosspiece at the top of the platform.

I cocked my arm and threw the Dragonshards. They spun through the air like the weighted rope I'd seen children throw to catch a bird. Only this time, a bird swooped beside the string of glass shapes, as if curious to see what this new creature of the air might be. Heads turned to watch the necklace and the jaffel soar. I caught my breath and cried, "No!" I hadn't thrown it hard enough. The Dragonshards arced downward. Then the jaffel pinched the necklace in its beak, flew to the fountain, and dropped it in Addy's outstretched palms. The bird came to rest on the top of the fish statue in the fountain and fluffed itself out as if proud of itself.

Addy flung Jaffen's hood back and drew his brother up beside him. He hesitated only an instant, but I saw it. Symond wasn't the rightful drake, but how sure was Addy that Jaffen was? How did he know the Dragonshards wouldn't burn his brother too? In an act of faith as true as any I'd ever seen, Addy looped the necklace around Jaffen's neck and fastened it. "I give you Jaffen," Addy cried loudly, "the true Drake of Kural."

In the square, there was a collective, indrawn breath.

"Let the dragon show us the rightful drake," the Sage said for the second time in a handful of heartbeats. Their voice shook but boomed into every corner of the square. Their intent gaze was on the Dragonshards.

The necklace glowed red, then yellow. Jaffen stood straight-backed, scanning the crowd, turning to let them see him. Ever so slightly, his shoulders relaxed. Slowly he smiled, and next to him, Addy broke into a wide grin.

"I don't believe it," a man in the crowd cried.

"What else could it be?" someone else said.

"People of Kural," Jaffen shouted, "I came to this island

in search of peace, and Symond played me false, as false as he played you. He killed his father, not I. I never even saw Drake Haron. I mourn him as you do. And I seek to rule you and serve you."

Voices rose over one another, louder and louder. Jaffen's crew tightened their half circle of defense. Addy's grin faded.

"People of Kural, hear me!" the Sage boomed.

Along with everyone else, I swung to face them.

"The Dragonshards have always shown us our true ruler," the Sage said. To me, they looked shaken by what had happened to Symond and was now clinging to what their faith taught all the tighter for it. "I do not believe they have failed us now. I recognize you, Jaffen, as the ruler of Kural."

A rumbling noise rose on the edge of my hearing. I scanned the sky, wondering if it was thunder. When I glanced back to the square, my eye caught on Jaffen. He'd lifted his face toward the Heights, eyes closed, mouth slightly open.

"Look!" someone shouted, and I raised my gaze to where the woman pointed. A man shouted, and people surged forward, their voices rising in a wave of fear gradually ripening to awe.

A wisp of smoke rose from the Heights and below it, a thread of fire trickled down the mountainside. Kural's dragon was stirring from its long sleep. And over the Heights, like a gigantic bird, a glittering red and black dragon circled, a thing of terrible beauty in the colors of Lyz. Its scream came faint on the wind, calling its brother awake.

The rumbling swelled. At the top of the Heights, rocks cracked and burst apart. A dark blur shot into the sky and spun, flinging off whatever had settled onto its scales over the centuries. Bits of mountain slid down the slopes in a crushing roar. On wings of blue and gold, Kural's dragon wheeled around Lyz's, both of them shrieking now. When I closed my eyes, I felt how wonderful it was to be free, to be alive, to be lifted into the skies and fly. No wonder Jaffen's eyes were shut.

Someone cried out in the square. An instant later, it sounded like everyone else joined in. I popped my eyes open to see the dragons rush at one another, claws out. They crashed together and tumbled in one another's grip. I clapped one hand over my mouth. They couldn't be enemies! Or maybe they were. Kural and Lyz had looked at one another with suspicion for long enough.

The dragons flipped over and when they steadied, Kural's was on Lyz's back. Their voices slid together and the shrieks shifted to a musical note. I blinked. Well, no. They weren't enemies after all.

Addy was right. We in the Dolyans had forgotten so many truths. Or maybe our ancestors had never told them because the people who knew them thought they were obvious.

Lyz's dragon hadn't been calling his brother. *She* had been calling *her* mate.

At that moment, pain wrapped itself around my right forefinger. Crying out, I dropped to my knees to cradle that hand in the other. Just when I thought I might pass out, the pain eased, leaving behind a ring that was part of my skin, a crafter's ring marked with the image of two dragons, intertwined.

Chapter 27

THREE DAYS LATER, I emerged from the glasshouse into the yard and settled on a bench to wait for the furnace to heat. When I'd left the Flame Testing, I found Miriv but no Dain in his house. She said Jaffen hauled Dain away. Beyond that, she knew nothing. Since then, I'd stayed with her there. Last night, I dreamed about Dain. At least I thought it was him. The figure was shadowy. And then my mother was there saying, "There's no use crying over spilled milk." I woke up with tears on my face, thinking that was well and good, but I was the one who spilled it. I pulled the covers up over Miriv, who slept peacefully beside me, and waited for morning.

The days of healing had left her stronger, but she was still pale and cradled the elbow of her hurt arm in the hand of the good one as if the sling she wore didn't offer enough support. This was the first time she'd felt well enough to leave Dain's house and go home, where I'd tucked her into bed and then come down to fire up the furnace.

I raised my face to the sun and closed my eyes. The rough stone of the glasshouse wall pressed solidly against my back.

At least we were sure the glasshouse still was our home.

Jaffen had denied Kedry's claim in his court. So now I knew a little better what kind of ruler I'd helped to take over Kural.

Not that I'd heard from him, of course. Since Jaffen's crew had swept him into the palace after the Flame Testing, he had made no effort to contact me or Miriv. Rulers were like that, I told myself. It was stupid to expect him to thank me. I hadn't seen Addy since the Flame Testing, either, and really that was fine, just fine. After all, he might not be a ruler himself, but he was the brother of one, and they usually weren't interested in people other than their fellow rulers.

I shook off a stab of loneliness. I still had my glasshouse family. Renie and Miriv would both feel well enough to work soon. Maybe even Gillis would come back, with or without Piret. We'd be all right.

Someone stumbled over the sill at the gate, and I looked up to see Addy. With a speed that dazzled me, happiness bubbled up in my throat. He wore Lyzian black and red today, which I had to say fit him well, showing things his baggy scholar tunic and trousers had hidden, but the colors made me swallow down that joy.

Careful, I warned myself. *He's still the drake's brother.*

He paused with his hand on the gatepost, then came slowly into the yard as if unsure of his welcome. "How are you? How's Miriv?" Then he added in a rush, "I'd have come before, but I didn't like to intrude at Dain's house when she might be sick, and then Jaffen kept coming up with things he wanted me to do."

I'd just bet Jaffen did. No matter how much he loved Addy, Jaffen was unlikely to let him be wasted on me. Addy might not realize it, but he was a card Jaffen might be able to match with one from another island.

"Miriv is better," I told him. At the news, he broke into a

wide smile, and I couldn't help smiling back.

From high overhead came the caw of Lyz's dragon immediately joined by the clear call of Kural's. I jumped to my feet and darted to Addy's side in the middle of the yard where I'd be able to see better. We both swiveled to search for them.

"There." Addy pointed to the Heights where the dragons circled and then plunged from sight.

Heat flared under the crafter's ring that had appeared on my finger at the Flame Testing. When I tried to rub the warmth away, the ring's surface felt uneven, slightly ridged beneath my touch.

"Does it hurt?" Addy asked, brow wrinkled.

I shook my head. "Not really. It's... uncomfortable, I guess." I studied the entwined dragons on its surface. "Do you think there are two because I'm both Lyzian and Kuralian?"

"What an intriguing question. Can I see?" He grasped my hand and squinted at my finger.

I sniffed softly. He still smelled of spice. It must be part of him, deep in his skin. Warmth crept into my face.

"You know what I've been thinking?" he asked, turning my hand over to look at the other side of the ring. "Maybe your mixed heritage is a good thing for your art. Maybe you can draw inspiration from both dragons." He raised his gaze to meet mine.

My stomach fluttered. I pulled my hand out of his grip. "What a lovely thought." It hadn't occurred to me that my unconventional glass work grew from double dragon vision. That was an idea I'd have to think about.

Addy shifted from foot to foot, readying himself to say something he was having trouble spitting out.

He's leaving, I thought, blinking hard. *Just get it over with.* "What's Jaffen going to do?"

"He'll leave once things are settled here, and he's found a governor both he and you Kuralians trust. He's serious about becoming Great Drake." Addy sounded sober, as well he might, since he was talking about something dangerous.

"And you?" I asked lightly. I didn't look at him.

There was an instant of silence before Addy said, "He wants me to come with him."

I faced him. "You're going, aren't you?"

He gave me a crooked smile. "He says he needs me."

"I told you that already." I was glad for him. Truly I was. I'd been foolish to make what had happened between us more than a chance meeting of two people with the same goal who would now go their own ways.

In the distance, the dragons called to one another.

For a moment, we stood in awkward silence. My throat felt raw. Surely we could stay friends. I started to say that, but Addy said something at the same time. He gestured for me to go first.

"I'm glad things worked out for you and Jaffen, but I hope you'll still come and visit Kural sometime." Though I knew it was selfish as well as stupid, my stomach was sick with misery.

He looked away, seemingly absorbed in the sight of a white butterfly in the weeds along the fence. "Visit?"

"I like hearing you talk about lore," I said. "Well, sometimes anyway. And you'll have things to tell. You wouldn't begrudge me that, would you?"

"Emlin—" His voice cracked. "I wouldn't begrudge you anything." He bent, and, softly as the first flare of a candle in the winter dark, he kissed me. My heart stopped, then started again, wild with joy, like an otter at play, like a jaffel soaring toward the sun.

"Jaffen won't like it," I breathed, my lips a finger width from his. "He'll have plans for you."

"Jaffen will get used to it."

"You have to go with him, Addy, and I can't stop making glass. It would be like ripping out my heart."

"Of course not. It's what you were born for. I'll bring you dyes you've never seen. There are dragons aloft, and you're blessed with some of their knowledge. The Dolyans are changing, and you and I are going to help Jaffen lead the way."

My world opened with glimpses of new possibilities.

Addy's mouth drew near again, but, being Addy, he was still talking. "You'll have to work here first though." His lips barely brushed mine. "I asked, and Jaffen wants a window with the jaffel and the Dragonshards flying together – a sign of new things."

In a flash of color, I saw it – the red of the jaffel, the rainbow swirl of the Dragonshards, the upturned faces of the dazzled people. I inhaled sharply. It would be difficult beyond description to capture that vision. Excitement flooded me. My hands flared with heat from my wrists to my fingertips.

I realized that Addy was still talking. I laid a finger over his mouth to silence him. This close, I saw that his gray eyes were flecked with bits of black. "Concentrate on what you're doing, scholar."

He kissed me harder this time.

I tightened my grip on his shoulders and kissed him back.

Dear Reader

Thank you for reading *Glass Girl*. If you enjoyed this book (or even if you didn't) please consider leaving a star rating or review online. Your feedback is important, and will help other readers to find the book and decide whether to read it, too.

Acknowledgements

This book has been a long time coming. I have drafts dating back to at least 2017. Luckily, plenty of people have supported me along the way. Thanks to the following:

The Wednesday night group of the Barrington Writers Workshop: Keith Mulford, Lance Erlick, Alex Oleksiuk, Kathy Mueller, Thom Pharmakis, Janet Souter, Sung Kim, Carol Cosman, Art Cannon, Mike Kreusch, Cynthia Miller, Tamara Tabel, and Mary Klest. I'm probably missing people because writers came and went over the years, but I owe thanks to all of them for the serious consideration they gave my work.

My fellow Dragons of the Corn: Sarah Prineas, Deb Coates, and Lisa Bradley. You were always fierce, and sometimes, you bit, but you made the book better.

Kelsey Blickenstaff, for her perspective on how a teen reader might react to the violence in the opening chapter.

The Purgatorians for their help with the blurb, and particularly to Kelly Andrews, who read and responded to an earlier draft.

Sara-Jayne Slack and the rest of the team at Inspired Quill, including Sannah Rabbani. Sara, your editing was insightful, but your support and high ethical standards were even more important to me.

About the Author

At one time, Winsor taught technical writing at Iowa State University and GMI Engineering & Management Institute (now Kettering). She then discovered that writing fiction is much more fun and has never looked back. If you visit Winsor's blog and sign up for her newsletter, she'll send you a free short story.

Dorothy A. Winsor writes young adult and middle grade fantasy. Her novels include *Finders Keepers*, *Deep as a Tomb*, *The Wind Reader*, *The Wysman* and *The Trickster*.

Find the author via her website:

www.dawinsor.com

Or tweet at her: @dorothywinsor

More From This Author

The Wysman

"The Grabber is just a fright tale."

Former street kid Jarka was born with a crooked foot and uses a crutch, but that no longer matters now that he's an apprentice Wysman, training to advise the king. When poor kids start to go missing from the city's streets, though, Jarka suspects that whatever's causing the disappearances comes from the castle.

Now he needs to watch his step or risk losing the position he fought so hard to win... but when someone close to him becomes the latest victim, Jarka knows he's running out of time.

His search takes him from diving into ancient history, to standing up to those who want to beat or bleed the magic out of him.

Will Jarka succeed in uncovering an evil long-hidden, or will he see friends and family vanish into the darkness?

The Trickster

"When it comes to family, you're rich... and I'm dirt poor."

Amid the intoxicating chaos of Winter Festival, attendant Dilly and Hedge Mage Fitch cross paths.

After surviving Rin's wretched streets, Dilly aims to prove herself to Lady Elenia, who brought her back to Lac's Holding and blessed her with a new life of comfort and luxury. Fitch seeks vengeance for a loved one, killed by a liquor that makes one vulnerable to suggestion.

But their separate goals are derailed when Dilly discovers Elenia's secret lover is the head of a too-ambitious kinship, and Fitch finds his own smuggler-family pressuring him into using his unique nudging abilities for mutinous deeds.

When murmurs of treason break out in Lac's Holding, it becomes clear that only Dilly and Fitch know the truth.

The question is how they can save the city when those they're loyal to stand in their way.

Available from all major online and offline outlets.